advance praise for
The Old Moon in Her Arms

The Old Moon in Her Arms is a gift of storytelling magic. Lorri Neilsen Glenn delivers the reader into a dimension where the past is the present is the future. Early on, she writes, "If I knocked on your door today, you wouldn't believe how many women would be standing there." By the end, we do believe. And we want her to knock on our door, so we can talk on the porch, that liminal women's space that is, what Lorri calls "a means to be both in the house and connected to the community." This book is like the best porch visit, where you are heard, your spirit and mind are enlarged and transformed by the power of story. I am so grateful for this writer and this book.

SHELAGH ROGERS
former host of CBC Radio One's *The Next Chapter*

The Old Moon in Her Arms is an extraordinary literary artifact, at once a memoir, a discourse, and an investigation. Lorri Neilsen Glenn guides the reader through the landscapes—historical, geographical, domestic—of a life, her life, its "200-year living present." Her prose is richly textured, lyrical at times, and plain-spoken when it needs to be. This is a book to be savoured, like the best of nourishments, to be held to the light for its hidden secrets, its beauty.

THERESA KISHKAN
author of *Blue Portugal and Other Essays*

A book that probes and explores and resists, by a poet, feminist, academic, wise woman who asks hard questions about the world we live in and our place within it. There are no easy answers and if we, the reader, follow the genre-bending trail she makes for us, if we open our hearts, we can absorb the knowledge she has gained by tracing her own lineage and the mythologies that speak to her. In the deeply contemplative writing Neilsen Glenn so generously offers us, this is one of those rare books a reader can linger over and return to.

SHEREE FITCH
author of *You Won't Always Be This Sad*

An inventive, lyrical compendium of memory and imagination, moving quietly from past to present, and delivered with care and compassion. We are thirsty for both in these noisy times.

SYLVIA HAMILTON
author of *Tender*

Lorri Neilsen Glenn's *The Old Moon in Her Arms* delves into the knotty complexities that make up a life—her parents' fraught marriage, a loss that finds her splayed across the hood of a car, an aging mother who wants her hair cut off—yet laughter simmers just below the surface. The past is offered up in fragments that become, in Neilsen Glenn's hands, rich and layered poems. This is a book of light.

ANNE SIMPSON
author of *Speechless*

"We think back through our mothers if we are women," wrote Virginia Woolf, and in this thinking-back book, Lorri Neilsen Glenn reaches skyward and seaward to parse her peripatetic feminist life, guided by her own curiosity about the women she became along the way to now. Looking forward is an acrobatic art, and Neilsen Glenn finds a future by setting the past in her sights. *The Old Moon in Her Arms* "gets the goddamned work done" with light and fire.

TANIS MACDONALD
author of *Straggle: Adventures in Walking While Female*

The Old Moon in Her Arms is a beautiful and profound reverie on a life spent hungering for understanding, meaning, and connection. In lyrical prose, Neilsen Glenn revisits her roles—daughter, mother, writer, teacher, wife, sister, friend—to reflect on what matters most. This is a brutally honest and emotionally transcendent memoir from the liminal place of advancing age. In a youth-obsessed world, it feels refreshingly real and important.

PAULINE DAKIN
author of *Run, Hide, Repeat: A Memoir of a Fugitive Childhood*

The Old Moon in her Arms swells and churns with memory and wisdom as Lorri Neilsen Glenn contemplates her life's path while offering insights on climate change, feminism, the creative process, aging, ancestry, and place, all observed with steady attention. With wit, anger, awe, intelligence, tender and terrible grief, she chronicles her experiences, her old age, and her many selves in the settings she loves—wide Saskatchewan prairie and vast Atlantic Ocean—through a flow of entrancing, ever-shifting prose. This memoir, a gorgeous offering to the literary world, will remain with me for a very long time.

LAUREN CARTER
author of *Places Like These*

Here Lorri Neilsen Glenn turns her ethnographer's lens on the people and places that have shaped her, resurrecting vivid memories of the timid child, the independent young woman, the creative teacher, the loving partner and parent, all folded into the woman walking the Nova Scotia shore today. It is a delight to share both her journey and her enthralled inquiry as to how and who to be in our tragic but beautiful world.

SUSAN GLICKMAN
author of *Cathedral/Grove*

In her memoir, Lorri Neilsen Glenn moves us from the Homeland of the Métis Nation to the East Coast, from maiden to crone, determined to write and mother and teach, to be and know and play. This is a migration in time and place but also in terms of how Lorri understands herself and, by extension, the world.

ARIEL GORDON
author of *Treed: Walking in Canada's Urban Forests*

the old moon in her arms
women i have known and been

Lorri Neilsen Glenn

NIMBUS
PUBLISHING LTD.
—— NIMBUS.CA ——

Nimbus Publishing Limited
3660 Strawberry Hill St, Halifax, NS, B3K 5A9
(902) 455-4286 nimbus.ca

Editor: Whitney Moran
Cover design & artwork: Jenn Embree
Typesetting: Rudi Tusek
NB1677

Nimbus Publishing is based in Kjipuktuk, Mi'kma'ki, the traditional territory of the Mi'kmaq People.

Library and Archives Canada Cataloguing in Publication

Title: The old moon in her arms : women I have known and been / Lorri Neilsen Glenn.
Names: Glenn, Lorri Neilsen, author.
Identifiers: Canadiana (print) 20230590780 | Canadiana (ebook) 20230590799 |
ISBN 9781774712696 (softcover) | ISBN 9781774712887 (EPUB)
Subjects: LCGFT: Essays. | LCGFT: Creative nonfiction.
Classification: LCC PS8577.E3373 O43 2024 | DDC C814/.6—dc23

Nimbus Publishing acknowledges the financial support for its publishing activities from the Government of Canada, the Canada Council for the Arts, and from the Province of Nova Scotia. We are pleased to work in partnership with the Province of Nova Scotia to develop and promote our creative industries for the benefit of all Nova Scotians.

Contents

prologue

With every step, the world comes to the walker.
Trinh T. Minh-ha

Today I walked on the ocean floor. On days when the tide is especially low, the dog and I step down over boulders and layers of shale to reach the basin of the bay. Here the gun-metal greys and bright ochres come alive. We cross the spot where a small stream rinses through the rocks before it's soaked up by the sand and the seaweed. Around here, that seaweed is called rockweed; its biological name is *Ascophyllum nodosum*. But do I need a name? Names can be a comfort, yet my wonder about the outside world increases with age, and language seems to limit my awareness as much as it expands it.

While I play at philosopher and step carefully over the slippery rockweed, the dog rolls in ecstasy in the slithery mass, her small sturdy frame flipping, writhing, snorting. She'll smell of the ocean now, which I think is the point.

I bend down to search for tiny periwinkles, most the size of a highbush blueberry. Some ooze meat from their opening. Their shells open in what I think of as a lament, but if today is a day for grieving, it's anticipatory grief—life is too short, I know nothing, everywhere is beauty, and I don't know how to appreciate it without breaking my heart.

Today is the summer solstice and, in Canada, it's also National Indigenous Peoples Day, a day to think of beginnings. I feel spent and raw, however, wavering between the desire to write and the need to be by the water.

And so I walk on the ocean bottom where low tide has exposed a wide swath of rock and sea life. I see subtleties in umbers and greys, splashes of yellow algae that carpet the shale. This bay is free of old beer cans, stranded flip-flops, and all the usual detritus from a summer place. Canada's Ocean Playground, say the tourist brochures. A summer place—my mind goes directly to the wistful strains of Percy Faith's old tune. Youth is filled with that kind of ache, I think. Now that I'm beyond child-raising and constant caretaking, the ache returns, but it's different, something between yearning and mourning.

The dog has poked her cold nose into the back of my knee and now looks up, waiting. I throw a stick about twenty metres out into deeper water and she plunges in, returning in no time, gasping, triumphant. The stick lands at my feet and my skin feels the cold spray from her full-bodied shake.

Tomorrow, the Earth begins to tilt away from the sun. When the dog and I walk back from the shore through the woods, the high sun shreds its light through tree branches, throwing tatters across the green.

I take pleasure in my transformations. I look quiet and consistent, but few know how many women there are in me.

Anaïs Nin

Each morning I carry into the day ancestors, my birth and immediate families, friends and acquaintances, those who taught me, loved me, pushed me, hurt me, inspired me. I carry my strengths and sorrows, faults and quirks. If I knocked on your door today, you wouldn't believe how many women would be standing there. And tomorrow? A slightly different group.

The Scottish ballad of Patrick Spens includes the phrase "*A saw the new muin late yestreen / Wi the auld muin in her airm*"—"I saw the new moon, with the old moon in her arms." Promise and poignancy: the new moon enters, carrying her pasts and, we hope, her wisdom. For 4.5 billion years, the moon has shown us all her faces: new, quarter, waxing or waning, crescent or full. An orange ball on the horizon to my Australian friend Lekkie; a pale thin wafer to me in the northern hemisphere. Over time and circumstance, haven't we all been various?

What have I learned under all those moons? Lately, the deaths of friends and family, along with my own compromised health, have made the "big chill" a daily companion. A cliché, but true: nothing like death's door to wake us up. Some turn to a god, some retreat from the world, some bide their time until the last door opens. As for me, I want to take stock: Who and what have created the person I am? What learning awaits? And so I write. If writing is a long goodbye, it's also where I often find the answer to "what's next?"

I was part of a typical working-class family in one of the little boxes Malvina Reynolds sang about in the 1960s, each with our own lawn mower and private sorrows. With age, I have welcomed complexity, the many ways we are—I am—human. And I have learned our ancestries, as poet Joy Harjo suggests, are more than people: we come from landscapes, ideas, customs, and places we cannot begin to chart.

The Cree concept of wahkohtowin refers to our interrelationship with all of creation, including the earth itself. Our lives and systems are interwoven in this kinship; we are responsible for each other. Western societies tend to value the individual over the collective, yet none of us arrived at this particular bright morning on our own. Our relationships with the land and one another create and shape us, help us survive.

The past is spectral, often ineffable. Although I knew I had forebears from France, Scotland, and Ireland, learning of my Indigenous ancestry late in life gave me a footing on the earth I'd not felt before. We all have thousands, millions of ancestors. In fact, a computational biologist at USC Dornsife used DNA-based evidence to confirm the theory that everyone on the earth is related. In the same way, the salt water sluicing in and out of this bay flows to and from all waters on the planet.

Time can create distance, even from ourselves; no straight line connects then and now. This collection is a kind of *ana*, a collage of story, anecdote, and reflection that gathers up a woman's life to try to make sense of it. What and who matters? Why? Here the reader will find a kaleidoscope of prose pieces, mixtapes and mash-ups of earlier writing, journals, letters, online conversations, and more.

In many ways, I am a stranger to my former selves. As a result, early in the book, I address the younger me in second person as "you" and reflect on that young person as "she." Then, recounting moments in mid-life, I write in first person and reflect on the woman I was then in third person. The last section of the book is in first person; my past is integrated in who I am at this writing.

Like both memory and the moon, what's written here aims to shed what light it can, bringing it home to now.

origin stories

another country

Childhood is another country but also a waiting-room,
a state of accommodation and acceptance.

Antoine de Saint-Exupéry

Your early years are lost in the mists of the past and when you enter that country, you find a familiar stranger, someone with access to images and pivotal events abraded by time. Years separate a white-blond girl in the foothills of the Rockies from the young woman on the prairies and the grey-haired woman now standing on the shores of the Atlantic.

You've always believed a life extends beyond the dash in an obituary. Sociologist Elise Boulding describes the span of time spent with your loved ones as the 200-year present. You reach back to include your grandmothers, Ethel and Eleanore, then forward 100 years from the birth of your youngest son, AJ, to the year 2086. This span is what Boulding calls your "life space," the expanded space in time in which humans think, hope, and dream.

When Biff Loman argues with his father, he says, "Pop, I'm a dime a dozen and so are you." Willy, the tragic salesman, disagrees. In this curious state of being human, you are an insignificant, transitory fleck across a planet's immense past and future. Your mind can't even comprehend how tiny your human world is. Yet, here you are, like so many others, telling your stories as if you aren't a dime a dozen. Why?

Because you believe, like Willy, even ordinary lives are extraordinary, with their own magnificence and tragedies, meaning and purpose.

The term *kairos* was coined by Plato to describe "the opportune moment." Kairos speaks to our experience of a turning point, to a fitting time for change. In writing, kairos is fluid, shifting, being open to the right word at the right time.

Hermes, the trickster god and divine messenger, is said to show up in liminal spaces, as does the Cree trickster wîskicâk. Mi'kmaw educator Sylvia Moore says the trickster challenges her to "embrace opposites, contradictions, and ambiguities as catalysts for thinking in new ways."

You see turning points, pivotal moments, and the people who were there with you, only in retrospect. If you had any agency creating the twists and turns in your past, it had to have been subconscious. Some gut instinct, perhaps, or the work of a trickster. You were never the child with a road map, the adolescent with a firm life goal, the single-minded adult with a tidy bullet journal. You fell into your life and rode or dodged the waves, often at the mercy of the tides. You wonder if that was true, too, for your parents and their parents, those in your 200-year living present.

Virginia Woolf wrote that "all the lives we ever lived and all the lives to be are full of trees and changing leaves." Seasons, like the moon, changing but constant.

cutting out hearts

Time makes room
for going and coming home
and in time's womb
begins all ending.

Ursula K. Le Guin

Bone. Blackbird. Families of the Cree and Saulteaux hunted and traded nearby. West of Winnipeg and south of Riding Mountain, the Scots, Ukrainian, Irish, and English felled trees, hauled stumps, built mills, planted crops. You imagined their winters of fifty below, hard-rain springs, scorching summers, picnics at Salt Lake, chautauquas at the Bend. Medicine was a bottle of brew and a box of Aspirin tablets. Churches sprung up as fast as schools. The West, as the Europeans thought, was young.

In September 1918, a troop train brought influenza to Winnipeg, and within a year, sixty thousand Canadians died of the flu. Ethel Hogg, a nurse from Schreiber, Ontario, travelled to Strathclair, Manitoba, to tend to the sick. One of the young men Ethel nursed in the small town that winter was Bill Glenn, Carson Glenn's son. Carson had come from Haldimand County, Ontario, with his wife, Margaret Morrison, to farm 10-22-20 near Green Bluff School. Like Billy Beard, the local nail-warmer, Carson was one of dozens who built the town's structures, including the graveyard where they all rest now.

One day, you and your sister will scatter yellow roses on their graves. You'll lie on the wet grass, listen to spring birds, and watch cloud-ships, drunk on wine and searing grief.

Grace April, your mother, was born to Ethel and Bill Glenn on April Fool's Day. A young nun fashioned a box with a candle inside to keep the two-pound infant alive. When Grace was ten years old her father, Bill (your grandfather), left the hockey rink for the Strathclair Hotel to have a soft drink. It was February 14. Bill collapsed of a heart attack, was laid out on a pool table, and died early the following morning. He was forty-one years old. In his pocket was a Valentine card for his daughter.

Grace recalls in glimpses the day her father collapsed. The cold and bitter wind as Roy Cummins drove her and Jack to school in the sled, a hot stone at their feet and a blanket on their laps. Trying to keep her book dry inside her coat. How they cut out hearts that day at school.

Grace knew winter well, and more than seven decades later, she died on Christmas morning. She mourned her father's death all her life.

If this were fiction, you might have prevented your mother, Grace, from losing her father, and your grandmother Ethel from losing her husband, Bill. You'd peek into the lives of those children at Green Bluff School: the Glenns, Currahs, Cummins, and the Gibb MacDonalds, enough offspring to grow a town.

Green Bluff is gone now; only a cairn remains. One summer, you and your siblings will troop through the chest-high weeds to find the patch of field by the school where your mother once walked.

But this isn't fiction, and after Bill Glenn died, his brother told Ethel to take Grace and Jack and move out; the big house was his now and he wasn't about to feed any extra mouths, thank you very much.

Ethel, sick with tuberculosis, had no money, so she sent Grace and her brother Jack to live with her mother in Port Arthur while she went into the sanatorium. When Ethel recovered, her children returned to Strathclair to live with the Gibb MacDonalds while Ethel left for Winnipeg to work as a nurse. It was the thirties; people took in strays everywhere. Mrs. Gibb, a Maritimer, was the canning, baking, sewing, and gardening champion of Strathclair.

Grace was a quick learner and the two often returned from the Brandon Fair with ribbons for crocheting and for rhubarb pie. Grace thought Mrs. Gibb could do anything.

One night Mrs. Gibb woke Grace in a panic. Come down. Bring your pillow.

The wind was whistling, rattling the windows. The hot summer had parched the fields, and Grace could see lightning slice the sky to the west. Mrs. Gibb's husband was away and Grace saw the panic in her eyes. Grace, Mrs. Gibb, and her son Bob held their pillows against the glass.

It was never about the windows, Grace told you later. Mrs. Gibb was afraid of being alone in the storm.

When Grace's brother Jack's difficult moods became too much for Mrs. Gibb to handle, he went to live with Ethel's sister Eunice in Kamsack, Saskatchewan.

Grace finished school at sixteen, found a job at the Bank of Montreal in Winnipeg, then trained to be a nurse. All the while, she sent support cheques for her brother in Kamsack. In the Winnipeg General graduation yearbook, her caption was from Henley's "Invictus": "the menace of the years / Finds and shall find me unafraid."

And that's where your story begins.

While Grace was visiting Jack, she met a man just out of the Air Force. Elvin was the son of Eunice's friend Eleanore. If this were fiction, you'd dress Grace in something Rita Hayworth would wear, with padded shoulders to highlight her eighteen-inch waist; her hair would be softly curled back. Grace was a foot shorter than this man's six feet plus. She had a sharp mind of her own, but she was smitten beyond all reason.

Photos of this man show him to be lanky, with the dark Indigenous features he would never cop to, a square jaw, flashing eyes, a broad grin. He had a regular job on the railway, had been offered a raise and a transfer. He was ambitious.

Together they could leave dust and the Depression in the rearview mirror and see plenty of Someday ahead. The war was over, rich prairie fields were soon fed by rain, and CNR trains began to ship wheat beyond Canada's borders.

This man, your father, lit up Grace's horizon, and you wonder, finally, if he wasn't the death of her.

follow the years

Elvin married Grace in the middle of winter. He knew little of his own background; his mother, Eleanore, identified herself as French.

Yet her—and your—ancestry wasn't that simple.

In 1765, young Matthew Cocking of England was hired by the Hudson's Bay Company in York Factory to transcribe journals and handle accounts. His salary was twenty pounds for five years' work. After helping Samuel Hearne establish the company's first inland post, Cumberland House, he became the postmaster at Fort Severn, where his union with a Swampy Cree woman, Ke-che-cho-wick, resulted in the birth of Wash-e-soo-E'squew, later known as Mary Budd. When Cocking died in 1799, he left annuities to his "mixed-blood" daughters.

Thus begins the stories of generations of your Indigenous grandmothers.

Mary Budd had several children with a Cree man: one child, Henry Budd, became the first Indigenous Anglican priest in Rupert's Land. Another, Catherine, known as Kitty, is your three-times-great grandmother. By the time of the Red River Resistance in 1869–70, the descendants of Ke-che-cho-wick are known as Métis, some of whom live along the Red River in a settlement now known as Selkirk, Manitoba.

You have remarkable great-uncles, too: Henry Budd, of course, and the Métis translator, treaty negotiator, trapper, and buffalo hunter, Peter Erasmus, Jr. One sunny day, over a century and a half after Erasmus built his house in Smoky Lake, Alberta, your friend and her husband will drive you to Fort Edmonton where it had been moved. You'll touch the door handle, imagine him stoking the fire.

But we are talking about grandmothers here. From Norway House down to Red River: Ke-che-cho-wick, Mary Budd, Kitty, Sarah, Catherine, and Eleanore. Elvin's mother.

Eleanore is born in Red River, meets Charles, a man from the United States, and they move to Kamsack, Saskatchewan.

See how long it takes for any of us to become? In your case, you can account for 250 years and wish you could trace more. But that's not the point. Your point is you became a twinkle in someone's eye in Kamsack.

You feel the strength of your ancestors, but you know you're of the land as well. By the time you leave home at seventeen, you are of the foothills of the Rockies, the grasslands and the boreal forests of Saskatchewan, the harsh winters, thick woods, and cold clear lakes of Northern Manitoba. You are of long rivers, hot summers, bitter winds that pierce your eyes with snow in winter and dust in August. Of clouds of mosquitos, of thumb-sized horseflies, mayflies, meadowlarks, and crows. Of mud like cement and fields of wheat and corn.

And of high snow. Your aunt—was it Kay or Eunice?— followed your mother, Grace, on a cold November night as she waded through snow drifts to St. Boniface Hospital in Winnipeg. You'll catch your death from cold! your aunt yelled. You were born just after midnight. The next day, your father sent a telegram from somewhere out on the CNR line.

By the time you are old, you will also be of nor'easters and rain and the sea. Of beaches and mud flats, of cormorants and seagulls, blackflies and the taste of salt. Today you are of wind and whitecaps on a dark powder-blue sea. Like anyone's body, yours grows from the soil and water on which you were raised. An elder once said, if you grew on this land, the land is your kin.

the corners of her mind

The gravel road.

The grille of a large car.

Her mother screaming.

Something loomed large beside her body. Her mother heard car brakes and ran to scoop her up. She remembers the man yelling, probably something like, "Why can't you watch your kid?" Her mother would have felt shame, got her dander up and barked at the driver. As if every child hasn't vanished when we least expect it.

Does she remember this incident? She was a toddler and can't picture it. Her body, however, remembered the physical presence of that threat well into her teens.

Memories before the age of seven are said to be unreliable. Some say a child can't recall events until they have the linguistic ability to put them into words. Wittgenstein's claim that "the limits of my language are the limits of my world" held sway for years. But humans speak many languages that don't involve words. In later years, Wittgenstein softened his stance on the picture theory of language—a word only holds meaning if we can define it or see it in the "real" world—and recognized the role of context, the slipperiness of language itself.

Some phenomena are impossible to describe in any form. The awe she felt standing at the edge of the Grand Canyon, by the face of Uluru, or thirty thousand feet above the Rockies, for example, will always elude her ability to express it.

The human body registers the effects of a traumatic event without having to put the trauma into words. Is that why she's extra careful around idling vehicles? Did her body know that memory before her mother shaped it into words?

She places images of her childhood on the page—memories of friends, family, books, schools, and more—and wonders, why these? Only this moment she remembers her friend Joey St. Marie in Edson, born with what they called clubfoot, hobbling on his brown shoe with the high thick heel. She recalls their easy companionship on their walks to and from school. He died young, she learned later. She hopes she wrote him a letter when her family moved to Saskatoon, but she doesn't remember.

Researchers at McGill have learned our brains actively remove memories; they don't disintegrate or fall, like scree, off the ledge of recall. If we remembered every single detail of every single day, we'd suffer from what's called "overfit"—we'd be so cluttered with information we'd jeopardize our ability to generalize to new situations. The more we recall and re-store a memory, the greater the chance it will be consolidated, but why do our minds keep the memory of this moment, toss the next?

Memory sometimes favours happier times, traumatic events, and occasionally the quirkiest detail. We bury some memories to protect us and positive memories can mitigate painful ones.

As she pulls up memories from her small worlds and shapes them into words, she transforms herself in the process. Her mind flits across decades, landing on something in 1964 or 1959, then in 2010. She's doing this alone; if people in her past were here, together they would remember more, and differently.

o'clock

We are always walking with our younger selves.
Greta Gerwig

Your mother was likely next door at Lillian's as you and Jeanie bounced around in front of the record cabinet, yanking each other's skinny arms up and down, hop-hop, swinging your tiny hips. Jeanie and her impossibly wild white hair rising like a cloud as she twirled, and you, likely with barrettes pinching curls to your head. You had only the memory of the black-and-white images on the movie screen that afternoon, and a line or two of the title song. Was it Patti Page, or the *Oklahoma!* soundtrack on the player? It didn't matter. Any music would do. You leapt about, hollering Rock. Around. The Clock. Tonight. This dance, this cry, felt vital.

You and Jeanie had walked down to the Nova Theatre that Saturday—in those days, townspeople pronounced it *thee-AY-tur*— for the weekly matinee, clutching your fifteen-cent allowances and five cents more for popcorn. Neither Jeanie's nor your parents could afford a television, so it was the theatre's monthly showbill that offered a glimpse of the world beyond the foothills of the Rockies.

Beyond. You remember this moment because you were roused by a clear, bright restlessness you feel to this day. The poster—*it's the whole story of rock and roll*—and images of a couple in a deep dance dive, her head near the floor, leg high; a man and a woman on a beach towel; dancers in gravity-defying, skirt-lifting positions—all were clues. These bodies in motion, their flips and twists, were a far cry from the pump-handle hee-haw country waltz grown-ups danced at the Legion down the road. Or at the parties in small living rooms with ashtrays and brown bottles, piles of coats on the bed in the next room where you often hid.

You'd bolted home after the movie, flyer in hand, hoping to remember Bill Haley's tunes long enough to try out the steps. You tilted up the lid of the laminate console, locked its hinges in place, slipped a 78 on the spindle of the turntable, and waited for the needle to electrify the air in the room. You remember baggy socks, the slippery wood floor, the fear your mothers next door would hear the noise. Did you try the under-the-legs swoop or the over-the-shoulder flip? You doubt it.

Neither of you had even thought of boys. This—this was about something new, something beyond the Western Canadian cloud-ships sailing above your houses. One, two, three o'clock. It wasn't even about the music.

After was coming and you were going to be part of it.

the one driving

What the—?

The windows of the Studebaker are closed, but dust seeps in. All you see are pines and billowing clouds. Your father's back is a bull's-eye of sweat and he curses the road crew: What the hell do they think they're doing? Jesus Christ.

You're too close, Elvin. This is the wrong way. She sucks in her breath when he's driving, as if she is being stabbed in slow motion. You wish she'd put her blouse on.

And what other goddamned way would you suggest? There is only one highway to Edmonton, Grace.

You think I don't know that?

I'm the one driving.

Right into the construction. And we need to stop. The kids are hungry.

Your father doesn't answer. He's focused on changing gears, grinding them in his haste, muttering. He doesn't look at your mother, whose flowered blouse is tucked under the visor as a sun shield and who is now opening the cardboard box. Egg sandwiches wrapped in waxed paper, and, you hope, those marshmallow puffs with chocolate tops, even though they're expensive. Please, not Fig Newtons. What if the highway crew sees her half-naked?

Out of the dust clouds: a yellow road grader. Its wide, insistent blade.

Well, isn't this fun, she says. Carry on, Mr. Know-It-All. I'm feeding them. She opens a mason jar filled with celery sticks and pickles.

This bastard's pushing me off the road. He yanks the wheel to the right.

Your mother's hands fly up; the jar's contents scatter. The grader blade is as high as the hood of the car. Something—a pickle?—ricochets off the dashboard. Your little sister, Punky, jerks to attention, rolls with the car into your brother, ripping his brand-new comic book in the process.

You three are a tangle of legs and arms against the back door, the ripped and crumpled comic between you. Dust everywhere. The car is atilt.

All you see is a crooked world.

what she doesn't know

> *I*
> *write because*
> *I would like*
> *to be used for*
> *years after*
> *my death.*

Eileen Myles, "Peanut Butter"

She knows the houses of her childhood, the one near the train station with an outhouse and a large backyard where her father used the garden hose to pour her a skating rink, the one farther up Main Street with the back stoop and a coal shed she and Darlene liked to jump off—next to the doctor's house—and finally the one up by Hinchey's and the water tower, close to the woods, where she and Jeanie played in all kinds of weather for hours on end until dark. She has flash memories of that time, along with a few black-and-white photos.

Her first teacher is Miss Best, whose kind ways allowed her shyness. She learned to "look and see" and "come and go" along with Dick, Jane, Sally, and Spot. When she is eight, she walks up to the front of the room to tell Mrs. Ringstad she can read the newspaper and her teacher's reply—So?—burns her with shame. Before her family leaves Northern Alberta for the Paris of the Prairies, she reads the Star Weekly and mail-order encyclopedias; she listens to the radio, the news, Howdy Doody, Clarabell the Clown, along with Maggie Muggins and Mr. McGarrity. She will prefer radio to any other medium her whole life. The store on Main Street sells 7Up for seven cents and Archie and Veronica comics for ten cents, and if she and Jeanie blow their allowance at the theatre, they'll have to wait until the following Saturday to buy them. The boundaries of her world include the water tower, the school, the woods near Jeanie's and the train tracks six blocks away at the bottom of Main Street. They include her family, schoolmates and friends, her cat Snowball.

The Queen of England is younger than her mother, and the large blue commemorative book about her coronation has pride of place in the living room under the radio cabinet. She will find the book years later in her old blue metal trunk with the brass clasps, along with dried flowers and her wedding dress. The Switzer girls across the street die in their burned house. And one day, as she listens to the clock in the kitchen, she is stabbed by the awareness that time ticks on, and her *own heart will stop one day. She doesn't know what she doesn't know. It is a wonder to be able to read, a way to live many lives. Words reveal, but also conceal; there is so much out there to learn. One day she will write, too, but she doesn't know that yet. One day she'll marvel at the extraordinary chance to breathe, move, think, dream, suffer, play, grieve, laugh, love. Her whole life becomes a why.*

a hole in the head

Aunt Eunie's short grey hair accentuated the dent. The first buzz cut you'd seen on a woman and you couldn't stop staring. When Eunie saw you, she bent down. Go ahead, touch it, she said. It doesn't hurt. The hollow looked like the depression in an underinflated ball. Your family had just moved from Edson to Saskatoon and she and your uncle Stan lived above the arena where you took skating lessons. At her fiftieth birthday celebration she yelped, I'm a half-century old, and laughed her big laugh. You are struck dumb by the thought. That year, Stan and Eunie sat in the cold bleachers to watch the carnival, hundreds of young skaters in costumes, a production that filled the arena. You recall the icy feel of your home-sewn black satin pants with a military stripe, the pinching chin strap on your toy soldier hat. Your new white skates with sharp toe-picks.

Neither Eunie nor Stan is bothered by the long drool and the rancid farts their two Great Danes produced. You loved her cheerfulness, how she made you feel you belonged. Eunice and Stan had introduced your parents years before in Kamsack and now, here you were, all in the same city. After Eunie's brain surgery, people said she was different. It wasn't that her mouth drooped, they said, but she seemed simple. Except for the dip in her skull, you thought she was fine. You wonder if you and Eunie inherited your loud laugh from Gram Glenn's side of the family. You'll take that over a tumour in your head any day.

starting over

On Saturdays, the girl pedals her CCM from her house on Main, up Clarence, across the 25th Street Bridge to the old brick library building downtown. She fills her basket with Nancy Drews, the Annette series, and books about horses. Heidi's story makes her long for a bed in a hayloft and makes her think a girl could survive most things. Spyri's original Heidi, she learns much later, is less cloying.

She reads all of the Anne of Green Gables series, but it's another book by L. M. Montgomery she remembers for its melancholy. Jane of Lantern Hill is the first book she reads that feels real. She checks out poetry, loves wordplay. Some Daphne du Maurier, her mother's monthly Reader's Digest books. After a battery of tests, she has to ride her bike farther from home—their second of four houses in the city—to Victoria School, where Miss Campbell will guide her so-called gifted charges through four grades in three years.

She becomes distracted by movie magazines and television shows such as Riverboat and The Ed Sullivan Show, the Disney rotation of Fantasyland and Frontierland. Her father says he has a crush on Connie Francis. She can sing every word of "The Purple People Eater" and "Witch Doctor." She tapes pictures from Photoplay and Teen Screen to her bedroom wall, sketches women with wasp waists in flowing evening gowns, makes clothing for paper dolls. She teaches the little ones in Sunday school. Her mother winds curlers in her hair in

front of the television on Sunday nights. Her braces hurt and she's em-
barrassed about her glasses and the clothes her mother takes pains to
sew for her on the Singer machine. At school, she makes white sauce,
baking-powder biscuits, and custard and, like the other girls, sews her
own apron and tea towel, stitches herself into the culture of woman-
hood. She and her friends Carolyn and Claire aren't the popular ones,
but they're not unpopular either. Her heart thumps in her ribcage when
she has to speak in class. In her last school year in Saskatoon, the girls
make their own grade-eight graduation dresses. In the photo she's a
scarecrow with bangs wearing a godawful rose floral getup.

In a future trip to Saskatoon, she'll call the elderly Miss Campbell
to say hello, to thank her. Her old teacher tells her Jonathan became a
Member of Parliament, and what has she been up to all these years,
married? Children?

She can draw and paint, do a mean hula hoop, skate and swim
passably. Almost a teenager, she can't figure out how to walk, what to
do with her hands in public. Her father will soon take up a new job with
the CNR in Northern Manitoba and they will live on the banks of the
Saskatchewan River, across from a reserve. She doesn't realize she has
relatives there; she only knows people walk across the bridge above their
railway house to get to town. That summer, when her parents pack for
the drive north to their new home in The Pas, she asks to take the train
on her own. With the new baby, there isn't room in the family car any-
way. The trip north, a milk run, seems endless, but she's on her own, and
she is going to start over. Starting over will become a life-long practice.

unlit

The stage was dark and you were terrified of forgetting your lines.

You didn't have many. As Elizabeth, the maid, you were described as a stout, amiable, subservient woman of fifty. When the curtain rose, you stepped into the parlour with a tray, set it down, then left and closed the door. Later, Mr. Manningham called you back and asked if you noticed anything amiss in the room. You looked around, then spoke your first line.

Nothing, sir. Except the picture's been taken down.

You were thirteen or so. It must have been the English teacher's decision to stage this play. An odd choice, given the innocence of the cast. For years you kept the Samuel French copy of *Angel Street* in a trunk that held memorabilia.

This play was the first, but you acted in high school and community theatre productions until you were in your late twenties. Stage fright? No, people fright. If you were acting, you didn't have to be yourself. You could wear a serviceable black dress with an apron and carry trays, or wear layers of makeup, a back-combed updo and a waist-cinching gown. You could lie across railway tracks, which you did once in a comical melodrama in Winnipeg, holding the back of your hand to your forehead while you wailed, "O, woe is me, O, lackaday." In high school, one of the Shakespearean characters you played was Hippolyta, Queen of the Amazons, possessed of her father's war belt.

But that first time on a stage, as the maid Elizabeth, you knew only you were in an old play, written in 1880. Mr. Manningham was playing tricks on his wife and Mrs. Manningham was always upset. She thought she was going mad. You don't recall what you thought of the story, only a hazy image of the dimly lit stage. The gloomy setting didn't dampen your excitement about being part of something that forced you out of your shell.

While the play was the first time you put yourself out there, it was also the birthplace of a term you and so many women would use decades later. First performed on Broadway in 1938, *Angel Street* later became known as *Gaslight*.

finding the words

Your first poem was about a storm. You were twelve, and in Mr. Komenda's grade nine English class in The Pas, Manitoba. You thought your ending had a hopeful note: "and stillness reigned." It was easy at that age to be sentimental, even mawkish. Later the poem appeared in the coil-bound yearbook between ads for Trager's Fashions and the Cambrian Café. Your first publication.

Mr. Komenda asked you to come up to his desk to talk about what you'd written. You tingled with apprehension. He pointed to the phrase about shadows and suggested you replace it with a single word. You wished he would whisper for god's sake.

You know the word. He looked up, waiting to see a light bulb. You know it, he repeated.

He was so keen to help.

It's in the title of that song by The Diamonds. You stood at his desk, your brain frozen. Others were looking at you. Finally, it clicked: *silhouette*.

At university, you wrote doggerel that swung between dewy-Disney platitudes and earnest folk-music bromides, but wrote no more poetry until you turned fifty. At a writer's retreat at the Trappist abbey in Rogersville, New Brunswick, your friend Joan Clark read fledgling drafts of your short essays.

Some of these could be poems, she said. Why aren't you writing poetry?

That summer, you went away to the Fundy Shore, watched the tide go in and out on the red mud twice a day, and pulled dozens of tottery poems out of memory and landscape. After years of academic writing, you felt an unfamiliar freedom. It's an old story, but true. When the words come, it feels like coming home.

homeliest gal

The train takes hours to pass by your house on its way to deliver grain to the Churchill port on Hudson Bay. The rural railway network in the early 1960s is more than twenty thousand miles long, transporting grain from five thousand elevators and two thousand delivery points. This is peak time for grain export in Canada.

You walk to school on the tracks, place a penny on the rail to see what will happen to the Queen's head. You slide down snowbanks in your fur-lined mukluks, and meet friends at the café in the Cambrian hotel for cherry Coke and fries. You look forward to the Trappers' Festival with its ice sculptures, pole-climbing, log-throwing, and leg-wrestling.

Like you, the Native students at the back of the class rarely speak. You hug the wall at school dances, where Conway Twitty once sang before he became famous. Your mother sews you a felt circle skirt, and one weekend you take the rail-liner to Flin Flon and buy a mohair pencil skirt with your own money, then take it in on your own, crudely basting the side seam. The next morning your horrified mother pulls at a stray thread, opening the seam as you head out the door for school. The perm your mother wanted you to have stings and stinks and, despite many washes, your hair springs back into Orphan Annie coils.

Your grandmother visits from Winnipeg and your mother is angry. Gram helps you make a corsage and a box lunch for the Sadie Hawkins dance, a mortifying event organized by the church. Poor Sadie, known in the comic strip Li'l Abner as "the homeliest gal in all them hills." Both you and Billy Knox are mute with shyness the whole evening and will never speak to each other again.

At Christmas your parents surprise you with a portable record player and a gaudy striped sweater you'll never wear. The plastic cap on your hair dryer has a hose that burns a red mark into your neck. Your younger sister sneaks into your room and tries on your clothes. You memorize fifty Latin roots and their derivatives and Mr. Fasano scolds you for not living up to your potential. You have no clue what your potential is. You listen to a song about "personality" and you don't understand what that is either, or even how to get one.

You hear the hit parade from southern US stations because the signal arcs over the Earth's curve and lands clear and loud in Northern Manitoba. Johnny Tillotson's song "Poetry in Motion" is your favourite, but the line about seeing "her deddle sway" makes you wonder what your deddle is (your first mondegreen; it's "her gentle sway"). You play music on your transistor at night to fall asleep, depleting its batteries, a habit you'll pick up again when you are your gram's age.

When another promotion comes up, your father goes on ahead and your mother packs up once more, arranges for schools, Cubs, Guides, and music lessons, attends to a toddler, and finally unpacks boxes in a tiny wartime house three hundred kilometres south along the CNR line. She often sits in the living room in the dark, smoking. That first winter in Dauphin, you and a boyfriend stand in the snow under your bedroom window while he smokes. You wonder if you'll grow breasts like Bonnie's. Reg has hair like Bobby Curtola, turns his collar up on his leather jacket: the Fonz before there was the Fonz. Dyeing your hair red is a disaster. Before long, your family is moving back to Saskatoon.

shine

Today early winter light bejewels the water. How can she describe that sparkling ribbon on the horizon without falling into cliché? It's like a piece of hematite glistening in the sun. A wet leaf gleaming in the inky dark of the forest floor.

Or—well, keep trying.

In an old radio interview, Alice Munro spoke of her youth, when the worst sin anyone could commit was to try to shine. The girl has felt that shame. "Who do you think you are?" her mother often said, long before Alice Munro had published her book. Also: "Get off your high horse" and "Stop showing off." Once, after the girl snuck into the house past curfew, her mother stood above her bed in the dark and hissed, "Who the fuck do you think you are? You're not nearly as smart as you think." She'd never heard her mother speak that word before.

Toward the end of her life, the girl's mother often told her how proud she was of her. Which version to believe? By that time, the daughter knew enough about the lives of 1950s mothers, postwar women who couldn't shine, whose daughters had so much freedom. She wonders if her mother, like Mrs. Gibb, feared being alone during the storms of her life.

The moon sheds her light like clothes at night, but oh, the shame of a woman daring to stand out.

Even at her advanced age, the woman is conflicted. She loathes drawing attention to herself. She wants to support people and to have her writing matter, but if she could manage that from a remote cabin, she would. It's ridiculous, of course. She needs and wants the company of family, friends, and writer companions to survive. To be part of something bigger than her own concerns.

In Sunday school, the girl sang the words "this little light of mine, I'm gonna let it shine." She was sure it was about her light, despite her mother's scolding. Later, she learned the Civil Rights Movement gave the old gospel song new life and meaning. It was never about any single light. It's about being among countless lights, about collective resolve and purpose.

Outside her kitchen window, she watches the tips of waves catch the sun on the restless waters, harvesting light.

Harvest, yes, that's the word.

laugh

You remember Sandra, older than your six years, walking past your house on Main Street in your small foothills town, her feet pointed outward in a V. What was she doing?

Sandra was the doctor's daughter, and your mother, a nurse weighed down with young children, admired Dr. Begg. So this must be how to walk, you thought at the time—and you began to emulate her.

What are you doing? your friend Darlene asked at recess. You look stupid.

You did. You weren't comfortable. Or balanced: you couldn't break into a run from a waddle. And how would you manage double Dutch or salt-and-pepper with your feet toed out like a duck's? Also, people would laugh.

You thought of Sandra the other day when the orthopaedist asked you to walk down the hall. Swing your arms, he said, walk the way you usually do.

As a young girl, you always watched to see how others walked, talked, or moved. What if you did things wrong?

When you left the tree-climbing, bike-racing, book-inhaling stage of childhood, you entered a tentative phase, a time when your reliable and energetic Gumby of a body began to surprise and betray you. Your chest became tender; your feet felt like untethered oars. And although you were morbidly shy, you became even more self-conscious. You stood in front of the magazine aisle examining photos of Sandra Dee and Kim Novak to see how they curled their hair or dressed. And why would they wear those pokey bras?

You and your friend Linda practised kissing on mirrors or, chastely, each other, curious how it was done in the movies without noses colliding. You spoke little, and suddenly you stopped laughing. You'd laughed all through your childhood, but your braces invited teasing, so you kept your mouth closed. You began to notice girls were judged more than boys were.

The early years of television offered a few models. How did Betty Anderson on *Father Knows Best* manage to giggle so gently, a cascade of liquid sugar? In the beach party movies, Annette Funicello dropped her jaw when she laughed, fluttered her eyelashes as she looked up at Frankie.

This becoming-a-woman thing threw you, and you were in flux. You tried the trill; the trill with the whoop at the top, like a cherry; the heh-heh-heh chuckle with the closed mouth; a whinny that belonged more in the stables than the back of the gym at the Friday night dance. You were a body on its way to becoming, and it seemed you had to get this right. Never mind the exports of Switzerland or quadratic equations, for a month or so, your most important homework became how to laugh.

And then, just as suddenly, that all fell away. In a rush of years, you were a high school drama club member, a university student, a wannabe member of the counterculture, a young married woman, a teacher, an artist, a mother. You muddled through your body's changes with as much angst and as many insecurities as your friends had, but you survived. You'd been a tomboy as a child and a quaking wallflower in adolescence, and you landed in the sixties where you treated makeup like a foreign substance. By the time you reached motherhood and middle age, you hadn't even stopped for a pedicure. You celebrated your fiftieth birthday by getting your ears pierced.

But you do remember this about laughing. In your forties, you were with friends at a gathering by the ocean. You had guitars, sang loudly and badly, hollering at one another, collapsing in laughter.

A friend made her way through the crowd: There you are! I knew I could find you from your laugh.

It's distinctive all right, someone said.

It's loud. But spontaneous, she rushed to add.

Yeah, I could hear you down the hill.

You hadn't been paying attention.

new skirt

Last exam. Grade eleven. Hot June day, the first day of your period, a pinching garter belt, painful twinges down below, and a pad that feels as though you are bringing a small ham to market between your legs. You're wearing your new skirt from the Simpsons-Sears catalogue. It's your last summer in Dauphin before you move back to Saskatoon.

You are on the far side of the room by the windows and as you finish the test, you feel it: the surge, the warmth. Of course. You look around, but everyone has gone.

Through the window of the classroom door, you see your friend Abbie waving, Hurry, come on. The teacher doesn't seem to notice her.

No, you shake your head and arc a quick c'mere with your fingers. Abbie frowns, and mouths, why? You point down below and grimace.

Just at that moment, the teacher looks up. Are you finished yet? You nod yes.

Well, bring it to me.

Can I leave it on my desk?

Why? Are your legs broken?

You feel dizzy, you say. Lying is easier than admitting you've ruined your new white skirt, and you've probably stained the seat of this old oak desk.

He purses his lips. Well?

Is it all right if Abbie comes in?

Now he looks suspicious. He pushes back his chair, opens the classroom door for Abbie, walks down the aisle to take the test from your hands, and returns to his desk to sort papers. He probably understands what's going on, and you're grateful he says nothing.

Abbie shuffles behind you as you make your way past his desk and out of the room, a girl sandwich, so close together you'd expect top hats and jazz hands as you head for the exit.

help yourself

When you and Patsy arrived at the party cabin, the only person there was a beefy guy with a shock of blond hair. He was vaguely familiar—perhaps you'd seen him last year on the football field as you jumped up and down cheering for the Bowman Bears.

You said six o'clock, Patsy said to the guy.

Around then. Don't worry. They're coming. I was just going to head up to the store to get a box of Old Dutch. I have lots of beer.

I'll go. I'm out of smokes anyway.

And she was gone. You sat on the sunken couch in the porch and watched kids on the dock next door splashing each other. Horseflies buzzed around the screen door. Beefy guy disappeared into the kitchen for another beer.

Summer had just begun. Grade twelve was behind you. Your canvas sneakers were still white.

Patsy had invited you to her cabin at Waskesiu, north of Saskatoon, and it was the break you needed. Her parents were friendly and relaxed and the family joked with each other all the time. You were shocked you could take anything from the fridge without asking. At sixteen, you'd rarely consumed alcohol, and definitely not in front of adults, but you remember the extravagance of several whiskey bottles on the counter and tall glasses filled with ice. The steaks on the barbecue were as large as pies. Here, you didn't have to hold your breath, fear the anger. When Patsy asked her parents if the two of you could go to the party, they waved you off with no mention of a curfew.

Want a beer? Beefy guy was now back in the porch looking freshly shaved; he held out a sweating brown bottle. You didn't want to offend him, so you took it.

How do you know Patsy? you asked, wondering if anyone else was coming.

He plopped down next to you, pulled on the bottle until half the beer was gone, set it on the floor, and in one swift movement, grabbed the beer from your hand and pushed you down on the couch. His armpit odour rose from under the reek of his cologne.

Decades later, you can't recall his name—you remembered it for years, but it's gone. You remember the shock, however, and the weight of his body. His hands up behind your shirt, trying and failing to find your bra strap. You remember being more angry than afraid. This guy doesn't know you, and Patsy is due back any second. Is he stupid?

You try to squirm out from under him, jabbing and shoving him until he swears and sits up. He's ripped your shirt and wrinkled your new summer shorts. Worse, you wear the stink of his disgusting cologne. You can't recall what happens next. Like every girl on the Canadian prairies, you'd been told sex for men is imperative: blue balls are lethal, apparently. But beefy guy's hard-on was not your concern. Where you grew up, girls were either respectable with a steady boyfriend, or whores. Be nice, you were told. Look pretty, but don't be loose.

Up to then your boyfriends had been small-town guys as innocent as you were. You necked with Garry until the car fogged up and your lips were wreathed in raw pink. You and Reg stood outside in the cold smooching chastely.

That day at the lake was the first time you realized that, as a woman, you were born wearing a sign: *help yourself.*

And you didn't have the language to describe it, but you realized something else: you feared others' opinions as much as the stinking weight of a stranger.

meanwhile

She sings along to "Kind of a Drag," "Penny Lane," "Something Stupid," "Respect," "To Sir with Love," and "Ode to Billy Joe." She wonders what he threw off the Tallahatchie Bridge.

Her mother might be reading:

Ladies' Home Journal, *April 1967: "A Doctor's Sure Cure for Housewife Fatigue"; Women's Day, May 1966: "Crocheted Handbags for Town and Country, Festive Shrimp Recipes, The Coming Crisis in Medical Care, How to Cook Chicken Superbly, Decorative Table Settings, The Glamorous New Look in Dark Glasses, A Cook Book Full of Pies."*

She might read:

On the cover of Time *magazine, April 7, 1967: "The Pill." The Star Weekly August 26, 1967: "Rock & Roll Comes of Age: When the Jefferson Airplane zoomed into Toronto's opera-and-ballet palace it signalled the day rock left behind the Monkees and the screaming teenies and—POW—turned on the young sophisticates."*

She'd have read One Hundred Years of Solitude *and* Rosemary's Baby, *and for school,* The Stone Angel. *On TV, she watched* Bonanza *(proud that Lorne Greene was Canadian),* The Beverly Hillbillies, *and* Ironside. *Oh, and that show where the cop says, "just the facts, ma'am."*

In 1966, Margaret Laurence wins the Governor General's award for fiction for A Jest of God. Rolling Stone *magazine launches, the Middle*

East is torn apart in the Six-Day War, Dr. Christiaan Barnard performs the first heart transplant. Otis Redding dies, and the musical Hair opens off-Broadway.

The summer after her first year of university she worked at the psychiatric institution in Weyburn, Saskatchewan, her boyfriend Bob's hometown. She had no idea Abram Hoffer, a doctor her mother had once worked with, had been at the institution doing groundbreaking research into the use of hallucinogens in treating mental illness. All she recalls of her workdays on the psych ward are the long steel tables, patients masturbating in the corners, and the impassive faces of those brought back to the ward after shock treatment. She washed her uniform every night, applied clear nail polish to stop the runs in her white nylons.

Pierre Trudeau comments, "There is no place for the state in the bedrooms of the nation" and she thinks he's right, but she knows so little about sexuality, even her own. Headlines about protests in Greenwich Village filter through the news. Something about Stonewall, something big.

Everything important seems to happen elsewhere, not on the prairies, not in small-town Canada. One day she'll visit New York and Hollywood and London and Paris where real life happens.

One day, she'll learn otherwise.

drive

As soon as you pass driver training at sixteen, you take your friends on a Sunday joyride in your family's salmon-coloured Pontiac, roaring through puddles in the 8th Street mall's empty parking lot. At the Preston Avenue intersection the car dies, blocking traffic. By the time your father arrives in the neighbour's car, white-lipped and silent, your friends have coaxed the ignition to life. Back at the house, your father throws you across the kitchen table and you land in the corner behind overturned chairs.

Don't ever embarrass me like that again.

The next summer, you move out of your parents' house and stay with a friend near the university. Your brother Brian calls around midnight. You have to come, he says.

Now? You should be in bed.

They won't stop.

Someone drove you—a boyfriend? You don't remember. It's a clear night and Brevoort Park looks desolate—a struggling sapling on the front lawn; the boxy four-bedroom in a new subdivision. Your father took every promotion he could at the CNR to buy this sixties marker of success. Your mom has packed and moved your belongings at least six times since those years in Northern Alberta. When you left home, you also left your sister, Allison, whom everyone calls Punky, and two brothers, Brian and Colin.

From the street, you can hear shouting. The kitchen light is on.

You open the back door to Brian's wide brown eyes and horn-rimmed glasses. Around the corner, your mother sounds as though she's speaking in tongues. You are used to shouting, cupboard-door and pot-slamming, then hours of eerie calm. But this incoherent, raw-throated screeching is new.

A chair falls. Glass breaks. You hear your father's low growl, then abrupt silence.

You peek into the kitchen to see the table, overfilled ashtrays, a few bottles. Your mother stands by the sink, a small carving knife in her hand.

I'm going to kill one of us.

Gracie. Your father's voice is firm. Put that down.

You whisper to Brian to run upstairs, get Punky and Colin, bring blankets, and leave through the front door. Neither of your parents seems to notice as you reach around the fridge to grab the car keys, rummage in the hallway closet for children's jackets.

Outside, Brian has opened the garage door. Colin looks dazed. He climbs in the back seat of the Pontiac with Punky, a pillow in his arms. You shift the car into reverse; Brian pulls down the garage door, hops in the passenger seat. Later, Allison will tell you she wondered if she'd ever see the house or your parents again.

We can listen to any station we want now, Brian says, and reaches for the radio knob.

We sure can, you say. We might even go to the Dog n Suds, if they're still open. Did you bring your allowance?

You drive the dark streets of the subdivision to the sounds of the Beatles' "Hey Jude" until early signs of light appear in the sky.

how love fled

You were almost home. It had been weeks and your body craved Gord's with an ache you'd never felt. He was the first man you'd ever loved.

You dialled his number from the pay phone at the truck stop in Davidson.

But it was his father who answered. It had been a long drive from Montreal back to the prairies. The day was hot and dry, everyone bleary with fatigue. A stop for gas and lunch in Davidson, little more than an hour outside Saskatoon. When you heard the news, you left the receiver dangling from the wall, walked out into the sun, and lay across the ticking hood of the car, somehow wanting its heat to penetrate you, brand your skin with the shock. It's not real. It's not. By the time you pulled into the city, his father's voice was still in your ears. Who would you have called then? You didn't know his parents well enough to drop in. Would his friends have already heard?

Usually you two were inseparable, but that night Gord was more than an hour late. You and Joyce arrived at the rink early and joined the campus crowd. Finally, you recognized him from a distance by the animal design on his Cowichan sweater.

Where have you been? Are you all right?

I don't know what happened. I passed out.

His speech was slurred. You sank into the shoulder of his sweater, smelled the oil of the wool. This has happened before. Should you be marrying this man? Does he drink that heavily?

You recall the funeral, everyone's clothing whipped by the prairie wind on the lawn of the cemetery out of town. You recall the gathering afterward at his parents' house, sneaking downstairs to his room, sitting on his bed, inhaling the scent from his pillow. You took something—his deodorant? His aftershave?—and tucked it in your bag. You recall his mother's face, how impassive it was. You recalled more details years ago, once you'd escaped from the fog of grief, but they've evaporated now. You turn to what you wrote about those days, your bond, his suicide, to refresh your memory; or to be more accurate, to refresh your memory of your memories. It's all simulacra now. Flawed memories of incomplete accounts of a time you return to fifty years later. Images lodged in your gut.

A campus dance at the Bessborough. The beautiful green velvet dress your mother made for the occasion. Your Shalimar perfume. The two of you booked a room, so you wouldn't have to drive afterwards. You left the room to retrieve your wrap from the coat check and didn't take the key. When you returned, you stood hollering at the open transom, but he'd blacked out. Surely he hadn't had that many beers, had he?

You two had already chosen a ring. When you went on that long summer trip to Quebec, you exchanged letters almost daily and talked long distance every night. But for several days, your calls went unanswered. No more letters came in the campground mail.

Then you called from the truck stop at Davidson.

Gord is gone, his father said.

Gone?

Yes, he's dead.

You don't remember now if those were the exact words. Something about life support, something about organ donation. Something.

The confusion: how can someone pour out their heart in letters and then put a gun to their head?

Twenty years later, you learn a colleague at work is a friend of Gord's sister. You track her down. She tells you the autopsy had revealed a large mass in Gord's brain that would have caused severe depression, blackouts, and speech problems. Many years later, Gord's niece contacts you and sends along photos of her boys. You see Gord's features in their young faces.

More than a turning point, Gord's death was an axe to your psyche. By that age, you'd mourned the loss of a grandparent whom you barely knew, your aunt Eunice, a friend and her boyfriend who died one winter from carbon monoxide poisoning in a parked car. One or two pets. Sad events, but not like this. The first tragic death of a loved one is significant; its message lasts a lifetime. You don't know it yet, but the grief that slices open your rib cage and yanks out your heart can teach you to live.

Years on, long after you married Allan, had a child, and moved to the Maritimes, Gord's younger brother finds you on social media and sends photos of his life in BC. He says he thinks of his brother daily. You realize now Gord's death taught you about an afterlife, not the hereafter found in faith systems, but the one in human memory. Who will be the last to remember Gord, or anyone you've loved?

And you've learned something else since then. You prefer not to hide from grief, but invite it in. Look at it straight on, hold it, feel its contours under your fingers, sense its exquisite misery and beauty. Because grief is love, as everyone knows, and we embrace it where we can.

Whenever you return to Saskatchewan, you drive out to the cemetery outside Saskatoon, walk the site until you find his grave, sit or lie on the grass and talk to him. As the years go by, it seems to take longer to find the grave marker at the cemetery, even when you remind yourself it's below the religious statues—the Apostles, apparently.

Greek: *apostolos*, meaning "messenger."

take down this book

She begins to read again. Books from her courses in the arts, books by long-dead authors. She often skips class to meet with friends and talk books over coffee and cigarettes, although an early-morning cigarette makes her dizzy. She should quit; she smokes so little, why bother? Around that time, "the problem that had no name" appears in a book by Betty Friedan.

She reads the book the summer she moves in with a friend from Miss Campbell's class. More than thirty years later, she'll learn her friend's mother died and, unbeknownst to the family, left a trunkful of diaries documenting the frustrations of being a faculty wife, a mother of six, and a volunteer. The feminine mystique indeed.

Her own mother, Grace, is a working-class version of the women in Friedan's book, but if she sent her a copy, it would only make her angrier. When her father leaves her mother, she will send a book to give her mother comfort, only to have it returned swiftly, with a note: "You think you know everything; I don't need this book." When she reads Simone de Beauvoir's The Second Sex, *she finds it—what's the word?— defeating? Dreary? Friedan's book feels more relatable. She's unaware of "the Other" de Beauvoir writes about, and of the role a philosophy called phenomenology will play later in her life. Perhaps she's not smart enough to understand* The Second Sex. *She reads* Silent Spring, *which causes her to think about the planet for the first time. It can't get worse than Carson describes, though. Surely, someone will do something.*

Then there's Ken Kesey, James Baldwin, and Salinger, and on the radio, Vietnam protest songs like "For What It's Worth." These people aren't much older than her and are coming together over something they're passionate about. She finds herself sitting on the basement floor of the Administration Building at the University of Saskatchewan, reading flyers by the Students for a Democratic Society, planning a campus-wide sit-in. They sing from a booklet titled Songs of the Workers: To Fan the Flames of Discontent *published by the Industrial Workers of the World. Workers? By now, she's worked in a grocery store, a jewelry store, a stationery store, and on a teletype machine at the CNR yard east of the city. Hardly seemed like work, and certainly nothing to rise up against is there?*

Someone hands her a pin that says "Sterilize LBJ: No More Ugly Children" which she finds hilarious. She finds the pin as she's culling her belongings for a move fifty years later, and wonders why she laughed at others' expense. Especially women's. Was it years of her mother's barbs, her father's constant teasing? Women are always an easy target, but what did Lynda and Luci Johnson have to do with their father's war decisions? How can she contribute if she fears putting herself out there? She's complacent, and ashamed of it. As Tish Harrison Warren said, "Everyone wants a revolution. No one wants to do the dishes."

Years later, she'll read Joan D. Chittister's words about women: "…usually tolerated in life and often loved, they are seldom respected for themselves, for their opinions, for their talents, for their perspectives… Women live knowing that inside themselves is a capped well, a fount of untapped treasure, a person gone to waste."

A capped well: that's her mother, for sure. But it won't be her, will it?

paris

You crouched on the floor hugging your backpack, waiting for the clock in the square to strike five. Two more hours to go.

His steady snoring vibrated in the air.

You breathed without a sound. In the dim light, you counted the number of steps to the door. You imagined rising quietly, tiptoeing down three flights of stairs. If you planted one foot on the floor and leaned in, you could rise in one swift movement. But your pack was heavy and you could lose your balance.

You were twenty-one. Your first night in Paris, the city known as La Ville Lumière.

You and your travel companion had parted in Spain. She boarded a flight to London and you took a train to the Gare du Nord. You'd graduated from a small prairie university; it had been a year since your fiancé died by his own hand and you were trying to join your friends in their enthusiasm for the future. Your parents had moved to Ontario; you were finally on your own. You stuffed clothes in an army-green canvas backpack, a journal in the outside pocket, and flew to Europe with your friend.

It was past midnight when you arrived at the station; you stood next to a pillar checking your guidebook under the dim lights for the address of the hostel. He came up behind you.

Canadienne?

Oui. He had soft eyes, a gentle bearing. You must have looked lost. The station was crowded despite the time of night.

Je cherche l'auberge de jeunesse. Your enunciation was awkward.

He ignored the guidebook you held out, pointing at a phrase.

Mes amis sont Canadiennes. Dans une auberge près de moi.

This was a lucky coincidence.

Oui. He shrugged.

You recall feeling spent, and you might have been cold. You couldn't say now what you were wearing, what corner of the station you were in, your exact words. What you later wrote in your journal were brief phrases that bloomed into images for years afterward. You remember being embarrassed about your French.

Allons-y. It was a struggle to pick up meaning in the river of his words. He had Canadian friends staying at a hostel near his house, and he knew how to get there. That much you did understand.

The Gare du Nord mystery man handed you a Metro token, shrugged off your attempt to repay. He was thin, with a distinctive Gallic nose and a solemn bearing. Was he a student, or perhaps a writer? Several stops later, you came up from underground to a long cobblestone street dotted by lampposts and glistening with water. Your pack felt heavier. Now out of your travel fog, you felt uneasy.

Where are we? You asked him. How much farther? You don't remember his answer, only that he reassured you the Canadians were nearby. After making a couple of turns off the wider street, you reached a house that looked quintessentially Parisian: one of many in a row, peaked roof, a gable window, crumbling brick. Your worldly knowledge as a small-town Canadian was what you gleaned from textbooks, two television channels, and a newspaper. You remember a stab of panic when you saw dark windows. He unlocked the door.

Vous habitez ici?

Oui. Avec ma grand-mère.

No Canadians then. Your legs felt like wood. You tried to breathe, but your ribs shook.

Chut.

He took your backpack as you climbed the stairs. Should you turn around? Where would you go? The subway had shut down. He opened the door to a small, spartan room with only a cot, a chair, and a chest of drawers. He lived with his grandmother? More likely a landlady. The bathroom was across the hall, and when you motioned to go in, he said chut again, miming not to flush. When you returned, your pack was on the floor and he was on the bed. You remember vowing you'd make it through this night intact. You would be fine. You would be fine.

He was the only person on the planet who knew where you were.

You twisted and fought back as he tried to undo the zipper on your worn jeans. He was insistent, and although you didn't understand his words, you knew what he was saying. Soon his pleading—a duck-lipped simpering—turned to anger and hissing. He wasn't much bigger than you, but he was strong. All of this in whispers. Non, you repeated. Non.

Je crie, you said aloud. Then louder. Je crie. Votre grand-mère. Réveiller.

A shriek and his hand was instantly over your mouth. If only you could have called down all the women in the world then. Generations of grandmothers, mothers, sisters, and friends who have had to live through moments like these, women from Paris to the Middle East to Africa to Winnipeg to Northern Canada, from everywhere, afraid, angry.

Enough.

Years ago, the young woman you once knew curled up on the floor of a small dark room in the suburbs of Paris, clutching her backpack, shaking, gagging into a tissue, too wired and enraged to sleep.

Waiting for the clock to strike. To return to the Gare du Nord and start again.

You think of her now with tenderness. Like so many women, she did what she had to do.

shiksa

His hair and eyes look right, at least.

You're sitting cross-legged by your upstairs closet in Hubbards, Nova Scotia, culling memorabilia stuffed in boxes. Why, after forty-plus years of marriage, have you kept these things? Because, if you throw them away, you fear you'll lose the memory too.

The drawing was in the box of your old art supplies, and the paper still hadn't yellowed.

Ah yes, this man was the master of why the hell not? When you first met, he'd jump through the basement window of the 4th Street

SW apartment in Calgary you shared with three other women from Saskatchewan.

Quicker than the door, he'd say, and grin as Brenda and her sister Linda, in their pyjamas, gasped and folded their arms across their chests. Lynn, your freckled friend with the deep voice, laughed every time. That summer, you and Lynn had driven to Alberta in her Mustang to start your first teaching jobs in the fall. Four young teachers in a basement apartment.

It would be two years before you moved again, back to Manitoba, where you met Allan, the man you'd marry.

You don't recall how you met Ira, but you remember waking each morning in Calgary to songs such as "Good Morning, Starshine" and "Moonshadow" on repeat. You and Ira planned the day's adventures while your roommates clattered in the kitchen.

We're off to Vancouver, he said one day. Pack your stuff. You drove all night through the mountains in his friend Bobby's convertible and found yourselves the next morning in Gastown. You walked the streets, he, determined to find the friends who'd promised a bed somewhere and you, intoxicated with freedom, delighted to feel a spontaneity you'd never known growing up.

From an open window, the sounds of—Ginger Baker, maybe? On the street, buskers wore tie-dye. Beaded curtains hung above a shop door. Macramé was everywhere: flower pots, bags, necklaces. Macramé and the smell of weed.

And so when you find the sketch of him that day, you track down his number. Why not?

Ira was in British Columbia and seemed happy to hear from you. After a few pleasantries, though, he asked, So, why are you calling?

Why, indeed? You weren't looking to rekindle anything. But you've always wondered what happened to people who mattered to you. He was a carpenter, he said, had two children, was divorced, and now lived on Vancouver Island.

You recall the night he closed the door to the apartment and walked to the highway to hitchhike father west. You'd started teaching and loved it; he wanted to buy a bus and travel with you around the States. It had been a year of sheer fun, a surprise a day, but now you craved security. And you were still mourning Gord.

When you think of that young teacher walking in Gastown, though, you smile. Your long denim skirt was wrinkled from the drive, and you needed a shower. Before you left for Vancouver, you'd ripped apart the seams on an old pair of jeans and stitched in flannel from an old plaid shirt to finish a full-length skirt. A maxi. Your bottle-blond hair reached your ass; you needed no makeup. His friends called you his shiksa: forbidden flesh. You were performing flower child, a young teacher unaware how mainstream she was.

seveners

A teacher ought to be a stranger to the desire for domination, vainglory and pride.
Amma Theodora

The seveners, you called them. Little wide-eyed impressionable people whose first days in a junior high school both delighted and terrified them.

As their English teacher, you tried to match their enthusiasm. Starting at a new school in Winnipeg in the first year of your marriage, you were going to make this the best year ever. The principal was severe-looking, grumpy, and your neighbour across the hall, a thick ruddy man more than six feet tall, wandered the halls with a yardstick he slipped up girls' skirts as they reached into their lockers. The teacher down the hall often threw a book at the head of any student who spoke out of turn. Next door to you was a passionate and highly strung older woman who insisted on bringing you small gifts, along with regular advice at inopportune times.

You'd made a friend who taught English to the ninth graders, and if you could find a spot at the staff room table not taken by men playing Yahtzee, you and Sharon swapped stories. You trusted her advice, and you loved her grounded sense of proportion. Every noon hour, the principal raced in, scowled at the table, retrieved his lunch from the fridge, and disappeared.

They're cute, and they try hard, you told Sharon one day.

They want to please, she said. Wait a year or two and they'll be cynical.

Nice and *good* seemed to be the only adjectives the seveners used in their short writing assignments. The cat was good. The vacation was nice.

You had work to do.

That early fall day, you remember the sun shone through the windows on the back wall.

The rows were straight, the students were quiet, far different from the motorcycle crowd you'd taught in Calgary. No one here was in the habit of punching the person next to them or competing in the belching or snot-throwing Olympics. A few of those young men had been wise beyond their years; the others were walking accidents, but you loved their energy, their defiance, and their creativity. You met one of them years later when he and his wife came to Halifax; a smart, kind, thoughtful man with a successful career.

No terrible teens here. This grade seven class was the epitome of good behaviour. You looked at the eager faces in the front row. Two girls in particular watched your every move and often came up after class to make sure you knew they wanted to do well.

Like raw clay, they were, and they stirred in you an ancient human impulse.

Okay, you said. Here's a test. Help me think of a word, any word, that you could use instead of *good*.

Nice? Said the blond boy with glasses.

Okay. Keep thinking. If the apple in your lunch was good, what else could you say?

Delicious! Someone yelled from the back.

Yes! And what else..?

Silence. A long silence.

Here's what I'm going to do. I'm going to face the board and count to twenty while everyone comes up with another word for *good*. When I turn back around, I want to see all your hands up.

All. Each one of you.

In the front row, the girls held your gaze, wide-eyed and nodding.

C'mon. You can do it.

You have always used a mixed bag of techniques when you teach but you weren't sure if this challenge would work. Nor did you realize you'd remember that moment to this day. You counted to twenty slowly, and turned around.

Backlit from the sun, most of their faces were hard to see, but not their hands. Each of them, all thirty-six or so, had raised their hand. The room was silent with anticipation. And compliance.

You felt ice in your gut as you looked at all those expectant faces. What had you done? This was wrong. So wrong.

It's okay, you said. It's okay. Put your hands down.

when you are old and grey

Something happens to the woman's head when she does the math. Her parents were born in 1922, she was married fifty years later in 1972, and now, more than one hundred years from her parents' birth and fifteen years after their death, she has been married more than fifty years.

What?

Well, her hair is fully grey, so the passage of time makes sense. She thinks of her paternal grandmother, Eleanore, who moved from Red River to Kamsack, raised five children in a clapboard house her husband Charles built. Eleanore's status in the census ("half-breed") changed when she moved to Saskatchewan. She doted on their last child, the only boy after four girls. Years later, Elvin's sisters Kay and Lillian say their mother let him get away with anything. His whole life, her aunt Lil insisted. Spoiled rotten!

Eleanore had watched her own mother, Catherine, burn to death in a riverboat off the wharf at Warren Landing at the top of Lake Winnipeg. The tragedy made international news. Eleanore had been working with her father and brother when her mother took the steamer SS Premier north to Norway House to visit them. There was no body to bury.

Almost eighty years later on an Easter weekend in Hubbards, the woman's infant son, AJ, almost dies in a house fire. Her own mother's stillborn child was placed in the hospital furnace. Does fire follow her family?

When the woman was a newborn, her grandmother Eleanore insisted she be baptized in a Catholic church or she would disown her parents, Elvin and Grace. She didn't want the baby to go to hell, at least that's how Grace tells it. Grace cursed the Catholic religion for decades.

How anyone can be certain heaven awaits a baby, or anyone for that matter?

The woman can dip into the shallows of the years, but she'll never recall the feeling of holy water on her skull: memory, like faith, goes only so far.

That skull has a shock of long grey hair now, like Eleanore's.

Whether or not heaven awaits, years leap ahead.

orbits

soft sand

The cool sea air and the glassy water of the cove tell her the heat has broken.

Finally.

She fills a thermos with coffee and drives to the beach. Only two cars are in the lot. A couple with a dog is at the end of the beach by the cliff so she turns in the other direction to make her way across the rocks to the sand, relieved she brought a walking stick. She stops to watch the water, unable to find words to describe it. Hasn't every cliché in the world been used? Diamonds. Sparkling sequins. Gah.

It's said writers live life twice, or perhaps three times: as a participant, an observer, then as the one who documents the event. Years as an ethnographer trained the woman in the art and science of participant observation. Now, she just thinks of it as being a writer.

The tide is going out and the sand is soft, making walking difficult, so she takes her time. She reaches the large rock at the end of the beach and sits for a moment, taking in blue veils of sky, the swish of water. She closes her eyes, breathes the air, and realizes she can't hear any birds. In previous years, aside from gulls, she'd spot starlings and grackles, crows, occasionally an eagle. She'd follow their shadows above the water and along the sand. Rachel Carson was right.

As she heads back to the car, a woman in a long blue shirt smiles and waves. Isn't this amazing, the woman asks, and sweeps her arm toward the water.

Yes. She waves back. Exquisite.

Because it is. It always is.

Writing about the past, she thinks, is like digging in soft sand. You can go on forever. The more she remembers, the more she can remember: Strega Nona's pasta pot of story. Images trigger grief, regret, and fear; trauma and suffering reach out from the past with their lessons, as do joy and tenderness. Memories churn daily now, surprise her: the colour wheel she laboured over in art class, the pneumatic tube machines that sucked her customers' payments up to the top floor of Birks to be returned with change. Climbing with Sharon to the tea house at Lake Louise, her first-born's feet dangling from the carrier. Decades later, in her Nova Scotia kitchen, her struggling newborn upstairs, scolding relatives who were filling the house with cigarette smoke.

She's no Jungian, but she can't help wonder what's in the shadows.

As the poet Gwendolyn MacEwen wrote, there is "something down there," and she wants it told.

the ocean beside me

When September arrives, I think of the beach as ours again. Those of us who show up in all seasons to appreciate what it offers, I mean. Right now, someone remembers that summer day they swam, threw a Frisbee, ate sandy snacks until their bodies shivered in the late afternoon sun and they carried wet towels and folding chairs back to the car. The beach in peak summer is a singular experience in Canada, a seashell of a memory to hold through the winter. Canadians, after all, are known to don shorts and loud shirts in a snowstorm to board a plane for Cuba.

I swim only when I need to cool off, but I'm drawn to the beach any time—in storms, at dusk, at low and high tide. Once, as I walked in pouring rain, the wind was so strong it held up my body when I let go. Another time, my husband and I walked the shore using only the moon on the incoming waves to guide us.

Today, the water hisses and shushes, waves are uncharacteristically shallow, and the sea moves like sleep-breath.

Today is our wedding anniversary.

How did this happen? I was the junior high art and French teacher, both of us new to the Fort Garry school, both of us quick with a retort. He thought I was a hippy; I thought he was a smartass. He stayed late the cold March night I hosted a staff party in my apartment off Pembina. When everyone left, I made him a grilled cheese sandwich and we listened to Neil Young's latest release, "Heart of Gold." We were engaged within weeks, married in six months.

The dog bolts from my lap toward the boardwalk. The air hangs like gauze; I can sense the sun's warmth behind the mist. Along the beach, figures appear as dark daubs in an Impressionist study. The moods of this long beach differ daily. Today brings a softness, a haze that quiets the land, but out on the water, the sun's rays light up the sea like pocked silver. Without a view of the hills at the end of the beach, I feel insulated.

Our wedding reception was at the Fort Garry Hotel. I wore a floppy hat; the bridesmaids wore autumn colours. Afterwards, we were so caught up in it all we forgot to say goodbye to his parents, a major faux pas. We drove around Winnipeg for an hour, had a nip and chips at the Salisbury, then returned to the hotel, guests now gone, and crashed in our room, exhausted from excitement and guilt.

I am three times the age I was when I met Allan. The thought gives me vertigo. Who would I have been if I hadn't met him? I might have had other lovers and other children; my sons would not exist. What forces in our separate personalities continue to shape us, willingly or by resistance? What character traits grew or were muted as we learned to live together? I'll never know who I wasn't. A marriage is a threesome. Two people and—as my friend Jane Silcott has described it—"the space between." You, me, and we, in other words.

He is fair, funny, and kind. He's thoughtful with loved ones. He enjoys running errands more than I do. He brings me coffee and tea, talks easily with anyone, the extrovert to my introvert. A voracious reader, talented photographer. A guy's guy. An excellent ball player before his knees betrayed him. At times it's been rough. But we're lucky; we know our luck wears overalls.

Fall quiets the birds, slows the grass, turns bushes by the boardwalk shades of red and brown. Some days the beach is scoured so deeply the ribs of an old wharf—or perhaps a ship's hull?—appear as large dark teeth along the sand, grooved by decades of waves and silica. Other days rocks hurled up on shore make for unsure footing. One day I'll walk a pristine shore and see only a glossy pebble or two; the next, piles of kelp and seaweed are strewn everywhere. If I set up a time-release camera, I could watch the change.

What would a camera show of the changes, the moods and shapes, of a fifty-year marriage?

The sea, the land, the air, always moving moving moving. Anyone who spends time near the ocean knows a restlessness that both quiets and soothes. The steadfastness of a moving, breathing phenomenon.

When we were still unfamiliar to each other and to ourselves, my husband and I addressed cream-coloured wedding invitations that included the phrase "always changing, forever constant." I wasn't pre-scient and I certainly had not heard of Heraclitus at that age. Until we moved to the East Coast, I hadn't lived with the gravitational pull of the moon. I hadn't experienced the rhythm of the tides.

But here we are: the two of us, an ocean.

drive south

Although he loved cars, highway travel flummoxed my father. Road trips in my childhood always ended in wrong turns and bad deci-sions; he'd infuriate my mother, then drive in icy silence. Driving around town to see holiday lights killed the seasonal mood. Our trip to Expo 67 in Montreal was a comedic sketch involving map-folding, -tossing, and -ripping; long stops idling at the bottom of exit ramps; and—our worst fear—the need to turn the trailer around, a laborious exercise involving steering in the opposite direction, craning to read large mirrors, and trying to decipher my mother's peevish and abrupt hand motions. She shrieked "stop!" a lot.

When my parents decided to visit Allan and me in graduate school in Minnesota, I was filled with dread. We were renting the main floor of a house north of downtown, a huge space with easy access to the campus and the main highway. The bar across the street was a favourite haunt on weekend nights. Cheap and delicious Middle Eastern food, a rarity for us, and regulars who became friends. Our own Cheers years before the sitcom aired.

Uh-oh, I say to Allan. It's already dark. They left Winnipeg at seven this morning.

They'll be fine. They probably made a lot of stops.

Allan has no idea; how could he? I am not worried about an acci-dent, but the rage that's going to spill into our living room.

Finally, the phone. Springsteen is on the record player singing about broken heroes and I turn it down.

What is wrong with these goddamned Yanks? my father yells over the sound of traffic behind him. Where the hell is I-94?

You're probably on it, Dad. I think: to get to Minneapolis, you drive south from Winnipeg, then turn left. Jesus.

Instead, I say I-94 runs into the 52. We're just off that. Describe to me where you are and we'll find you.

I'm not an idiot. His voice is muffled. He hisses: Grace, stop talk-ing. Christ.

Ten years later, when my parents visited us in Nova Scotia, Dad rented a car to travel around the province. After a week of their serial fights on the road, Mom landed in the hospital with what doctors called a "cardiac event." I felt helpless. Dad spent the remainder of his time cursing bumpkin drivers, bad signage, insufficient Halifax parking, and bad road conditions.

My father never returned to Nova Scotia, but continued to love driving, swearing the whole time, until illness caused him to quit. He died before cars came with navigation and backup assistance. He would have loved those. I once heard him say that every car has a blind spot.

Sometimes it's the driver.

frail things

Friendships, even the best of them,
are frail things. One drifts apart.

Virginia Woolf

We had met in a course about the Bloomsbury group. K, fifteen years older than us, was a straight talker, practical, and was returning to school now that her children were grown. D was a poet. Dennis, whom we called Dents, was the resident scholar of Victorian literature and a quick wit whose off-hand comments could double us over. Two years of parties and word games and hijinks and dances under disco balls at Sutton's downtown. Allan and I were childless then, and so we studied hard and played hard. It was the freest time of our lives.

A couple of years after Allan and I were married, I followed him to graduate school in Minneapolis, because why not, and found myself addicted to learning. My mind caught fire.

Dents, tall and gangly with a huge grin and extravagant gestures, was never without a cigarette or a gay partner. He often spent Sundays at our apartment where we played music, cobbled together brunch, and argued about topics such as the Oxford comma and British spelling. K ignored the speed limit in her Volvo, dazzled as a host, and often invited groups to her large and comfortable suburban home to play murder in the dark. Twentysomethings hiding in closets and behind couches: the screams, the hilarity, the wordplay. Bizarre and goofy, I think now. Such luxury to be so oblivious.

We called ourselves Doonsbury and quoted Virginia Woolf to one another. I teased Dents about being Lytton Strachey. He had a biting wit and shared my love of puns. We were entirely full of ourselves.

That was then, as they say.

K developed dementia and died early in her seventies. The others became writers and doctors with talented children. Dents became a much-loved professor of literature in the South. And, despite several relationships, he was recently living on his own. He came to visit us once in our house overlooking Hubbards Cove, but he was used to big-city life and its amenities and I didn't expect to see him again. I read online of his efforts to establish a library program for incarcerated people.

A few years ago, the internet brought Dennis and me together again and I joined an online book club he'd started. The wordplay and literary discussions were reminiscent of our old days, with the emphasis on dead white British novelists, which didn't interest me much anymore. The group talked about cheeses they imported from Europe, pop culture phenomena, and recent purchases. Dents was seeing a therapist—I don't recall his ever not seeing one—and was frequently upset about things, but he kept the details private.

In 2020, the pandemic hit. Shortly after, Nova Scotia suffered the worst tragedy in recent memory, the horrific murders of twenty-two people. It devastated families and communities, and left the province reeling. I stayed offline for several days and when I returned to the discussion group, I found the chatter frivolous and grating, privileged. Was Dennis always like this? Was I? I mentioned the tragedies in Nova Scotia, which by this time was international news, and only one person in the group had heard of them.

There was no response from Dennis. Then: tripwire. He lashed out about the lack of appreciation for his efforts on behalf of the group. What had I said? I wrote Dennis privately, thanking him for his ongoing friendship, and told him I was leaving the group. He responded with generosity and love, asked me to stay, said he'd been so tired lately he was prone to hissy fits.

I was hurt, but Dennis was beloved and I'd always felt we could pick up where we left off.

About a year later, Dennis's named popped up on social media. He was dead. He'd had late-stage lung cancer and called 911 after a bad reaction to chemo, but died before the paramedics arrived. I was gutted.

Reverend John Watson, writing in nineteenth-century Scotland as Ian Maclaren, wrote, "Be pitiful, for every man is fighting a hard battle," a phrase I always thought was Plato's. Dents's death was painful proof.

Like most, I've been on the receiving end of unkind comments and rejection, and they've buckled me. Usually, I retreat, say nothing. But we can lose loved ones in a trice; any conversation could be the last.

The other day, culling old recipes I keep in a tin box, I found a stained index card in Dents's careful script: *Life is Vapid and Meaningless Omelet.* I smiled. I'd added *te* in pencil to the end of the word.

she wrote

She returned to Calgary, this time with her husband, and when she wasn't teaching, she sat in the tiny office of the Alexandra Centre with her friends Edna and Joan, poring over submissions for dANDelion magazine or she picked up books from the Calgary Herald offices to review them. She learned quickly that a word limit is the best editor and continued to publish commentary or features in magazines, including author profiles. Later, when she looked back at those days, she realized she had kept herself on the periphery of writers and writing, writing-adjacent if you will, but not producing her own work.

The year before, she'd taken a course in Minnesota for her master's degree, and the instructor, Miss Fergus, had encouraged her. Just write, she had said; you're good at this. She drew on memory, hammered out essays using carbon paper and Wite-Out, and discovered a fluency with words on paper she'd never had when she spoke. She excelled in the course, but once she completed her degree and returned to Canada, she put the folder of essays at the bottom of a drawer. Who would want an essay? And where would she begin to publish one?

She knew so little. She relished the chance to read journal submissions. The one time she attempted to write a short story, she became stuck: what would her character do next, and why? Believing at the time fiction must be entirely made up, she was devoid of inspiration. Like many, she confused the fictional with the false, believing imagination to be an exercise in creating whole new unfamiliar worlds. She certainly wasn't about to use her own life in fiction. Later she realized the obvious: fiction writers draw on what they know and can imagine, as well as on research about what they learn. How ironic. She'd thought putting herself in fiction would reveal too much, yet she wrote personal essays that dug deep into her and others' lives.

She wanted to read and to write "true" stories. They felt vital and they fed her curiosity about people. But Canadian writing was in its adolescence; no one she knew talked about life writing, and aside from the occasional celebrity memoir or biography on the newsstand, she found few examples of writing that weren't either fiction or poetry. She also didn't know where to look. She loved writing, this she knew, but was only beginning to see its power.

waxing

Sap flows when the moon is waxing. Moisture is pulled up. Plant above-ground vegetables at this time, the almanac says: beans, peppers, tomatoes. Leafy greens. Garden by the moon.

When I moved to Calgary for the second time, I was married. We both immersed ourselves in teaching, our first son was born, we hiked and skied in the mountains, ate around friends' tables every weekend or they ate around ours. Months rolled into years, a flip-book of photographs.

A birthday party, fifties' theme, pigs in blankets and pinwheel sandwiches, friends in beehives and crinolines lip-synching "My Guy." A hike to Athabasca Falls near Jasper. Visits with Vietnamese refugees known as "boat people" as they settled into new lives in the city, their young son Kenny the age of ours. Graduate student gatherings and pots of chili, evenings throwing clay into pots, the first babysitter to watch our son. Dancing. So much dancing. Board books and lettered wooden blocks. My wedding band, gone from the bedroom when I returned one night. Rinsing cloth diapers into smelly pails. Books and classes and rock concerts, a city swollen with the promise of oil, the odour of avarice. Start-ups and BMWs on every downtown street. A first word. A first step. Visits into the foothills, campfires and tents, and busy children. Mount St. Helens erupts, as does the Middle East. Booster seats, high chairs, handmade Hallowe'en costumes. Hot Wheels. A one-kilometre jog along John Laurie Boulevard, then two. *9 to 5* opens in theatres. Trays of cookies and yards of wrapping paper, raucous parties with sticky plastic cups and slab cakes with blue icing. *The Muppet Show.* Maurice Sendak. Holiday to-do lists. Mac and cheese. "Another Brick in the Wall." New Balance and a headband. Five kilometres, then ten. One small rented apartment, then another, a duplex, then a first home. A mortgage. "Slow Hand." Wakened the morning before my first 10K by Vangelis on the stereo, full blast, my husband grinning: "Ready?" Auntie Martha, Jasmine, confident women who care for children. "The Tide Is High." Hand-knit sweaters in Winnipeg parcels. *Enjoy it. It goes so fast.* A tricycle to the park two blocks away. First trip to emergency. Second trip. A cut, badly stitched. Years later, the doctor's ex-wife: "He had no dexterity." Prairie road trip: the Christmas Day two-step across Winnipeg streets to gift-bulging trees. Aching hearts, hard smiles, bitten tongues. *Enjoy it: it goes so fast.* First daffodils by our front step. Long talks with women friends. One foot in the dark, one stray Lego block, seven thousand nerve endings. Annie Lennox, her sweet dreams.

It's spring, a new moon. Once more and once more. A first garden. So much seeding, tending. Watering. Mountains in the window. Prairies in the distance. The East Coast calling.

Harvest beyond.

trailways

The trip back to my student quarters in Durham, New Hampshire, took about ninety minutes, but that night, time flew. I was studying ethnography at Cambridge, courses not available in my program at the time, and the first class left me electric with excitement. This was research?

I'd rushed to the second-hand bookstore for one of the required texts and started it under the dim lights on the bus. *Street Corner Society* read like a novel. Before I knew it, the driver was calling out to me. We'd arrived in Durham; the bus had already emptied.

When Allan and I returned from Minnesota and settled in Calgary, I taught English for a few years at what was known then as Mount Royal College. Like other sessionals, all women, we applied for every full-time teaching position that opened up. And, like other sessionals, all women, we watched as appointments went to men with doctorates. Clearly, there was no future there for me.

A colleague and I decided to leave the college and teach writing in Calgary's oil industry and in local government. For two or three years we found steady and sometimes lucrative work pitching the elements of report writing, the value of a good executive summary, the benefits of the active voice. Yet, our experience at Mount Royal College seemed to repeat itself in the oil industry; larger, more secure contracts were awarded to male competitors, many with what I called drive-thru doctorates.

After five years in Calgary, Allan was invited to teach a summer course at a university in Halifax. That summer, we travelled around Nova Scotia with our first-born son, finding beautiful landscapes and friendly people around every turn. And there were turns; so used to driving straight roads on prairie grids, we'd be astonished when a hundred kilometres took two hours instead of one; more than thirteen thousand kilometres of coastline carved by coves and bays and inlets.

This is a place to live and raise a family, we said. People are down-to-earth here, we said. Let's move here as soon as we can. And we did.

About the time we moved from Calgary to Nova Scotia, I realized my mind was starving for stimulation, for a challenge. I was tired of losing contracts to men with doctorates, eager to learn more about writing. During a chance visit from a friend, I learned her university was starting an innovative doctoral program in New Hampshire. But our son was only five, about to start school in Nova Scotia; could we manage it all? Together, Allan and I decided we could. I applied and was accepted.

And so back to the States I went, this time to the East Coast. Here I could study linguistics, sociolinguistics, creative writing, and the psychology of reading all at once. I'd studied experimental research in Minnesota, but for this degree, I wanted a different approach to study the process of writing. I'd found the language of experimental research off-putting—isolated variables, validity threats, bias, mortality. The enterprise seemed to follow Galileo's credo: measure what is measurable and make measurable what is not.

Some of the faculty in the new program were using ethnographic methods: interviewing, documenting behaviour in situ and in great detail. Participant observation. But no ethnography course was available there. I signed up for one at Harvard, a bus trip away.

That night, as I walked from the bus stop back to my room, eager to finish the book, I was charged with excitement about learning. My backpack held other ethnographies, enough to keep me busy until next week's class. They read more like the works of Joan Didion and Michael Herr. I couldn't wait to start.

William Foote Whyte's *Street Corner Society* was a go-to text in sociology courses for some time. Later, critics voiced legitimate concerns the work simplified a complex society. The world of sociology was soon shaken by needed correctives in how we represent class, race, and gender. People began to ask the question: who's telling whose stories?

But the day I discovered research as story, as a way to tell stories of real people living ordinary lives, the world opened up. My insatiable curiosity about people and our behaviour found a home.

no cry

Forty-two weeks. At the last checkup, the doctor measured my belly and muttered something about a small baby. She was new to the clinic, young, but seemed to know what she was doing. At thirty-nine, I was a woman of "advanced maternal age" and worried daily about my baby's health. You'll be fine, she said, and I drove the hour back to our house overlooking Hubbards Cove. But I'm at forty-two weeks, I thought. That night I felt movement briefly, but it stopped. Allan was out of the province and I debated the wisdom of driving back into the city on dark, snow-slick roads. Who'd watch our seven-year-old?

Days later, I am in the OR. The atmosphere feels charged, urgent: my doctor's averted eyes, the intent focus of the anaesthesiologist.

I am on the surgical table with a barrier—a sheet?—at chest level. Swishing movements, faces in masks, instruments clinking. My husband's breath at my shoulder. I am disembodied, a slab of meat laid out on a table waiting for the knife.

Quiet. Rustling fabric. No one speaks. I am waiting for a cry.

There is no cry.

AJ is at my breast, days old. His wrinkled skin, large watchful eyes. Old eyes, we said. A five-pound sage whose emaciated appearance took people's breath away. My heart cramped in anguish: will he be okay?

When AJ was a few months old, the pediatrician told me AJ may never learn to read or write. I stared at my wide-eyed baby who was staring at the doctor's stethoscope. The doctor added, He may need to be institutionalized.

Institutionalized.

I'd been reading about Erik and Joan Erikson's newborn son, Neil, whom they sent to an institution, telling their other children he'd died. Instead, he lived another twenty-two years and the Eriksons, celebrated psychologists of the day, didn't return from Europe for his funeral. Neil was born in 1944, when it was common practice in North America to send disabled children to mental institutions. In the 1800s, communities "warned out" disabled people, sending them away to other towns. In some cases, disabled people were sold to those who'd provide cheap care and maintenance. Bearing such a child was a source of shame; what is wrong with you that you could produce such a defected creature?

Even now, well into the twenty-first century, stigma and an-
tipathy persist. I will toss aside a book or turn off a program if the
R-word is used. No exceptions.

I wish I could find that doctor now. I want to tell him within a
few years, we'd be in awe of AJ's remarkable memory, the internal
GPS that amazed us as drivers, his ability to read faces and emotions
in a room. I'd tell him the man AJ has become is kind, thoughtful,
witty, and caring, despite it all. Or perhaps because.

But all I could do then was look at the doctor, his dangling stethoscope, the ease with which he could utter the word *institutionalized*,
and turn away.

threshold

When our first son was born, my mother called long-distance to the
Grace Hospital in Calgary. As the doctor debated whether to use for-
ceps, a nurse came into the delivery room with a portable phone.

I just had a sense, Mom said.

I pushed. Hard. He was born strong and robust. For months, he
thrived on my breast milk, but soon squirmed out of my arms at
every turn, as though my love was radioactive. When he could walk,
he pushed a chair to the door, unlocked it, and ran naked down the
street wearing only a Superman cape. The milkman brought him
back every time. We revelled in his curiosity, let him crawl under
stalls, walk on raised walls, put things in his mouth. He talked constantly. Once he bit me, hard, and on impulse, I bit him back. We
never spanked him. He resisted time outs; if he was going to his room,
it was going to be on his terms.

In high school, he grew his hair to his shoulders, gained thirty pounds, joined the drama club, and ate only pizza. The basement room was a graveyard for forks and plates. He and a friend filmed their own version of *Pulp Fiction* and wrote comedy sketches. His imaginative drawings were strewn on the floor. He grew silent. Chores took weeks. He hit golf balls into the yard of the self-righteous neighbour. We urged him to stop (secretly, I was amused).

He and his father bared teeth like dogs. Once he slammed the basement door so hard the hinges broke. One day, in a rare moment of talkativeness, he asked: If you wanted to dry something slowly, like herbs, how would you do it?

Lay it out on a cookie sheet and put it on low heat, I said, before the penny dropped. I used to think my parents wouldn't notice the watered-down Scotch. The next day I told him to burn it all in the wood stove, a free high wafting in the air for the neighbours.

You have to go, we finally said. The kitchen was a war zone; his younger brother's intellectual disability meant he needed attention, a stable climate. I became ill. I devoted my energy into AJ and my teaching, kept mum with shame. I winced reading friends' holiday letters about their children's sports trophies and piano recitals. What would I write? What kind of mother was I, anyway?

But his story is not mine to tell. I can only tell my own.

If you don't leave, I will, I said. I'll take AJ and you and your dad can battle it out.

You grew up in the sixties, he said. You smoked weed, and you both drink. You have no moral authority.

What had we done? Where was the spark plug we once knew? He moved into the city, enrolled in an arts degree, lived in a cramped house by the bridge I feared was a hotbox. He dropped out of school, found low-paying jobs, was always short of money.

My mother visited us in Nova Scotia during this time. You're my first grandchild and I'm proud of you. I love you, she said to him. But you have to straighten up and fly right.

He looked confused—an old Nat King Cole lyric was not on his radar.

One day, he packed up, leaving the basement room empty. We swam in grief and worry.

When he boarded a train west, I followed his journey in my mind. Now he was checking his bag—tickets, passport, gum for his woolly mouth. Now he was waking to prairie light, now the train rocked him toward the mountains. I waited in our home overlooking the cove, where the greying deck was cracked from skateboard crashes. Where the forsythia bloomed on the grave he'd dug for our first dog, Buttons.

Fearing a midnight phone call, a stranger speaking of him in the past tense.

Months went by. A year. We heard he was in Canmore, moving from one McJob to another. In one of the dozen places he lived, he paid rent to sleep in a broom closet with a folding door.

One December, we bought him a ticket home. He was rail thin and distracted. He spent time emailing a girl from Canmore's rave scene and left words on the open screen about his family's boring life, our too-earnest attempts to talk. How he loathed us.

When he returned to the Maritimes, he moved to the cabin for a few months, forgot to pay rent or we kept forgetting to ask. I found Gram's bone-handled knives, blackened, and called the police, thinking it was a break-in. I insisted on family counselling, and Allan opened up about struggles with his father and I with my mother. Our son went to one session.

We'll never know what we should or shouldn't have done. Did we hover too much? Not enough? Is my anguish self-indulgent? Children are their own beings, after all.

A friend whose son struggled with addiction says our children will never understand or believe how profoundly their behaviour affects others, not while they're in the claws of their demons.

We've since learned how many stories echo ours. We were among many parents whose hearts were breaking, but we didn't have the courage to talk. Recently, a writer posted about her son's lethal over-dose, and my gut churned. My worst fear, realized.

What our son learned in those years we'll never know, but he's transformed into an empathetic, caring person, married, with a steady job and a host of friends.

Those years were a turning point, however; I learned fear and shame grow silence.

I learned nothing is stronger than the love for your child.

I learned we think we are alone, but we're not.

real women drive stick

My father loved cars—the old Studebaker, the new green Mercury he bought when I was ten or so. I remember Saturdays outside 1131 Main Street in Saskatoon; he'd wash down the whitewall tires, take a chamois to the grille and bumpers while I poked 2,4-D into the lawn with a dispenser and piled up the dead dandelions in the alley behind the garden. The sickly smell of the herbicide; the tangy lemon of the car wax; the heat of early summer sun.

When I was fifteen, my father took me south of the city to practice steering and gear-shifting on flat roads, then across to Saskatoon's north side to find a decent hill. Parallel parking was easy, but Dad cursed while I wrestled with the clutch as cars whizzed by close enough to whack off the rear-view mirror. It was important to him I master this. Perhaps my mother was right—he wished I'd been born male. Not once in my childhood did my father warn me about climbing trees or sheds, or whittling with a knife. When I asked for a cap gun and a holster at six, he didn't bat an eye. When I reached driving age, he seemed pleased his daughter might do him proud, after all: drive stick like the best of them, and finish high school early. Later, his encouragement landed me in flight school at the local airport. I took the test, but without the money to log hours in the air, I never earned a pilot's licence. I have, however, always loved driving old trucks and shifting gears.

Why, I'm not sure. It could be my love of small towns and rural life or my comfort with my working-class roots. Perhaps I think I'm in a country music song. Or, maybe it's because a basic used truck is functional, serviceable without the flash, power, or price tag of the monsters I see in ads. Maybe my rusty used truck is me, whether or not I want to admit it.

After I'd left home at seventeen, my Dad had a late-sixties Dodge with a push-button start, perhaps a Buick or two. His Chrysler 300 with a 383-cubic-inch engine pulled a trailer across Canada to Expo 67. He always wanted newer and bigger, anything that seemed like an upgrade. I didn't share his love of gas-guzzlers or big fins and grilles.

The eighties Chrysler lasted a surprising fifteen years, all through the lengthy divorce proceedings with my mother. The thing was a boat, low-riding and wide, an insipid taupe marketed as gold. After Dad had disappeared for years with his new girlfriend, my brother spotted him on a Winnipeg street. My sister then used her research skills as a banker to track down his whereabouts.

One winter, visiting Allan's parents in Winnipeg, I decide to call my father. He'd yet to see or even acknowledge his three-year-old grandchild, AJ; did he want to meet for coffee? I didn't have a car but I could meet him somewhere.

How did you find me? he whispers into the receiver. I'll pick you up in an hour. We'll go to a Tim's. He is furtive: the call lasts only a few seconds.

When I see the old Chrysler drive up, a knot forms in my stomach. In later years, he'll claim my mother's demand for $150 in monthly spousal support was the reason he'd had to drive an old car.

We are ready at the door. AJ, bundled in his red parka, bounces down the icy sidewalk and runs toward him. Grandpa!

I stand at the bottom of the steps, watching.

My father emerges from the car slowly, looks directly over AJ to me.

Well, you got fat, I see.

believing

Miss Fergus, the English instructor whose essay course gave her assurance she could write, died in 2007, the same year her parents died. The woman wishes she'd tracked down Miss Fergus after she left Minnesota to thank her. As a teacher herself, she's deeply moved when former students contact her, yet back then she was off into her own life, oblivious to what a note of appreciation might have meant. Patricia Fergus, like most teachers the woman admires, played the believing game. She treated writers with respect and took their work seriously.

Everyone has a story about bringing home 90 percent on a test and being asked where the other ten points went. So much of the woman's education was marked by what writing teacher Peter Elbow called the "doubting game." It's based on the assumption we can achieve perfection, and as a result, learning becomes an error hunt. While critique is often necessary in learning—and usually welcomed by seasoned writers —novice writers need someone who sees past their flaws to the potential beneath. Every teacher who helped her son AJ succeed in school believed that he could.

Simplified, it's the glass half-full, half-empty notion. Sceptics often deride it; they think it means "anything goes; everyone gets a medal." But it's not about unwarranted praise. And it's not a game, she thinks. More a philosophy.

In the scholarly life, she learned to doubt. Put an idea up on the wall and brace yourself for the fault-finders and the yabbuts who relish playing gotcha. Plain old academic one-upmanship. Being open, flexible, supportive, cooperative, seeing strengths is often considered wishy-washy, soft, flakey. To critique, to doubt, to pick holes in an argument shows rigour; we need standards after all or the world will fall apart.

The world won't. But there's a good chance someone's spirit will suffer.

When the woman works with adult writers who fear approaching the page, she finds most have a history of essays returned bleeding in red ink. Their work has been made an example of what not to do.

She doesn't golf—she likes the hitting but not the counting—but *she recalls a former boyfriend trying to coach her. By the time he'd corrected the position of her feet, the angle of her arms, the flex in her knees, she couldn't hit the ball for love nor money. He never suggested she look at the point in the distance she should be aiming for.*

Confidence begets confidence, in the same way writing begets writing.

Dorothea Brande, Natalie Goldberg, Anne Lamott, and many others popularized freewriting, the act of writing to a prompt or as stream-of-consciousness without censoring ourselves, stopping to edit, correct, or "compose" our words. The Canadian writer W. O. Mitchell often used what he called "freefall" when he mentored writers in the early days of The Banff School. One version of freefall, which the woman has adapted with other writers, involves freewriting a draft, noting parts in the draft that have some "heat" or resonance, lifting out those parts, and freewriting on those alone. The process can continue indefinitely, the purpose being to write to the heart of what we're thinking. It's akin to psychologist Eugene Gendlin's notion of focusing, going deeper and deeper to explore an emotion or an event to find its core element. When Patricia Fergus encouraged the woman to write and see what happens, she was telling a novice writer she believed her writing had possibilities, she took her seriously, which, in turn, helped her not only to believe in herself, but to take risks with the work she otherwise wouldn't have.

However, she knows she's been lucky. She presented as white, cisgender, and school-smart with few negative stereotypes trailing her. How much more difficult is it for educators to believe in someone for whom society holds negative stereotypes? Or for that person to believe in themselves? Claude Steele's work shows how pervasive stereotype threat is, how it's internalized. Skin colour, sexual orientation or gender expression, religious affiliation, social class, and more: believing is potent. It's the light we see in one another.

traffic

When we downsized to a house in an older neighbourhood last year, I finally threw out the neon orange traffic cone. It was an early tactic to steal writing time.

Even now, if I leave my room to refill my coffee, my husband might not always read the distance in my eyes. A question about eggs or the power bill can break the spell.

When my brain switches to the household management channel, it can take an hour to be immersed again in the writing. Decades ago, researcher Mihaly Csikszentmihalyi described the meditative, engaged state of immersion as the "flow state." Flow state grounds and soothes me; it opens time and lifts me from the quotidian world. Several days away from that immersive state and I am peevish and sour. In my early years, drawing and painting took me there; now it's writing.

When our son AJ was little, I bought a neon plastic traffic cone at a dollar store. At a time when being Mom made me the family's main throughway, I was desperate for focused writing time. When you see the orange cone in front of the door, I said to my family, that means I'm busy writing. Please do not interrupt me unless your hair is on fire or you've cut off your arm.

I faced a tableau of shifty eyes and blank faces. Everyone nodded slightly.

AJ opened his mouth to speak.

I mean it, I said.

The following afternoon, after a quiet hour or so, it seemed the cone trick might be working. But when I lifted my fingers from the keyboard, I heard breathing on the other side of the door.

Then, a gentle tap. I ignored it and returned to the poem I was struggling with.

Another tap, this time more insistent.

The door opened a crack. Um, Mom?

I stared at him.

See? Hair not on fire. AJ pointed to his blond mop and smiled. I sighed, ate my lips, and looked into those steady eyes. Silence hummed between us. I didn't dare speak for fear of losing the words I'd been about to type.

And my arm is good.

I could feel the vapour trail of my idea dissipate in the ether.

What is it? I finally said. His face fell; he could read the frustration in mine. I smiled. I wanted to ruffle his soft hair then, but I also wanted peace and quiet.

Um, can I— His speech was often halting. Finding words took time.

Can I have the last Fruit Roll-Up?

The cursor blinked, waiting.

handicap

AJ was so frustrated trying to make himself understood, he'd often crawl under his desk. School in our small community was torture for us all.

One winter, after a day on the ski hill, I asked AJ about his friends at school.

I can't even say it.

What?

You know. *School.*

The word came out as a watery slush in the back of his throat. To this day, when I hear someone say *dishtracted* or *shtreet*, I wince.

They laugh at me, he said.

I stirred milk on the stove and added cocoa. And so it begins, I thought.

Okay. I set down the cup of cocoa. Have a sip. Let's do this.

I opened my mouth as wide as I could.

Try this, I said.

Front of mouth. Teeth. Ssss. Ssss. Then back in your throat. Sk. Sk. Sky. Sky. Skoo. Skoo. School. School. Then Ssss. Ssss. St. St. Story.

That night, he fell asleep practising this new-found skill, eager for Monday morning. I lay awake wondering why I hadn't done that sooner. Was I in denial, thinking he'd learn by osmosis? Now in grade one, his speech was behind according to school norms. And he was smart enough to realize it.

"Handicapped" is now an outdated and offensive term for people with mental, physical, and other disabilities. We have come a long way from the R-word, "crippled," and "feeble-minded." "Special needs" is used so often it has become somewhat of a joke, a phrase abled people use to mock others. We're encouraged to use "person-first" terms: *a person with* special needs, *a person with* a disability, yet some prefer to refer to themselves as disabled: a disabled writer, a disabled activist. Activist Dorothy Ellen Palmer describes herself as "lame" and argues the problem isn't the disabled person, it's ableism and inaccessibility.

AJ has a language delay. When he was born, he was labelled IUGR, an acronym for intrauterine growth restriction, a condition that hampers the growth of a fetus. In those days, the R-word used wasn't "restriction"—which perhaps indicates a kind of progress.

I had eaten well, hadn't smoked or used alcohol, yet my placenta failed to give my son enough oxygen.

My husband and I had sailed through school. We devoured books. Our graduate work was all about linguistics and the psychology of reading and writing. But by the age most children begin to speak, AJ had learned only a few words. We read to him regularly, played tapes of stories at bedtime, and filled his brain daily with narrative. When he began school in our rural community, we worried. Overworked teachers had little time or patience for a child who was different.

At work I had conversations with graduate students about language theories; at home I became the student. Reading and writing made AJ so anxious he'd weep to escape to a video game. I had to park my hifalutin ideas about literacy in the abstract and learn to pay closer attention to my son.

Who had the handicap here? As AJ grew, he taught me to assume nothing, to tread lightly, to listen. To wait. What I learned from him soon spilled into my work with writers whose insecurities often torpedo their confidence and skill. But where does their fear come from? A judgmental parent or teacher? Society?

We'll never know the "what" of AJ's condition; as parents, however, we've had to learn to read him as well as he reads us. The French philosopher Simone Weil claimed, "attention is the rarest and purest form of generosity." It is also, I claim, an act of love.

With Allan's encouragement, I began to carve out an hour or two to write during school hours or late at night. I marvelled when I read about Lucille Clifton, a mother of six, who kept lines of poetry in her head until she had a moment at night to jot them down. I traded sleep for poetry, gathered enough work for a manuscript, and applied to a five-week writing residency in Alberta. When Don McKay, the mentor, called to tell me I'd been accepted, I broke into tears. The call broke a dam, touched a raw need I hadn't realized was so deep.

I saved money to travel to places to write: a retreat in a prairie abbey, a New Brunswick nunnery, a borrowed cottage, a hostel near Inch Beach in Ireland. I accepted writer-and scholar-in-residence positions in Canada, Australia, and New Zealand both to write and to teach writing. Allan urged me to make time to write. As AJ grew, so did I.

When AJ was about ten, we applied for grants to send him to a school dedicated to supporting disabled students, and in the meantime we asked for changes in his local school to benefit not only AJ, but all local learning-disabled children.

After years of family read-aloud nights of entire fantasy series, video games, and later, anime series and a smartphone, AJ learned to read adequately. By then, schools were adapting to learning differences. With adjustments to the curriculum, AJ finished a community college diploma in baking when he was twenty-four. He's taken countless work-preparation courses since then.

Now in a place of his own, he has support workers and his parents to help him meet the daily demands of adulthood. His reading and writing continue to improve. He has defied everyone's predictions.

AJ has learned a lot, but so have his so-called well-educated parents. We are still learning.

not for her

As a child, she sat at a piano in front of an examiner every year, poised to play. She forgot about the fun of making up songs at home and concentrated instead on perfecting every note, every pause. A slip of the finger or a brain freeze could end it all. It was high stakes.

Decades later, she had to present a proposal for a huge sum of money. She and a colleague in BC led a project to connect students online with students across the world, a first for Nova Scotia high schools. It was the days of text-based internet, before the World Wide Web was available. The project, Learning Connections, focused on non-university-bound students; their excitement was infectious. But the success of the project found the woman appointed to a national research consortium, prepping a presentation in Alberta to secure millions of dollars in funding for technology in schools. Her friends in Calgary, away on vacation, offered her a place to stay. The night before, as she tried to finish her presentation, the keys on her paver-sized laptop were sticking. Lint and crumbs, perhaps? She brought out the central vac. At 3 A.M., in the bowels of the house, she was rummaging through the vacuum canister for an A or a T or a B, any laptop key she could find. The next day, she was the classic fish out of water. The entire team blew the presentation and slunk away. Thankfully, although she often feels insecure, she trusted herself. Fail better, said Beckett, and she did. The corporate and bureaucratic life was not for her; she wanted to teach and write, not vie for brass rings in someone else's carousel.

She was in her forties before she realized she'd absorbed everyone else's expectations and criteria for success: parents', friends', colleagues'. She doesn't regret the piano lessons or the professional humiliation—it's all learning, after all—but she regrets not trusting her heart, not listening deeply to what she wanted and needed to do.

When the woman began writing poetry and creative non-fiction in her early fifties, she knew immediately it was where she wanted to be. Writing and teaching can invite anxiety and uncertainty, too, but she thinks about women like Georgia O'Keeffe, who persevered despite being "absolutely terrified every moment of her life." Shoot for the moon, she thinks, when it's something that matters.

homing

Each day, about an hour before sundown, crows fly across the Bedford Basin on the way to their night roost. Look up and you'll see a scattering of black here, then another few, and another, thicker each time, strewing the sky with wing and intention. Once, during a wild storm that lashed trees with sleet and snow, the birds dipped in and out of view, tenuous and fleeting as thoughts. I imagined their hearts muscling the effort, prevailing against the bitter force of another nor'easter.

Crows, reviled by many, are clever, resilient, faithful, crafty, devoted, curious, and true to their nature. Like their cousin the raven, they are revered trickster figures: Hermes with beaks and attitude.

They represent what disrupts our lives, cracks open ideas, appears in threshold spaces, times when the weather is rough and the path unpredictable.

Land near us was first settled in the late 1800s by the Sisters of Charity. When their numbers dwindled, the Sisters sold the grounds of their seventy-plus-acre property. A developer razed the grounds, hauled away logs from two-hundred-year-old trees, destroyed cairns and statues, then left the fields to languish. The devastation felt like murder.

After the deforestation, the crows seemed to disappear.

At fifty, I began to write poetry and was soon drawn to lyric prose. The word *lyric* comes from the story of Hermes, Apollo's wayward brother, who stole his brother's sheep and hollowed out a tortoise to make a lyre. When Apollo demanded Hermes bring back the herd, Hermes sang to him, and Apollo, enchanted, agreed to give up his herd in return for the lyre. In this way, the myth goes, lyric—the singing of the self—was born.

As an academic, I was skilled in writing to argue a point, to tell someone what to think and do. But that kind of writing didn't feel like me and still doesn't. When I immersed myself in poetry as a form of inquiry, I saw it as philosophy, perhaps even a form of prayer. Poetry demanded I learn to pay attention, listen, stay awake. Poetry became my trickster; writing it, my crow time. Now I write more prose, but poetry will always feel like singing myself into an understanding of the world.

Poets—all writers—write alone, but, like crows, we love to gather. Countless opportunities—in friends' living rooms, writers' retreats, programs by the water, in the mountains, or on the prairie; church basement workshops and conferences—all provided the community I sought when I began to write. Occasionally, I saw rivalries and ill will, but in general, the writing community has been far more hospitable than the academic one I left.

Which leads me to an Old English word, *gelang*, meaning "together with." Belonging to a community means I am part of something complex and slippery. I have to check my personal failings and challenges, my willingness to please, and my tendency to be cynical.

A celebrated writer whose workshop I attended about twenty years ago shamed and derided writers in the group and violated every teaching principle dear to me. I wanted to defend our gathering from her bullying, and wrote a scathing poem about her. My anger was a turning point, and I kept the poem to myself. By exposing her, I'd expose my own failings. Her actions were unkind and damaged the spirit of belonging. Leave these things to karma, I tell myself, although I know that doesn't always work.

As Rilke said, "There is no place that does not see you."

The crows on the grounds hadn't disappeared at all.

Within a year, insistent saplings were the height of a human, and wildflowers and long grasses grew up through the wood chips and rubble. One afternoon, as the sun began to set and the dog rolled with delight in the fresh snow, I heard a few crows call from a small grove of trees at the end of the field. The branches were knuckled with them. They were back home.

Crows can't help but assemble. They muster (from the old French word *moustrer*, to show up). And like humans around a kitchen table or a campfire, crows tell stories. Gathering before dusk allows them to share information about predators, sources of food, and other wisdom we humans are not privy to.

Crow time, I whispered, when I saw them. When I look in the trees at dusk and see them, common tricksters in their blue-black form, I am strangely comforted. Like us, they need their kin.

that's you (yaass)

That's you? My son stares at the large glossy black-and-white in the Greystone yearbook. You were a queen?

Yeah, I don't know why, I say, and take the volume from him. I'd been looking for photos of a university classmate whose name I'd heard on the news. The book is heavy and must have cost a fortune to produce.

It was a thing, then, I finally say.

Long live the queen.

I'm embarrassed, in the same way I cringe when I admit I was a cheerleader in high school, doing jumping jacks in a short, pleated skirt for the Bears, one of whose team jacket and adhesive tape-wrapped ring I wore for a brief time. Dave was thick and sweaty with a kiss that felt like cold Alphagetti. My last year of high school put me at a crossroads; my heart and head were with art and writing and drama, but I bought the lure of sixties markers of popularity, including team sports, where girls were a side benefit. A commoner's star system, where beauty and local celebrity are prized.

My son AJ, who wasn't even in school yet, wouldn't have been interested in a conversation about the gender politics of beauty contests.

He only wanted to know if the photo was of me. In my youth, contests were everywhere. Somewhere in a box in the house there's an engraved silver tankard with a glass bottom, a gift each college queen received at the year-end dance where one of us would be crowned All-Campus Queen. Among the many dances during the year was Ag-Bag-Drag, sponsored by the Agricultural College Student Association. Guys joked or bragged about which bag would be their date. The Ag-Bag is known as a storage system for feeding farm animals, but that product wasn't developed until 1978; before then, I was one of the bags who attended with my pharmacy student boyfriend. Hay bales, cowboy hats, and the odour of beer in the barn were everywhere. Yee-haw. The dance thrives today—unironically, I assume.

As I write this, Queen Elizabeth has recently died. The singer-songwriter Liz Phair lamented the loss, for which she was excoriated. An academic publicly cheered the Queen's death, hoping it was excruciating.

Phair, defending the Queen, said, "she knew with exquisite precision the bounds of her tricky role, and I adored her for maintaining it so elegantly."

The legacy of the monarchy is like that of some global religions; it includes genocide, slavery, abuse, greed, and financial corruption. Yet children grow up in a culture saturated with glass slipper fairy tales and heteronormative Disney confections. Decades ago, both my sons were helping Mario save Princess Peach.

And even now, well into the twenty-first century, little girls want to be princesses, despite many parents' best efforts. Up until 2019, Nova Scotia's Apple Blossom Festival crowned a Queen Annapolisa and we continue to read about queens of various domains, from mystery novels to fashion to casseroles. Serena Williams is called "The Queen of Queens." A movement of right-wing populists claims their leader is the Queen of Canada. And who is Beyoncé if not Queen Bey? Drag queens have always been among the most creative and entertaining people among us. Gay men sometimes simply claim the title "queen" for themselves.

Being queen carries a kind of magic, especially when you're young and impressionable. That 4 billion people watched Queen Elizabeth's funeral in 2022 suggests it still does. Monarchies, real or imagined, have outlasted their function. But as a young woman, flattered to be chosen, I bought into my own objectification. I played queen.

All I can do now is resist. And hope my sons do the same.

the moon inside

Someone accompanies every soul from the other side.

Joy Harjo

It's heavy.

It's made of cedar. Look inside.

Yes, but it's damaged, and it's taking up space in the shed.

I know, but it was Gram's. Maybe we can repair it?

As a child, I watched as Gram's glasses magnified her watery eyes, making them look like oysters on the half shell. She pulled a tight elastic band around her knees to hold up her brown stockings. She was always dabbing her eyelids and her cheeks with a handkerchief. If we were lucky, Gram put on her sturdy black shoes and her Persian lamb coat and we'd take the bus downtown on a Saturday to the Paddlewheel Restaurant in the Hudson's Bay building. It was exotic —to reach into the case in the cafeteria line and choose a dessert cup filled with cubed Jell-O, whipped cream on top. To have real battered fish instead of fish sticks. My siblings and I were in heaven. It's only now I wonder how she afforded this. My mother's mom had retired early from nursing and lived with her sister-in-law in Winnipeg on their government pensions.

After her children, Grace and Jack, were off on their own, Gram Glenn spent much of her time in Ontario where most of her brothers and sisters knew her as Effie. I was relieved to learn recently their families all adored her, just as we had. Yet when Gram visited us in Edson or The Pas or Saskatoon or Dauphin, her visit was never long enough for us or short enough for our parents.

One year Gram taught me how to crochet. Because I am left-handed, it was a long and frustrating session, but she was never impatient, never critical, and never raised her voice. I was her first grandchild and I loved her completely. Until I left home in my late teens, Gram tucked ten dollars into every birthday card. She shuffled about the house in her slippers, rocked back and forth on the chesterfield on a Saturday night, smoking and cheering for the Toronto Maple Leafs. The large beige hearing aid wasn't much help; "eh?" marked all our conversations. When she was transfixed in front of the television, her cigarette dangled above her clothing, its ash growing to half its length before she tapped it into the amber glass.

For several years after I'd left home, I kept her tatted doilies and handkerchiefs. A rag rug or two, a paper wastebasket constructed of magazines rolled around wire coat hangers. All that's left now is her cedar chest.

Shortly after I moved to Nova Scotia, during the years my mother wasn't speaking to me, my father called to let me know Gram had died. I rarely cry, but I sobbed for an hour that day. Psychologists say a child needs only one person to love them unconditionally. When I began publishing poetry, I took Gram's last name, Glenn. Even now, I can recall a parcel arriving in Edson from Winnipeg when I was about six. Cradled in a large silk-lined box was a doll, wearing a crocheted figure skater's dress and a hand-stitched fur-lined hat and cape. All white, like Olympian Sonja Henie's costume, the star of the movie I'd seen that year. (I had been learning how to figure skate.)

I picture Gram at the mirror in those days, dressed in her fur coat and thick-soled shoes, pooching out her lips. She runs her lipstick across her pursed top lip, then bottom, so when she breaks into a smile, it's red rickrack.

correspondence

Subject: RE: mothers
Date: Sunday, May 21

Good morning, Lorri,

Well, the sun has come out and the wind has finally subsided, so it looks as though we might actually have a pleasant long weekend. I'm woken every morning by birds, and the crabapple outside my study window is full of deep pink blossoms. Life is good. Your son and I have been making plans to transplant his dill and try various locations for other herbs. He tells me you have pots of herbs on the back deck in Hubbards and he seems very drawn to bringing growing things into his own life. It's nice to have an enthusiast around, since I generally do these things all on my own. Things seem to be doing well with your son and N; they keep the basement area relatively tidy. They are getting used to the crush and pace of Calgary, which is not easy. I don't see a lot of them, but I enjoy their company.

Oh, Pat, how you tried to set him on the right track, to support him. I know it was for me and our lifelong friendship, and I know you never held me accountable, but thinking of those days hurts.

And as for mothers...

Ah, yes, our mothers. This was about the time my mother was fighting my father in court for support, and your mother, like mine, was now on her own. You were dealing with your shocking cancer diagnosis and the long end of your own marriage.

What happened with your mother's appeal? Lorri, I cannot imagine your own mother's rage seeing her ex-husband in Pleasantville, refusing to support her, smug and assured all is well while her own world shrinks. My mum has been wrestling for four years with the question of where to live next, since she is becoming increasingly frail and finds the demands of cooking, shopping, and keeping a life going difficult to meet on her own (all the while, of course, feeling guilty she isn't also looking after my father in the mix). Last night she marched into a new complex where the old YMCA used to be in downtown Saskatoon and put a deposit on a little bachelor suite. The building is designed for seniors, with all meals served in a dining room on the ground floor. There are large common areas for reading, recreation, television and all that, but her personal space is now going to be about four hundred square feet. Having made the decision, she is shaking in her boots. Since she has retired, every move has been to something smaller, and she is well aware how huge a step this next one is. What's so hard is there is little in her growing up and in the culture that was available to women of her age to talk about the spiritual growth that can come with the shedding of things and of old ties. Mostly she just sees it as a loss and tries to brave it out.

Yet your mum was strong, Pat. You were gone by the time she died, but you'd be pleased to read this excerpt from her obituary: "Educated at Bellahouston Academy in Glasgow, Jean then went on to take training as a shorthand typist. During World War II, she served as a private in the Auxiliary Territorial Service of the British forces, typing coded military documents that included the orders for the D-Day invasion." So much about the lives of our mothers' generation hid behind tomato soup, laundry piles, and others' needs.

When I was in Halifax, I went to Pier 21, which is where Mum landed as a war bride. It was moving to be there and see how much of her story is the story of thousands of women of her age: the war, marrying a Canadian farmer with no sense of what that actually meant, heading out in the winter on the Atlantic, travelling by train across the country with her pregnant sister, arriving in Regina in February. She says she doesn't have a sense of being caught up in history, it was just what was happening to her as she tried to live her life, but I find it compelling now. I grew up with the stories, but who cares what your parents talk about when you're little?

Now, I talk with her about her fears, about her sister who ended up having twins on a kitchen table in what passed as the hospital in Drumheller at the time, how she lost both of them to SIDS.

She felt she couldn't live up to all the images—the Donna Reed and Ida Lupino, as you say—or to my dad's German family ways.

The fact her life before Canada was doing secret things to prepare for the Normandy invasion meant nothing to him beside the fact she couldn't cook.

Yes, the pressure. I remember my mother trying not to catch her arm in the wringer washer, foul-smelling diaper pails, how my father would walk home for lunch to have a square meal, one of three a day. Women in post–World War II North America were homemakers, that rosy-tinged role that smells of talcum and breast milk and looks like servitude.

I remember all those years when Mum went to doctors to get stuff for her nerves. In that Arborite world, demons grew in the dark.

Love, Pat

scars

A scar opens a story. See this white line on the shortest finger of her right hand? As a child, bored with cleaning silver, she tried to fit her pinkie into the opening of the metal Silvo bottle; a doctor cut the bottle off her hand. She has dark marks on her face and back, probably from slathering on baby oil and iodine and lying in the sun as a teenager. Or from trips under the brutal suns of Koh Lanta or Australia's Kakadu Park. On her lower abdomen is a two-inch white line from an emergency appendectomy, a longer line from a C-section, allowing AJ, deprived of oxygen in her failing uterus, to be born alive. There's the tiny line from a foot operation, and a white bump on her cheek from a monstrous stress pimple in her thirties. Like anyone's, her body wears both insignificant and momentous events.

For years, she's asked writers to freewrite about their scars, visible or invisible. What pours from their pens are fears, turning points, tragedies, and unexpected insights. The French word blessure *means wound. To bless in English is to make something holy. Rumi wrote that the wound is the place where the light enters you. The woman wants to think the more scars her body gathers, the more light blesses it. Not in a religious sense, but something better: the sheer light of being present in the world.*

Spanish poet Rosa Chávez calls scars "cartographies/carved with destiny's knife." She likes to kiss them:

there, where the skin grows tougher

there, where the memories are visible.

moments of glad grace

Heat rising today after a cold spring, and I am indoors and in my head. Squandering an early summer day is heresy in this country. God help me, I think, but if not, well that's fine too.

When I called Aunt Kay last night, she was making dinner.

How does one hundred and three feel? I asked. My dad's sister is the last of her family to survive. As always, she laughed.

I didn't expect to live this long. And, as always: When is your son getting married?

I yelled an answer.

When?

My voice cracked from shouting, and I coughed.

Are you fighting something?

Fear, I wanted to answer. I didn't tell her, but I'd called twice earlier; it rang and rang for minutes. No answer. I'm stabbed with the knowledge she could be down to months or weeks. She keeps up her small apartment, the fridge stuffed with morsels wrapped in plastic and rubber bands, the walls filled with fading family photos her daughter will one day take down. Tchotchkes, mementos everywhere.

I am not ready to lose her.

A bright yellow bird appeared on the deck yesterday, stunned from the impact of a crash against glass, ending its spring busyness. I picked up its cooling body, felt the miracle of its soft intricacies, whispered a blessing before placing the body under a budding bush near the shore.

Resurrection? Predator? It doesn't matter. The future is always a promise, and always fatal. The old apple tree, the bird's home, endures these absences year in and year out. At night, I fall asleep looking at stars, listening to the disputes of snarling raccoons in the yard, and I wake before dawn to the scent of lilac, the hush of soft green poplar leaves in the wind. Don't give up on the world, says the poet; keep going even when the going is slow, says Confucius. Everything a bumper sticker. Childhood is burnished with simplicity, and the gift of years, if we're lucky, is nuance, the lingering specifics of intimacies, gratitude for those we've walked alongside. Aunt Kay has always been in the world; I can't imagine her not being here.

Always there will be storms. And loss. The years in my body lean harder against the seasons. What else can I do?

Today is an ordinary spring afternoon in an ordinary life, one that reminds me any of us could live to one hundred and three if we don't take ourselves too seriously, if we wrap up tiny moments and store them, and when people ask how we've lived this long, we give them, as Kay always does, a different answer each time: I used to skate a lot. I've been a widow for decades. I walk around the mall in the winter. I don't let things worry me.

Up the hill, a machine digs a foundation out of the earth. The bus stops on the main road and from the window, I see the neighbour's son and daughter jump out, kick up dust along the gravel. I step outside to water a planter and check on the young prairie crabapple tree with its wind-cracked limb. Like my aunt, whose beauty is enhanced by her fragility, the tree makes me happy.

The sun warms my back. I bend by the flowerbed to look at buttercups popping up in the patch of alyssum, marvel at the way light cups them like an offering, as if to say: see, look, you are here at just the right time.

entangle

The mother of a friend was a well-known psychic. He, however, is a scientist. He spent years researching his mother's talent, hoping to understand its source. Science wants observable phenomena and finding hard evidence for a sixth sense or paranormal skills is difficult. Christian describes his mother as a "sensory savant" whose instinct—her ability to know what others don't—was something she was allowed to cultivate.

We can all cultivate these abilities, he says.

Author Patricia Pearson's own experiences prompted her to explore phenomena such as precognition, after-death experiences, presences, and other incidences that seem to defy the laws of science. Why does Western society dismiss, ignore, or deride these experiences? Why do some people report a bodily sensation of joy or grief, only to learn of a relative's news? Or know, without any tangible evidence, who is calling? Pearson's research reveals spiritual incidents have been common across many cultures for centuries and our "prove it," "pics or it didn't happen" demands for confirmation hold us back from our human possibilities. Palliative care professionals are familiar with such phenomena, but we second-guess ourselves when we experience a "visit" or a "sense" or a "vision," whether we're awake or dreaming.

And now, winners of the Nobel Prize have been awarded for their work on quantum entanglement. My layperson understanding of entanglement is this: subatomic particles can be connected to each other, regardless of how distant they are from one another. They're in relationship and one state can alter the other. Kinship, again.

And so theories arise: since the human body comprises subatomic particles as well, can our bodies respond to changes in others' bodies? What about our emotions, our responses? Could intergenerational trauma, shown to pass down from generation to generation, be encoded in those particles, invoking a response decades later? Certainly, evidence from Indigenous communities supports this. What if my friend's mother's abilities were a perfect example of quantum entanglement on a human scale?

For months after our first son was born, I felt as though his body was part of mine and when we were apart, I felt the absence viscerally, a kind of phantom limb phenomenon. When we first moved to Nova Scotia in 1983, friends invited me along to see a psychic who lived on the South Shore. I recall her emphasizing that a boy was coming into my life soon, and would need a lot of my help. One of the neighbour's sons, Jamie, often visited our five-year-old and stayed for meals. His mother and father were separated. Was this the boy who needed help?

A couple of years later, however, our second son was born, starved of oxygen and with a host of learning challenges we spent years helping him overcome.

When the phone rings, I usually know when it's AJ. Now and then, when I think of him, a text from him will pop up on my phone. Could I visit loved ones when I'm no longer around? Does entanglement also suggest my own consciousness could be part of a larger consciousness? Are we talking god here? I'm not alone in these thoughts, but I rarely voice them. Unseen connections between people across distance and time isn't a topic welcomed in a world that seems to value rationality and material proof.

And yet—

batoche

I park near the gate and walk directly to the site. Two half-circles with an open centre, the Métis Veterans' Memorial is imposing and beautifully conceived. Names carved in the stone don't seem to be in any order, but I find many familial ones nonetheless: my great-uncle Edgar Couture, several Fletts, a couple of Budds, an Erasmus. A woman asks who I'm looking for; she's driven from Ontario in a camper. She, too, is new to her Métis roots.

I've been researching my Ininiwak (Swampy Cree) ancestors for several years, and although their names appear in histories and archival documents, I claim my Métis identity proudly, yet awkwardly. I have French, Scottish, and Irish roots, too. I was raised in small northern and prairie towns and while we were not well off, I was never refused entry to a public place or derided for my background.

I'll likely never have to use my phone to record a nurse's mistreatment of me. No one shadows me when I shop, nor would they drive me out to the city limits in sub-zero weather on a "starlight tour" that will cost me my life.

My father's Métis features were distinctive if you were looking for them; like so many Métis have said, we simply hid in plain sight. Of my three siblings, one has lighter skin and hair and two darker. Many relatives have features I would call Indigenous; several, for example, look like a younger Phil Fontaine—steel-grey hair and high cheekbones. But physical appearance is only one possible marker, and it's minor compared to cultural practices, community, and language.

As my father aged, and well before the internet, he travelled across the prairies and into the United States to search public records. He'd made a note about Peter Erasmus, Sr. and his wife, Catherine Budd, but only to indicate they were his mother Eleanore's grandparents from Selkirk. He had no idea they were well-known Red River residents. Because his Irish father emigrated from south of the border, his interest was in claiming dual citizenship. My aunts Kay and Lil kept rumours of our background alive, and my mother's disdain for "Indians" piqued my curiosity. But how could I find out the truth? I hadn't a clue how to start.

When I began to read all I could about Red River history, fur traders, and the history of colonization, I saw close encounters I'd missed. In The Pas, our family attended the Anglican church founded by an ancestor, Henry Budd, and lived across the river from relatives in the reserve. At dances as a preteen, I was teased for using steps I only found out later were common to Métis jigs. As a young art teacher in Winnipeg, I was hired by a fast-food chain to design the interior of an outlet using the Red River cart, which I did, oblivious to the connection. Once, introduced to a friend's husband, a Cree man, he stared and said: Are you Plains Cree?

I am drawn to Cree beliefs, especially the emphasis on inter-connectedness. I have no idea what I've inherited genetically, and I am careful to mention such things; they can, of course, be explained by sheer coincidence or wishful thinking. We humans, after all, tend to find—or force—patterns after the fact.

I am not a pretendian, but I may be perceived as one. Debates about Métis identity began to appear in public discourse more than a decade ago. Indigenous commentators were justifiably angry about the many who "played Indian"; it seemed everyone wanted to call themselves Métis or Indigenous. They had cause: high-profile auth-ors, artists, and academics continue to be outed, their ancestry and their stories challenged. The search for my past corresponded with growing revelations about pretendians, and the timing was fortuitous: I was forced to be meticulous, diligent, and thorough in my research.

Métis friends and relatives remind me my past has been largely hidden from me—Indigenous people in Canada have experienced erasure for centuries—and my parents and grandparents had rea-sons to keep their backgrounds hidden. They might have wanted to protect their children from racism, or they had practical or eco-nomic reasons to pass for white. Growing up in small prairie towns, I witnessed the maltreatment and humiliation of Indigenous peoples daily. If you were Native, you weren't thought of as human.

Has much changed? As communities expose the horror of count-less graves of residential school children, many Canadians deny the graves exist, deny children were mistreated or murdered, deny the roles the church and governments play in attempted genocide.

Our history is important; looking at that history through Indigenous lenses and placing alongside—or supplanting—those conventional colonialist accounts can only reveal the humanity of those who've walked this land for thousands of years. Poet and scholar Marilyn Dumont recently attended a local event in Edmonton focusing on Indigenous issues. Peter Erasmus, Jr. is widely known in Métis history as a linguist and translator who played a key role in treaty negotiations, yet the speaker was unaware of Erasmus's legacy. How easy it is, Marilyn said, to diminish our contributions.

But here I am, finally, standing in the heart of prairie Métis history: Batoche. So much to learn, to question, and to grieve. Although I read and talk regularly with Indigenous authors, particularly Métis ones, I live away from the Métis homeland and am not surrounded daily with Métis customs and practices. Here at Batoche, I can soak in them. The campervans and F-150s are filling up the grassy area behind the buildings now, and people are beginning to mill about.

I see the canteen is opening. *Skoden*, I whisper. I leave the war memorial and head to the booth where the Manitoba Métis Federation is setting up its display. I want the company and the conversation.

the land is kin

We are born on it, die on it; we come from it and return to it. The land and the waters, oceans and rivers, are part of us, relatives and ancestors in a very real way.

Patty Krawec

When I say the land is my ancestor,
that is a scientific statement.

Keolu Fox

Starlings at the end of the beach are a cluster of dots, and in a flash they rise, quiver above the sand, and disappear into the cliff. My walks on Hirtles Beach on Nova Scotia's South Shore are always marked by moments of beauty: the sheen on ochre strips of kelp, striations below rocks written by wave action as the tide goes out.

At the end of our road, where one hundred-year-old fruit trees once flourished, storms such as Dorian and Fiona have clawed at the shore. Two trees and their massive root systems have washed away. Our yard has sunk the last few years, eroding from underneath as it makes its slow transformation from land into sea.

Yet, in a time of chaos, collapse, and climate catastrophe, I seek solace and beauty in the so-called natural world. And I'm trying to learn to walk differently. The writer and filmmaker Trinh T. Minh-ha reminds me that walking can be a colonial act. People "do" the Camino, the Bruce Trail, the Pacific Crest Trail; an achievement to cross off a list, an act, she says, of "consumptive spectatorship." Instead, she tries to walk so the world comes to her, so that she is open to receiving it, rather than aiming to conquer in some fashion.

When we receive the world around us, Minh-ha claims, we alter the way we walk. We have to park our ego, our instinct for naming and claiming; we tame our extractive impulses. We challenge centuries of considering the non-human world as other.

Since childhood, I've believed everything in creation (humans, animals, plants, water, earth) has both material and spiritual aspects. And because I believe in science, and because humans are of the

Earth, I consider the Earth itself to be an ancestor. Most Indigenous peoples on the planet, despite their differences in origin or histories, see the universe as a whole living being, and all of us, from rock to plankton to tiger to human, as kin. Just as the Cartesian distinction between mind and body is specious, so, too, is the belief that human-kind is separate from what we call the natural world. Once again, I invoke the idea of wahkohtowin, our interconnectedness and our responsibility to one another.

The Anishinaabe-Ukrainian writer Patty Krawec asks, "how might we become better relatives to the land?" When we acknowledge the land is kin, we are more likely to honour its rhythms, to think in terms of stewardship rather than ownership.

Even as I snap a photo of another bright rose sunset or shimmer-ing crystalline view of the ocean to post on Instagram, I recognize I am consuming. I can argue that I'm sharing beauty, celebrating the good fortune to be a witness to the planet's wonders. Or I could ask myself if I'm using the land's beauty to exert my own presence in the online world, a vast territory that itself can exploit and be exploited.

What if I sat outside, instead, listening to the sound of the water, alert to bird life and rustling leaves, and took it all in?

flow

When she drew, she could become lost in the pencil strokes, looking up from her sketchpad hours later to see the sun was setting. When she worked on the page, absorption was a kind of river that pulled her along, away from the sounds and sights and smells of the material world. It had energy, this fluid state of heightened awareness.

The same thing happened when she wrote. Some days, especially the days when she was on her own with no child or husband or pet nearby, she forgot about lunch or a to-do list and sat at the typewriter —later, the computer—attuned to words and their possibilities. The flow state. A kind of focus Buddhist scholars liken to a universal consciousness.

She doesn't think this is a mystical state or a woo-woo spell when magic pours from her pen. There is still a lot of work afterward—revising, restructuring, cutting, tweaking again and again. (And again.) But the flow state is a working state, productive, generative, and challenging, in which she dances the line between control and letting go. She is immersed in an activity both essential and important, something that provokes her and draws her in. It's a state of both ease and effort, pleasure and discomfort, reinforcement and reward. It is addicting and, like an addiction, can cause withdrawal. If she goes too many days or weeks without it, she becomes a bit flinty, off-kilter, unbalanced.

When she is in this bubble and finds herself in the kitchen pouring more coffee, she is still inside the writing. A phone call, a knock on the door can burst the bubble, pitching her rudely back into the world where she now sees the dog staring at her, hears the fridge humming and the garbage truck as it clatters down the street. But she'll be back.

Rapper Dr. Dre says, "When that flow is going, it's almost like a high. You don't want it to stop. You don't want to go to sleep for fear of missing something."

Edna O'Brien writes: "My hand does the work and I don't have to think. In fact, were I to think, it would stop the flow."

And perhaps it's the ecstatic, as writer bell hooks suggests. Ecstasy in its root form means to stand outside oneself. Like hooks, the woman finds herself "immersed so deeply in the act of thinking and writing that everything else, even flesh, falls away."

Nothing compares. She lives for this.

the golden legend

A hunter in a red tunic stares at a stag with a crucifix between its antlers. The man holds a silver blade in his outstretched hand; his lanky white dog looks up at him, poised to react. Off in the distance is a castle.

When I climbed into bed, the painting, framed in ornate wood, arrested me. Now what? it seemed to say. I was in the former abbot's suite and wondered what an abbot thinks of as he drifts off to sleep. Does he think about God? About Brother Michael taking the last piece of bacon again? Both?

Outside, the snow was steady, the wind bitter. The impenetrable sky suggested we'd be under a white blanket for a while. On the East Coast we have near-hurricane-force winds, sleet, rain, then ice pellets, layers of packed ice-snow and dirt that tax the blades of the mightiest road grader. This prairie snowfall was gentle in comparison.

At breakfast, the man next to me groused about the prospect of waist-high snow drifts and temperatures of thirty below. I dusted my oatmeal with brown sugar. Cold, you can dress for, I thought; snow-drifts you can move.

Regardless, we all want some kind of faith to carry us into spring.

When Ilonka and I returned from our walk, our legs were caked with snow. My aching fingers burned. Lil sat on a chair inside the vestibule, her snowsuit unzipped, water dripping on the institutional linoleum, snow shovel in her hand.

How you do it all, Lil?

I have a trophy, you know. Her eyes were bright and sweat clung to her curls. Abbot Peter had it made especially for me. It says "Snow Angel." She grinned. An eighty-year-old churchgoer volunteering to shovel every path after every snowstorm is another wonder of the world. And a reminder to me to keep moving.

Legenda sanctorum, otherwise known as the Golden Legend, is a collection of stories about the saints written by Jacobus de Voragine around the middle of the thirteenth century. Saint Eustache, formerly a Roman general, encounters a stag with a cross held in its antlers and is instantly converted to Christianity. The painting above my bed in the abbot's suite renders that moment: a man on the brink of belief.

I believe in the deer wandering in the snowy field at dusk, picking at garden stubble. I believe what's dormant is, in fact, alive: it rustles, bristling, waiting for the weather to change. I believe in Lil, the snow angel who shovelled while the rest of us stared at screens using whatever wits we can conjure to divine words. I believe the people of sturdy faith in this Benedictine community gain much from their devotion and their mission: "I was a stranger and you took me in."

That week I was reading about nehiyaw (Cree) world views and contemporary Western philosophers' foray into what they now call "vibrant matter," the idea that so-called inanimate things can animate, produce effects. Imagine! Fuck right off, I think. Are philosophers late coming to understand holistic Indigenous perspectives or are they hijacking them? Pass the dream catcher.

I've always been drawn to notions of interconnectedness, but I've never committed my inchoate thoughts to paper. And it's complicated: my great-uncle was the first Indigenous man to be ordained in the Anglican church in what is now called Canada. Yet I abandoned Christianity in my youth. How many lives have been destroyed by idols and crosses? How many Jean Vaniers and local parish priests have betrayed women and children?

Although I follow no organized religion, every clear night I look up and wonder what's behind the stars.

The god of my childhood saw my every move and, if I was good, could bring me a jackknife or a paint set. But whatever power created planets and worlds surely has other things to do. Einstein didn't believe in a personal god, a dispenser of punishments and favours, only a larger force. As an agnostic and one comfortable with mystery, I'm inclined to agree with the physicist who wrote, "if there is a god, we should not be able to find it." If something other than my consciousness flows through my fingers as I type this, how would I know?

We all long to believe something. In the painting at the abbey, the hunter tramped over the hills and stopped to behold the cross cradled in the animal's horns.

It's a sliding door moment. He was looking for dinner and he found a story.

stroke

Dave was at the door.

AJ, let's go, he said. AJ was trying hard not to stare at his dad who was now half-upright on the couch, uttering sounds that made no sense.

Dave and his wife, Donna, often took care of our youngest son, AJ, after school. They'd been devoted to him since he was a scrawny infant who resembled ET, struggling to gain weight. Donna made every dish AJ loved and Dave kept him busy, teaching him to craft a jewelry box for Mother's Day or to build a go-kart to enter in the local summer race.

It was unusual, however, for Dave to be at our house so early in the morning.

You okay? Dave looked at me, at Allan on the couch, then took AJ's hand. Let's get you to school.

What about the bus? AJ paused, eyes wide. He was dressed a bit haphazardly, his large backpack weighing him down. He looked confused and on the verge of tears.

Go with Dave, sweetheart, I said. I could hear the sirens coming up the road.

I'd lingered in bed that morning, listening to Allan and AJ moving about the house, when I heard a crash in the basement. Odd, I thought. Who's down there? Why was Allan doing laundry this early?

Everything all right? I called from the top of the stairs.

I heard Allan's voice, but it wasn't clear. It was a slurry of sounds, a note of anguish, some mumbling. I ran down the stairs.

AJ looked terrified. Something is wrong with Dad, he whispered.

Later, in the hospital, almost an hour's drive away, I walked in and was stabbed with alarm to see a phalanx of medical personnel circling Allan's bed. What was wrong? This looked even more serious than I'd thought.

The team asked him question after question, flipping the pages on their clipboards, nodding to each other, lips pursed.

You're so young, one of them said. We don't understand why this happened.

I sure as hell don't either. Allan's speech was now clear and direct. He held up his arm, wiggled his fingers. I took a deep breath and felt something like relief.

I was pulling clothes out of the dryer, he said, and I saw this arm. It looked like it belonged to someone else.

Your vitals are good, one of the doctors said. It's a TIA, but the results of the CT scan will tell us more.

For years afterward, the sound of the crash in the basement, followed by Allan's anguished sounds, haunted me. Even now, when I hear a loud noise from wherever he is in the house, I catch my breath. Scientists describe the startle response as "an extreme response to a highly novel and/or intense stimulus that carries potential major salience for the intact organism." Salience, indeed. A fortysomething man in perfect health collapses and begins to babble incoherently. Neither one of us has been the same since.

It happened again, years later, and left lingering effects. Two days after successful hip surgery, Allan climbed out of his hospital bed and collapsed on the floor. Afterward, as I sat in the dark beside his bed, I could hear the death rattle of the man in the next bed. It happens more than people around here will ever admit, the night nurse whispered. I mean, you're cutting bone and who knows where…. Her voice trailed off as she fussed about, arranging covers, tidying the table near Allan's bed. His eyes were closed; I hoped he hadn't heard her. I was confused, enraged, near tears. The room had no windows and smelled of despair and death, my request to have him moved either forgotten or ignored.

Earlier that day, the surgeon, a cocky cowboy with adoring female residents, strode in, chipper as all get-out. How are we doing now? The medical *we*, like the medical *dear* or *hon*, is enough for me to look around for a sharp object. In this case, it was particularly offensive, given this man's surgical skills could have been the cause of his patient's stroke. Impossible to prove, of course. What's done is done.

I can't remember what questions I asked, but I persisted. His answers were curt, dismissive. I hadn't expected anything less.

Well, it happens, he finally said, and turned on his heels. One of the dewy-eyed residents managed a shrug, wiggling her fingers bye-bye.

deer

The one time I hit a deer, I dreamed about the animal for months afterward. I was outside Halifax and, as can happen, a deer ran into the road before I saw it coming. Someone behind me stopped and called the police, or was it the wildlife division? In any case, someone with a gun.

I remember the eyes. They haunted me.

I drive differently now, especially at dusk and early morning when deer are likely to be on the move. Whenever I see one, I say a small prayer of sorts.

Deer seem to weave a path through my life. They've made short work of crocuses I've planted, and made the cedar trees their bonsai project. They sleep in the woods only a couple of hundred metres from the house and keep our area teeming with ticks.

But whenever I look out the kitchen window and see them, I catch my breath. They pause, stock-still, when they detect movement behind the glass. Up to seven will appear in the yard as they travel along the shoreline. Today, when the dog became frantic, I looked up and a lone deer in the yard, staring back at the dog. The dog wanted out, as always, but let the creature graze, I say.

The Swampy Cree word for deer is apisimôsos. Deer legends are global. In Celtic folklore, deer, often referred to as "fairy cattle," represent both the power of nature and the realm of the dead, the underworld. The red deer, the Highland stag, is an important Scottish symbol. In Christian lore, deer represent devotion and piety; some believe if you see a deer, God is around. In Buddhism, deer represent peace and harmony. In general, deer suggest gentleness, and for many, the embodiment of what's sacred.

In Nova Scotia, I don't look forward to hunting season, largely because it too often means an antlered carcass strapped to an F-150 and a good story over a beer. The Sinixt Nation in British Columbia is one of many Indigenous nations who've honoured the deer by ensuring nothing was wasted. More than food, the animal's hide became clothing, antlers knife handles and other parts of the carcass became jewelry or tools.

"A wounded deer—leaps highest," Emily Dickinson wrote. Around ten thousand deer in our province are "harvested" every year. I know nothing about culling herds, or wildlife management. But others do, people who never think of destroying wild animals or Disneyfying them, who respect their ways and manage their growth. They are kin, after all.

godmother

god·moth·er

> *noun*
> 1. *a woman who presents a child at baptism and promises to take responsibility for their religious education*
> 2. *a woman who is influential or pioneering in a movement or organization*

It's late April 2020 and the world is banjaxed with fear and uncertainty. I walk down to the shore as the light fades, grateful to breathe fresh air. Spring is coming, I try to reassure myself, since optimism is scarce nowadays. When I return to the house, I look at the dead leaves and old stalks of last summer's growth by the side of the door. I should find a rake in the barn and clear that out. My phone pings; it's a message from my cousin Ray's wife, Shirley, with a photo.

Ray stands outside our aunt's apartment block in Winnipeg, masked, two metres away from Aunt Kay who looks straight into the camera. It's her one hundred and fifth birthday. Her second pandemic birthday in a hundred years.

Aunt Kay has always looked fierce. Maybe it's her wild and shocking white hair, her square face and strong cheekbones. She is looking even more skeletal this year.

And I can't travel to see her.

Kay has been in and out of my life since I was born. I thought she'd always be there. When she attended the launch of my book about Red River women, Kay wore her toque and heavy coat and told anyone who'd listen she was my godmother. At my father's funeral, she said to my sister and brothers, I'll be your mother now that your parents are gone. In many ways, she was.

Born Katherine and often called Katie, she married Francis Reynaud in her thirties. Frank died at forty-seven, leaving Kay a widow with their eleven-year-old daughter, Eleanore. Kay lived another sixty years and hinted once, with a wink, that perhaps being on her own was why she'd lived so long.

Kay's mother, also named Eleanore, was my grandmother, a strong Métis woman. At the age of one hundred, Kay was curious about her mother's past, the tragedy that affected the family in 1908. At her urging, I spent years researching the events of our ancestors' lives, and what I learned changed my life. Kay changed my life. Although she was my godmother, she never talked about religion with me. My mother and I had a difficult relationship for most of her life, yet, between Gram, my maternal grandmother, and Kay, a paternal aunt, I always felt loved and supported. Kay sent birthday cards and notes until she was at least one hundred and three.

Kay outlived all her sisters. Iona was a quiet woman whose affair with a married man forced her to give up a child for adoption (that he found her late in life was a joy). Elaine moved to the States; I never met her. I saw more of Lillian, Ray's mother, who was candid, confident, and straightforward.

During the first year of the pandemic, Kay became weaker. Ray checked in on her regularly. She was alone in her apartment, stopped venturing out with her daughter to shop, ate less and less, and soon confined herself to her bed or her couch. I was thousands of kilometres away holed up in my home in Nova Scotia, masking and avoiding crowds.

No point, Ray said. What could you do here? Nothing.

I sit on the front porch, Atlantic winds blowing through my hair, and notice tiny green shoots of daffodil reaching up at the edge of the deck. Inside, I open Shirley's email again and look at the photo of Kay. Outside, the local porcupine waddles by the bushes, ignoring the rabbit sprinting out from under the shed. The snow is gone and a twinge that could be hope blooms under my ribs.

She's still here. Kay is still here.

herding

If my husband goes to bed before me, the dog ushers him upstairs, then comes back down to the living room to glare at me, as if to say, bedtime. Let's go.

She's a pack animal.

We all are. Time is short.

On this cool rainy day, I am in the closet unearthing a pair of wool socks when I pull out our boxes behind the clothes. Old papers I'd forgotten about.

It's the time of late summer when butterflies come, and when the waiting grows too heavy for the arriving to bear. I drop hours, like pebbles, into a jar, slowly... Hmm. An angsty attempt at poetry, I guess. No date.

Song lyrics for "Les fraises et les framboises." Ah, yes, my days teaching beginner French. I wanted to teach songs, but we had to stay with the Thibaut family. House. Come. Go. Voici, M. Thibaut. Répétez, s'il vous plaît.

Three poems and a song from Ivan, the fellow with the crazy hat and the Cossack boots who showed up after Gord died. I remember his Volkswagen beetle, and escaping from his car on a winter evening. Thirty below. It was a long walk.

Gordon Lightfoot's autograph. Secured the night he came to a friend's house on Osler Street in Saskatoon after playing at the university gym. He sat on a chair, looking morose and tired while eager young men offered him beer and young women like me sat, tongue-tied.

A letter from a man I met in Mexico, and the song lyrics to "Guantanamera" and the ribald "Los Hermanos Pinzones."

I dream of things as they could be, and say, why not? Kennedy's words written on a torn piece of foolscap. A photo of Pierre Trudeau in Saskatoon wearing his trademark rose.

A note from a grade six student in my first teaching placement: Blaine Lake, Saskatchewan. *What time is it? Thank you. Nathan Hollick.* The woman who billeted me served borscht, meat and potatoes, and pie at lunch and I'd trudge back to school heavy-footed and sleepy. To refuse would cause offence.

A photograph Sandra Semchuk took of me, soon after she had set up her own studio. Truth teller. She later left an abusive husband and married a Cree man who fell off a cliff to his death in the middle of the night. I saw recently her photographs are in the National Gallery.

A dinner invitation from Richard, written in German in his large, confident script. He wore lederhosen, served beer and sausages, and we laughed a lot. Twenty years later, we recognized each other on a ski hill in Alberta. He'd become a respected lawyer, and, I learned, had accidentally killed his friend when they were duck hunting. I've often wondered how he dealt with that.

A proficiency certificate from the International Order of Job's Daughters. Bethel No. 4, Saskatoon. What? A vague recollection of a room with lighted stations, women in gold-trimmed gowns, odd rituals, stylized movements. Had my mother's friends enlisted me because my father was in the Masonic Lodge? What was I thinking?

Ah, my father and the Masons. The card game he hosted in our rec room. My mother upstairs cooking, my high school friend and I dressed in go-go boots and short skirts at my father's request, serving cheese and crackers to leering men at a card table. Fuck, I'd forgotten that. It makes me think of Elly Danica, and I shiver.

Letters from Michael John. Our mock love affair.

Don't ever stop writing. Your letters are, as Baudelaire said, "an explosion of warmth in my black Siberia." Besides, you know Cree words. So, will you marry me?

A cardboard milk cap at the bottom of the box. Images of cold bottles, the freezing cream lifted off the tops. The milk bottle high above the Alpha dairy plant in Calgary, my first glimpse of the city from the back of my parents' car in the late fifties.

More letters. A teaching certificate. A contract. A letter of resignation. An application to graduate school. A satchel of correspondence between my mother and brother that sits like a resistant boulder. No stomach for those today.

I herd, it seems. I'm curious about those I've travelled with in my lifetime. Everyone has their own cast of people who made a difference, for good or ill. A personal human library with interwoven histories. Our kindred. Our pack.

And we don't forget, at least I don't. When RM, my boyfriend of fifty-some years ago, contacted me a while back, I'd recently watched *nîpawistamâsowin*, the film about Colten Boushie. The filmmaker, Tasha Hubbard, was RM's partner's daughter, I learned. How our worlds weave themselves together.

A former junior high student from Winnipeg recently wrote to thank me for my confidence in him. *You made me feel I was just fine as I was and that I was worthy.* The boy I'd remembered as Bob had tracked me down after fifty years and sent a gift he'd handcrafted. I was thunderstruck. Over the years, several students from the same era have been in touch over social media. It's heartening. Not only do these connections reinforce continuity in a life, they remind me we matter to one another. Some people have lifelong friends, others have friends for a time in their lives. Being stuck in the past likely isn't healthy, but going back now and then and showing appreciation for others must be.

grace house

will

We stand by the large Glenn stone in the Strathclair Cemetery on a hot summer afternoon at the turn of the twenty-first century. The stone pitches forward; the ground is uneven. Mom is wearing a blue bowler, a white shirt, and navy pants in that godawful polyester fabric that soaks up heat. She's wanted for years to come back to Strathclair so when I visited Winnipeg, I rented a car. She wanted to return after her divorce—she owned a town lot near her cousin Jean, but had to sell it to pay the lawyer's fees.

Let me take a picture, I say. Jean moves to stand by Mom.

This is where, Mom says, and points down. I've paid for the plot. It's in the will.

A flowering bush has dropped fresh petals around the gravesite. I hear only the sounds of birds and an occasional car on the highway nearby. A small hill to the west, large trees, a view of the prairie beyond. That Mom stands on the very spot she wants to be buried causes my stomach to flip. She's true to the quote in her nursing yearbook: *Finds and shall find me unafraid.*

Today on the grass; later below it. A whole world vanishing.

Back at Jean's we make tea, look at the photographs on the wall of children and grandchildren all distantly related to us, and then set out with Jean's husband, Peter, to meet the others at the restaurant in Shoal Lake for the Sunday smorgasbord. The room is a sea of grey hair; the pre-war generation of this farming community gathers here every week. Mom is shy, and I wonder if she feels embarrassed about her dark glasses and white cane. She sees well enough to recognize

another cousin, Viv, whose startled eyes are unfocused—a stroke?—
and Viv's husband, Doug Beamish.

Grace went out with my brother, Doug says to me. Grace, you
remember when you fought with Donald and jumped out of the
moving truck?

Never! she barks. Not me. He wheezes, tries to laugh, gently
places his thick fingers on Viv's shaking hand to calm it. Mom's smile
betrays her.

In a couple of years, when my sister and I clean out Mom's
dresser, we'll find a framed photo of Donald and Mom as a couple,
wrapped carefully in tissue.

Later that evening, Mom and I drive back to Winnipeg in the
singeing heat. Mom insists on stopping for a smoke at the Portage La
Prairie Petro-Can. When I return from the washroom, I find her in
the shade with her dark glasses on, laughing with a biker. They butt
out their smokes at the same time.

i'm sorry you don't like your life

The last time my parents and their four children were together was
in our parents' living room in Winnipeg. It was the night before their
youngest son's wedding. We were laughing over drinks when Dad
called me into the kitchen.

Pipe down, you guys. You're too noisy. He pulled his chair back
from the grey Arborite table and closed his arms across his chest. His
tie was loose and his shirtsleeves rolled up. His hair was now fully
white, a trait we've all inherited. He was smirking and his eyes were
hard. My stomach dropped.

This is the first time we've all been together for years, Dad. Years. It's Colin's wedding.

And it'll be the last time. I won't be around after this.

What do you mean. Are you sick?

I don't have to explain myself to you, missy. And he stood up, slammed his cup on the counter, left the kitchen, and walked outside.

It was the 1980s, a peak time for divorce in Canada. But my parents, after thirty-eight years?

Tammy Wynette's "D.I.V.O.R.C.E." was the kind of novelty song perfect for imitating a country twang. It was released in 1968, before she married George Jones, a man so desperate to drink he'd drive the lawn mower to the local bar.

Drinking and secrets can be lethal for marriages. Since my father wasn't a big drinker, something else was going on.

When my father said he'd be gone, I didn't take him seriously. He was being petulant, I thought, annoyed the rest of the family was having a good time. But he was a reticent man who often seethed in silence; to make such a forceful statement—cruel timing aside— he had to have meant it.

He'd been having an affair for years with a younger woman from the CN offices in Thunder Bay. At some point during Colin's wedding, I heard him say, That's it; the last one is married off.

He'd done his duty.

When he left, Mom's confusion, grief, and anger were profound. She wrote letters to me in Nova Scotia filled with invective I suspected was alcohol-fuelled, railing against my father's narcissism, cruelty, and arrogance. *He could barely get out of grade twelve*, she wrote. *He hated that I was smarter than him.* She called him a half-breed, which stunned me.

She spent a decade fighting Dad in court for support. The same man who'd wanted her to quit nursing—a wife with a job was an insult to a man—argued she was still young enough to get a job. Mom became a heavy drinker, smoked a package of cigarettes a day, and developed macular degeneration, which soon caused her to lose her sight.

If my father thought my mother could return to work and reinvent herself, he was wrong.

Tina Turner escaped Ike's fists and rose to fame. Nora Ephron used the ashes of her marriage to write *Heartburn.* When poet Sharon Olds's husband left her after thirty-two years for another woman, the book that followed, *Stag's Leap*, won the Pulitzer Prize.

My mother had neither the heart nor the strength to bounce back, recreate herself. She was broken. As de Beauvoir said, "her wings are cut, and then she is blamed for not knowing how to fly."

When Mom moved into an over-fifty-five high-rise apartment in the south of Winnipeg, I hoped she would meet friends, find some companionship.

She'd lost her beloved father at ten, and her mother left her and Jack at a critical time in their childhood. She became a nurse, a profession she loved, married a man she adored, and moved with him across the country far too many times. She'd had enough of reinvention.

And now this: the man she both hectored and doted on, leaves her for a woman only five years older than his daughter.

He was done, he said.

buying a piano

A piano! Pat noticed it in the front porch right away.

Right? Amazing. I called my brother and said, Brian, I bought a piano. But there's a catch, I told him. It comes with a house. In Saskatchewan.

Move it out of the porch, said Pat. She spoke firmly, as always. Her spiked and gelled hair looked like bedhead, and her eyes sparkled.

And I'd pop out these boarded-up kitchen windows, too.

She was right. I could open the space up to the light. Yes, paint the dark walls, spruce up the old bathroom, take down the heavy drapery, and install fresh, crisp blinds.

You could start your next book of poetry here, Pat. Come and stay.

Pat had just finished her seventieth chemo treatment. It's incomprehensible to write that number. Pat had been my friend since high school at Aden Bowman. Pat, Edna, and I were in the writers' club under the watchful eye of gangly Mr. Smyth, whom I feared. How we learned to love writing after working with him was a mystery.

It was Mr. Hinitt, our flamboyant French and drama teacher, whose creativity most inspired me. Monsieur, as he was called, was tall, red-haired, and often donned a Napoleon hat, climbed up on his desk, and marched us through a bad version of "La Marseillaise." His productions overtook the school—we skipped chemistry to dye bolts of fabric in the staffroom; we skipped English to rewrite scripts for production. Our troupe drove all night to the drama provincials, which we won. We folded, bent, and poofed pounds of facial tissue into flowers to bedeck the gymnasium. A plywood bridge, several mock-up chandeliers, and the vast expanse became the Palace of Versailles for our graduation. Even the rank odours of sneaker rubber and sweat seemed briefly to disappear.

When Monsieur turned seventy, we gathered in Saskatoon. The Castle Theatre attached to the school was to be renamed in his honour. Emails spanned the globe, and three hundred former students, including Pat and me, descended on the city one summer weekend to roast, toast, sing tunes, write send-ups, perform old skits or Shakespearean scenes, and to dance. Verna and I laughed about the morning we ran for the bus on an icy Saskatoon street and she slipped. When the driver opened the door, Verna's head was on the bottom step, her feet under the wheel well. Carol and Wayne were still together after decades. Irene, a talented pianist, was there, along with Mardi, a quiet blond with bright eyes who'd lived across the alley from me and dated Mel. Brian, the jock who crossed group lines and became a drama aficionado. Eddie, Monsieur's talented protegé, was now six feet tall and living as an actor and singer in Winnipeg. Shortly after that reunion, Pat called me. She had been struggling with her health and received a diagnosis: stage four ovarian cancer.

I love you, she said.

I love you too.

This is new territory, she said. I am so used to working twenty-hour days, fighting the good fight for kids in schools, and now I have more to learn.

And she did. Pat went to counsellors, to a shaman, to healers, and to friends. She gathered everyone around her who could make meals, weed her garden, find books to feed her understanding of how to live the rest of her life. She wrote poetry, which she had always wanted to do, and I was given the gift of editing her manuscript before it was published.

By the time I'd bought the little house in a small town in Saskatchewan, Pat's body had been assaulted by so much medication and treatment her very cells were bruised. But she said she felt cleansed; she was free of the clutter of two bad marriages, betrayal, and overwork.

We'd walked around the empty house that day, talking of its possibilities. Making plans. Next summer we'd roast marshmallows, we said, listen to meadowlarks, and watch the sky turn red.

We spent the two-hour drive back to the airport in Saskatoon talking about her next book, essays on what she'd learned these last few years as a cancer patient. Winter was coming; I had to return to Halifax and she to Calgary. I had a launch planned in Winnipeg, and she had another round of chemo.

How did this happen again? she asked. This house? I mean, you live in the Maritimes.

A simple quirk of fate. After the reunion for Monsieur, I reconnected with Ed; he'd inherited his father's farmhouse south of Saskatoon and invited Allan and me to visit. As I walked around the nearby small town, with its angle parking and flat movie-set store-fronts, I spotted a For Sale sign outside a blue-and-white thirties' style house.

Well, I love it, Pat said as I dropped her off at the airport for her flight to Calgary. Your little house on the prairie. You should give it a name.

I will.

I'm coming back.

I certainly hope so.

Within months, she was gone.

bad fiction

By the time her father sat her mother down in their Winnipeg living room in the summer of 1985 and told her, "I don't love you anymore. These things happen. I can't live a lie," her mother Grace had had two miscarriages, five births (one a stillborn boy her husband had the nuns incinerate in the hospital furnace while she was under anaesthesia), a hysterectomy, had been diagnosed with ulcers, angina, a myocardial infarction, diverticulitis, arthritis, hypertension, and a degenerative spine. She was sixty-three years old. Two weeks later, after leaving her a note on the fridge demanding that she "be back in his bed by that night" because "he was still a young buck and needed sex every day," he flew into a rage when she chose instead to stay at their daughter's house across the city. Soon after, he took most of the money from their bank account. When Grace began to rely on prescribed drugs and alcohol, he left AA pamphlets on the kitchen table, told his lawyers she was an addict, and after raping her at 5 A.M. one morning when she returned from her daughter's house for her clothes, he threw her on the floor when she threatened to call the police.

You're not good for anything anymore, he said.

Writers often draw on their experiences when they write fiction, but the events and characters have to be believable. Sometimes life makes bad fiction.

call

December 1.

Halifax airport. I pack lightly, except for my long green thrift store coat and sturdy snowboots with grips. It's been years since I dealt with Winnipeg winters. I'm ready to board when a 204 number pops up on my phone. It's my sister.

You all right, Punk?

Are you at the airport?

My plane doesn't get in until close to eleven, so don't worry about picking me up. Stay put.

Uh, well, Mom—

I'll handle the nursing home details when I see her tomorrow, I add.

She's not at her apartment. She went into St. Boniface this morning.

What?

It's her stomach again. All she's had for days is ice cream and tea. I'll wait up for you. I hope you have warm clothes.

I heard—thirty or thirty-five below. Is she all right?

Or more with the wind chill. High winds. We don't know anything yet. She's in emerg.

Does Colin know? And B? I spent all day yesterday researching wheelchairs and walkers and doing internet searches on Winnipeg seniors' homes. God.

And to complicate things, I have my own surgery next week.

What? In the same hospital?

Yeah. Gallbladder. Last week we tried to talk with her about moving into a home. She said the only way she's leaving her apartment is on a gurney.

God. Can she get referred since she's—

Who knows? Colin's made some calls, apparently.

Hang on. I see he's trying to call me.

December 11. She was in the ward then, 5B, surviving on ice chips. Telling us about playing basketball at a CNR party in 1968. As she talked, her fingers swiped from the nape of her neck to the top of her head, scratching, scratching. Her neck was a field of calluses and raw red lines. Every few minutes she asked us to shave her head. Cut it off! It's driving me crazy.

Basketball? Brian asked.

Naked, she said. And then she smiled her lopsided smile. Aren't you glad you didn't know me when you knew me?

The IV line continued to beep and Mindy finally came into the room, followed by a candystriper with wide eyes. Brian and I stepped aside. Mom leaned into Mindy as she adjusted the IV line—it kinked, setting off incessant beeping. Noisy Family on the other side of the curtain had been sighing and tch-tch-ing about how disruptive the beeping was.

Disruptive? Daily we'd had to listen to a large man whine to his tiny mother, Mary, with the thick legs and failing heart, and bicker with his wife, a woman who narrated every movement like a carnie barker: I'm taking the tomatoes out of the Tupperware now, Mom, and I'm moving to this side of the bed. I'm here, and where are your slippers, Mom, have you seen them, Harry, find them, I don't care what you think, you just show up for the easy parts.

Occasionally, I'd see my mother roll her eyes, grimace. Mom was blind, but Mary next door was not.

Noisy Family would have to deal with us, The Beepers. At least today the nurse found a vein. A hard poke, the nurses called Mom, and within days the flesh of her left hand and wrist were the riotous colours of a rocky beach. Sometimes I rubbed her skin softly, wishing away the bruises.

Let's not lose this, Mindy said to her. You have no more veins.

Do what you need to, Mom said. And began to cough again. It always started low, then built, until whatever was growing down there began to crawl its way out. Like slug slime it gathered in her throat, and one of us was always ready with a tissue or a warm wet cloth. Handwashing, warm cloth, laundry hamper, alcohol pump, warm cloth, repeat. Afterward, Mom leaned back, tipped her chin upward, and sighed. She was spent.

The hallway was filled with bent bodies and lost faces. The abandoned elderly, collapsing bonehouses of stories—the vital who once wore ties, splashed on Old Spice, and sprinted off to work, or sewed clothes or baked fifty birthday cakes a decade, who changed the oil in the car or dispensed cough syrup at 3 A.M. or slathered Vicks on the chests of their children lying near windows laced with frost. I never once saw anyone visit the hallway people. Slumped in their pale blue johnny shirts, bones protruding from skin the colour of a mouse's belly. They stared ahead or let their chins drop on their chest. I think of Willy Loman's wife, Linda: Attention. Attention must be paid.

Mom sighed again, turned her rheumy eyes to Mindy and the candystriper. Her face broadcast something alert, new.

Is she about to repent? This is what happens when you smoke, dears, she's going to say. At the same time I'm thinking—1968? Where was I while she was shooting hoops in the nude in someone's backyard in Saskatoon? University, I guess. Osler Street. Yes, that's where I was. Not long after Gord shot himself.

Mom leans in, as though she is about to share a secret.

Sotto voce now. Do you— She blinks.

—Do either of you have a cigarette?

Mindy smiled and pushed Mom forward gently, adjusted her pillow, straightened the sheets. I don't smoke, she said.

Well, someone here must smoke. I'll pay you twenty-five bucks for a cigarette. Right now.

You'll blow up the hospital, Mom. And besides, your wallet's at home.

Oh, I'll blow up the hospital, will I? And she stuck out her tongue like a three-year-old. There I go again, I thought, Lucy from Peanuts. Self-righteous know-it-all.

The candystriper burst out laughing, and Mindy winked as she opened the curtain to leave.

Mom's right hand flew to her head again. Snip, snip, snip! Cut it off. Cut it all off! I have scissors in my apartment. In the top drawer by the bed. Bring me the scissors.

An apartment she'll never see again, I thought.

Daily, she'd been flinging off the covers, trying to remove her johnny shirt. Helpless, naked, piping loud, wrote Blake of his birth. Did she want to leave the world as helpless and hairless as she came in?

This was a new mother. This was a new country. A place of no return.

Off! I want it off!

steal you blind

By chance, my brother Brian and I were in Winnipeg at the same time, and decided we'd try to visit our father. After my parents had divorced, my father and his second wife, M—Brian calls her the Mouth—had disappeared for ten years. Then, Dad made the occasional phone call to us in Ottawa and Halifax when M wasn't around; we weren't sure how to take this, and I, at least, wasn't sure I wanted any contact at all.

On that August afternoon, Brian and I arranged to meet them at a local restaurant, Maxime's. We were apprehensive. We decided to tag team it: one of us could listen to his wife while the other tried to have a conversation with him.

At the table, M sat across from me; I sat beside Dad. He's more work than I can handle, she began, looking directly at him, and then talked nonstop for an hour. My father, his mottled brown skin, grey vestiges of hair, his soft, crumbling voice: my father, now Man in Third Person. I looked at this woman's shiny manicure, her crusty-sprayed updo, her scaly yellow scalp. The scent of Estée Lauder was overwhelming. I stopped listening.

How are you feeling, Dad? I turned to look at him. He opened his mouth.

He's driving me crazy; we had the fire department in last week— I can't lift him anymore.

Brian began: Why not get one of those lifelines? He can push the button any time—

Are you crazy? He'd never manage that. Besides, you never know who's going to have access to your property then. They'd case the joint.

Brian and I locked eyes on that one. The sale of the family home, all his RRSPs, everything sold or moved out of reach or put in his second wife's name so that he could approach the judge and cry poor mouth: I'm sorry. I simply can't pay support to my ex-wife.

Case the joint. Good one, I thought, wishing Mom could hear this. My aunt had told me M's children refused to have anything to do with their mother. I wondered if she had any friends.

This is our table, M kept saying that day. They know us here, don't you? The waiter reached to take a plate. Did you hear me?

The wait staff were excessively, carefully polite. Your salad isn't as good today, she said—tell your cook. The waiter nodded, glanced at me.

Elvin, you're spilling. How am I going to get that goddamn stain off. See? She glared at me. This is what your father's like.

By the time Brian and I followed them back to their house and helped Dad to the door, neither of us had been able to have a conversation with him alone. It would be that way until he died.

Hope you're feeling better, Dad, I said at the front step, trying awkwardly to give him a hug. From inside, I heard:

Elvin, shut that goddamn door the flies are coming in.

It's Lorri, I say. Lorraine. My heart in my mouth.

Oh, you're back in Winnipeg, eh? M's voices grates. My heart thumps.

Yes, we're staying at a friend's house here.

From the window, I can see snow piled on the thick bushes. It's the second last Christmas season of my parents' lives, and I sense neither of them will be around for much longer.

All of us are here. Allan, me, the boys, I add.

Where?

Wildewood, Crescent Park area.

Oh, yeah?

God, she's crass, I think. And I'm disgusted with my father. My mother wasn't easy to live with either, but this was frying pan into the fire territory.

Silence.

Then: Well, he's not here.

I forge ahead. We'll likely never again be in the same city, I think. I knew that in my gut.

Is he free for coffee anytime in the next couple of d—

No, he's busy—doctors' appointments all week. No time at all.

Every day? I ask, separating the words. My jaw is clenched.

Shouldn't have said it that way; she'll take it as a challenge. Well, I say, we're here until after Christmas—we can pick him up anytime that works for him. And you, too, I add.

It galls me to include her in the invitation. I pace in front of the window, stretching out the curled cord of the phone. My stomach is cold and my voice is beginning to shake.

I said he's out—you can call later.

I take a deep breath. Okay, good. I will. We'd all like to see him. The boys haven't seen him for years. AJ is almost twenty. Can you believe it?

Oh yeah?

We won't need to take up a lot of his time. We could keep it short.

Silence.

We could take him to Tim Hortons. Even an hour, if that works. So he won't get tired.

A long pause.

Are you telling me that all you can give your father is an hour?

strawberries

Her head bends over the spinach and berry salad as she stabs wildly. When the fork impales a piece of spinach, a bit of onion, or a quarter-moon of tomato, I hold my breath; her unsteady hand can send it back to the plate. More than once she has bitten down on empty tines.

Whoops, she says. Oh, my.

Nice to see a strawberry or two in here, I say. The waiter fills our water glasses.

I'm glad we put some away today. It made me feel useful.

Ah, Mom—I look at the ends of my fingers, pink from strawberry juice: two quart baskets, hulled before lunch—you have this thing about usefulness. What's that about?

More than once, our cross-country calls have landed on that word. I'm no good to anyone anymore, she'll say, and I'll list all the ways that she is. Then I haul out some cliché—we're not human doings, we're human beings—or whatever pop-psych drivel comes to mind. What am I thinking? Afterward, I tell my husband: for Christ's sake, if I make it to eighty-five, don't humour me.

Maybe I'll give some strawberries to Millie when she comes to shop for me on Wednesday. She usually brings me pickerel.

From their cabin?

Yes. I don't have much to give to her.

Sure you do. Her husband—what's his name?—you were helping her deal with him.

She curls a lopsided smile. She is wearing a jacket and a hat, a boater. My mother's hats aren't coy fifties' things, like overturned nests, nor the large, floppy hold-on-to-yours that Maureen O'Hara, her favourite actress, might wear on a windswept hill, ribbons flying, violins swelling. Hers are Here-I-Am hats: the red one with a good brim, the sturdy navy one she's wearing today that matches her blue-checked jacket with the padded shoulders. Never mind that her black pants have an elasticized waist and are pocked with lint. From the waist up, she's an elderly woman to be reckoned with.

With her white cane, raised chin, and brown-tinted shades, she beetles her way through store aisles or, as she has today, through faux Greek columns and Homerian busts to reach our table. She's always straddled a line between confidence and defensiveness: here I am, world, what are you going to make of it? Once, as she came upstairs with her mail, a woman in the elevator told Mom her shirt was inside out. Well, Mom said, unbuttoning it; let me just turn it around. She held out her mail: here, hold this.

I look toward the door every minute or so, hoping like hell my father doesn't show up.

Gordon, she is saying, and I turn to look at her. She can tell I'm distracted.

Millie's husband. They took his licence away, and he won't cook, so Millie has to do it all. And now she's sick, blood where there shouldn't be. I told her to get to a doctor!

She looks up, surprised at the strength in her own voice, and puts down her fork. Her plate is a white moon strewn with rearranged spinach.

Behind us, a middle-aged woman cuts a chicken breast for an older version of herself. Here it's grey hair and Naturalizer shoes. Real linen and overpriced warm chicken salad served on excessively large plates.

For Mom, going out has usually meant her youngest son and his wife pick her up outside her apartment, take her to Smitty's or Perkins, and, she says, order a half-price coupon meal, an extra plate and fork.

And their home just sold for six hundred thousand dollars, she told me during one of our phone conversations, her voice rising to a squeak. Just once—just once!—I'd like to order what I want. Full price.

I look up again. At the entrance are a stooped man in a suit and tie and his companion in a turquoise leisure suit and flowered scarf. No, it's not him. Although with his Parkinson's, my father might well be that short now.

Earlier that morning, I'd asked Mom if she wanted to go for a drive to run an errand.

Or go for lunch? Her blind eyes blink a few times.

She purses her mouth. Where's that place your father had his eightieth birthday party?

Maxime's? You want to go to Maxime's?

Yeah. Yes, I do. She looks up. A sly smile. Well, I'm curious. Why is it so special? Did you go?

No—it's too far to fly. And anyway, I wouldn't come to Winnipeg without telling you, Mom.

I had called the restaurant that night, though, and the waiter handed the phone to my father. Dad managed about twenty words—one of his longer conversations—and asked if I'd like to speak to M. Maybe

Allison, I said. Or Brian. One way or another I talked with my sister, brother, cousins, brother-in-law, and nephew, everyone passing along the phone. I knew I was grandstanding, but it was a way of being there. M's voice bled through every conversation, dominating the table, hectoring Dad. Brian later told me he'd gone back to their house after the meal, and as Dad made his way slowly to the bathroom, M had hollered: And I suppose you'll be calling for me to wipe your butt. She laughed and turned to everyone in the living room. Can't even wipe his own ass. I didn't sign up for this.

Mom is quiet, picking at the salad, tapping the fork on the plate to search for larger, firmer chunks.

The stooped man and his turquoise companion pass by our table. It's getting late. We won't run into my dad.

But if they did show up—would I be up for that?

Oh yes. Yes, I would. Bring it on.

When I arrived at Mom's apartment that morning, Maxime's restaurant was the last place I thought we'd end up. I'd taken the elevator down with her laundry, and on the way up, noticed a hand-scrawled sign: *strawberries, 10:00 A.M.* I went back downstairs and bought two quarts off the back of a truck in the parking lot.

Oh, she said, when I brought them into the apartment. Oh, my. I wanted strawberries this year, and I would have missed them. While I rinsed them in the sink, she sat at her kitchen table, ready to slice the fruit into a bowl. It was a hot day and the apartment was stuffy.

It had been twenty-three years since my father sat my mother down and told her that's it. I'm leaving, I'm selling the house, so you'd better find a new place to live. Until you do, you can stay here. I'll give you $250 a month for groceries—and household upkeep until I sell this place—and one piece of tail a week.

How are you feeling, I asked?

Well, I can't walk very well. I need to get out, but I'm so tired. She was using the knife as deftly as if she had sight, her hands placed deeply in the bowl to avoid any spills. She'd been in the hospital the month before after a fall. She'd lain on the floor of her apartment for two days, calling out. Blind and weakened, she wasn't able to reach her medical alert or answer the phone. At some point that week, thousands of miles away in Halifax, I'd received a call from the florist about the Mother's Day flowers I'd ordered. Did I know where my mother was? They'd phoned, knocked, and called again. Was she in the habit of leaving during the day?

When I called my youngest brother, who lived ten minutes away from her, he snorted: pfft, she's probably just sleeping one off. I took a deep breath, felt the fury in my voice turn to ice.

That was years ago, I said. She doesn't do that anymore. Go over and find out where she is, please, and call me.

Later, the doctor said: I don't think I've ever seen blood results so nasty. Another few hours and she'd have been gone.

As I watch her cut up the last of the strawberries, sprinkle sugar on them, and shuffle her way to the refrigerator, I realize everything is taking longer.

Everything could be the last time.

You're tired because this is the beginning of the end, I think. Instead, I say: strawberry shortcake. You used to make biscuits and top it off with fresh strawberries in their own syrup, remember?

This might be the last time you and I putter in a kitchen together, I think. But I say: And sometimes the ones in the square cans with the metal ends.

Those were good for the winter, she said. But they're too sweet. Millie used to buy me fresh fruit and I'd cut it up and store in the fridge in that glass jar I loved. I had fruit every morning. Last year I broke it.

And you tracked blood on your carpet. That was scary.

I couldn't even see I was doing it. Couldn't feel the cuts. Oh my.

When she asked go to Maxime's for lunch that day, I was happy to oblige. We finished our salads and I could see she was tired; it had been a long day.

I wanted to stay in her company.

Would you like some dessert, Mom?

Do they have anything lemon?

I hope so. The waiter caught my eye.

Mom, remember when you took Allan and me and the boys to Perkins? You wanted to buy a lemon meringue and a rhubarb pie. To take home with you, you said. Then somehow you managed not only to pay for our meals—you gave AJ the pies to boot!

Are you still on about that? AJ got such a kick out of that. I tricked him. I loved it.

She looks around, and I think she senses the restaurant is empty.

You used to make that, too, Mom.

What?

Lemon meringue pie.

Yeah. I did. From scratch. You don't see that much anymore. Scratch.

You're right. But sometimes it was that instant filling too.

She turns her head sharply. Never! Well, sometimes, yes. She smiled.

The waiter removes her plate with the limp salad scraps. I've since wondered if Mom hoped she might see my father at the restaurant. Perhaps ask after her health. Or be remorseful.

As we sit there, neither knows that as soon as my father dies, M will leave for Hawaii, but not before sending all of his children a cheque for one dollar. Or that, after Mom's death, the frozen strawberries will still be in her fridge. All I know is Mom and I are alone together in a restaurant today and I want to take in every last detail.

Anyone looking in the window will see two diners sitting under cheap gilded mirrors beside faux Greek columns: a handsome elderly woman in a smart blue hat with her middle-aged daughter, enjoying a full-priced lunch late on a summer day.

A little salad with strawberry. The sweet tang of lemon.

winter in hades's bed

Persephone is gathering flowers in a field—some say roses and lilies, hyacinths and crocuses—when Hades, god of the underworld, carries her off. Some versions say she went willingly.

The poet Louise Glück wonders if the young woman cooperated in her rape

—or was she drugged, violated against her will,
as happens so often now to modern girls.

Persephone's distraught mother, Demeter, wandered over land and sea in search of her daughter. Some say Demeter's sorrow rendered the earth barren; others say anger made her spite the land by withholding seed.

Yet it's so difficult to find the truth in stories when they're curated by those who benefit from them.

In any case, winter. In Hades's bed.

Glück, again:

Persephone is having sex in hell.
Unlike the rest of us, she doesn't know
what winter is, only that
she is what causes it.

To save the earth, Persephone's father, Zeus, orders Hades to relinquish his bride and Hades, ever crafty, gives Persephone a pomegranate seed to eat to ensure her return for part of the year. And when he returns Persephone to her mother, Demeter, the fields bloom again, and corn is abundant.

When spring comes, Persephone arrives; in fall, she leaves.

The woman is on retreat in Saskatchewan; it's close to forty below. Tall pines glint in the sun. Hoar frost laces everything, renders winter enchanting. Animals come out to feed—deer on corn husks, birds on seeds, feral cats mill around the slop pail with the farm's kitchen scraps.

People die in this cold. Women die in this cold.

She thinks of her mother who wandered lost and in despair for years after the divorce. When she and her sister cleared out their mother's

apartment, they found surprises. Wigs: blond and brunette. Their
mother had never undergone chemotherapy; had she been playing
dress-up with others in the building? They laughed at the thought. Had
she snapped in rage after her husband left her and begun to stalk him?
A large white teddy bear her friend Millie bought for her. She always
had trouble sleeping, Millie said. Nights were long.

Later, after she went blind and stopped drinking, their mother
found a kind of grace for her remaining years. Embraced her daughters
again. Grew into her name.

Mothers and daughters, unmothered daughters, all left wandering.

Who among us hasn't been underground, hoping to survive our
own winter? Or is she indulging in the writer's fallback—wresting a
metaphor from whatever is at hand: a garden, a sunset.

A myth. A season.

Of course she is. A metaphor is another way to carry belief.

As Glück says,

What will you do,
when it is your turn in the field with the god?

victoria hospital

If you want to see your father alive you'd better get to the hospital.

She said what?

I've been visiting Mom in St. Boniface Hospital, returning at
night to her empty apartment. My brother Brian has flown in from
Ottawa and we have spent the evening with our sister, Allison, talking
about Mom's condition, unsure of what's next. Our younger brother's
call comes as a shock.

Colin's voice is strained. That's what she said. Dad's in the Vic and he doesn't have long.

Wait—Dad's in the hospital? Since when?

Saturday night. She didn't bother to let us know. And she wasn't even around.

Hang on. I don't understand.

She went away for the weekend. The health-care worker had to call an ambulance and go to the Vic with Dad.

She didn't leave a number with the worker? Where was she?

No idea. Can you contact the others? I'll meet you there.

My body is numb. The musty smell of smoke in Mom's apartment lines my nostrils and I can't think. I glance around: the brown florals and knick-knacks, her ashtray, the worn lounge chair.

We have to go to the hospital, I say.

I can't believe this, Brian says. What are the odds? Both parents?

Brian speeds through the night to the south side of the city, and Allison, Brian, and I troop into the hospital entrance. Everything feels as though I'm imagining it, as though I have to narrate what's happening to myself to believe it's real.

What are the odds, Brian says again.

We follow the signs to the ICU. We can hear Colin's voice in the distance. He's furious.

Why didn't you call? Why didn't you leave any contact information? Why did the hospital have to call Aunt Kay?

None of your fucking business, my father's wife yells. I don't have to answer to you.

Dad's been here for three days and you're only now letting us know?

M looks up, sees us, and turns toward her friend, a man I later learned worked with Dad for years. They look a bit chummy. Maybe that's where she was, I think.

When can we see him? We're his children, for god's sake. Colin is distraught.

I'll find out what's going on, a nurse says, and leads us all to a family waiting room. They're waiting for the priest, she adds.

We all exchange charged looks. Last rites?

Soon after, we hear garments swish in the hallway and see black cassocks turn a corner. Several minutes later, the nurse returns.

One at a time, she says. You have a minute or so each.

This is bullshit, someone mutters.

What will I say in this, my last minute with my father?

In the car, I'd asked Brian and Allison what they would say if they saw him.

How about, you broke our family and destroyed your wife. Was that woman worth it? Something like that?

How are we going to tell Mom this?

Are we telling her?

We are all ushered into the ICU and circle the bed. The only lights are from the medical equipment. M watches us from the corner.

When it's my turn to approach the bed, Dad seems to recognize me. I tell him Mom is in the hospital and it doesn't look good. He is tubed-up, with beeping monitors and a swirl of cords and devices, so only his eyes speak.

Is that concern I see? It's hard to tell. He looks at me and blinks rapidly. How do I communicate years of hurt, fury, disgust, and disappointment? My last words to him: a moment to sum up, to end, a life?

Venting twenty years of pent-up spleen would feel righteous, but what will that do? What do any of us want to hear as we leave the world?

I was seized with shock and my heart felt ragged, shredded. It ached. I might have said something like, *Go in peace. I wish you well.* Something anodyne.

After each of us has spoken to Dad, the priest and his assistant approach the bed. As soon as Dad sees them, his legs thrash and his body shakes. His eyes are small bright moons of terror.

It will be any time now, the nurse says as she ushers us back to the family room to wait.

An hour or so later, M comes to the door and Colin and his wife make conversation with her, a small truce perhaps, something about Dad's Air Force items. I don't have the heart to look at her. I could ask where all our family photos are, but I'd have to speak.

Another few hours and no word from the ICU. The family room becomes memory lane. My siblings and I reminisce about record collections, who played tricks on whom, the dreaded Swiss steak, tomato aspic, new bikes, old slights, and a secret or two. We laugh a lot. My sister admits sneaking into my closet to try on my clothes. First-borns are given the first of everything, she says, clothes and freedom, and I realize she is right. I didn't choose to be born first, I say, unsure if she is upset or if I should apologize. The last time all of us were in the same room together was the night my father said, "That's it. I'm done."

We wait until we can't. We are wired and spent. Another long drive on ice-packed Winnipeg streets back to Mom's smoky apartment where we wait for word from the hospital.

Dad doesn't die that night. He dies on the solstice, December 21st, when the earth is hinging from fall to winter, the shortest day of the year and the longest night.

The moon is waxing gibbous.

My mother never met M, my father's second wife. She never talked to us about any suspicions she might have had while they were married. Was she in denial, fearing abandonment? Or did she believe "my marriage, my problem"? He wanted to lose weight, so Mom cooked low-calorie meals. He went to Thunder Bay often to visit a sick cousin she'd never heard of, so she rearranged her part-time shifts at the hospital to accommodate his trips. Thousands of kilometres away, I was up to my neck in children and teaching and the daily urgencies of mid-life; what did I know of her struggles? A cousin indeed.

Over the years, I told her bits and pieces. The woman's appearance; her love of Vegas. Her complaints about the South Asian nurse tending to my father, the Chinese cardiologist, the Nigerian aide, all described in racist slurs. How none of us can bear to be around her.

You guys in Ottawa, she said to my brother one day on the phone, after taking the receiver from Dad. I don't get it. How about that Governor-General broad? What are they doing with a [n-word] for a Governor-General? She don't got no class at all.

My mother cackled when I told her this, incredulous. I watched her eyes go somewhere I can't go. Here is a woman who kept up on political issues, read books until she went blind and switched to audiobooks. A woman who gave no truck to fools.

Yet stood by, held out hope. The following December, two days before her own death, I will be at my mother's deathbed and she'll read my body language. Did he die? she'll ask, and I'll understand her question, even though her teeth are out and a tube is down her throat. Yes, he did, Mom. Yesterday afternoon.

How do you feel about that, she asks me. I don't know, I say. It's complicated. He was my father. But I can't say I loved him. I can never forgive him. But you. How are you?

I don't know. Her eyes are to the wall.

Do you want some time alone? She nods.

I straighten the sheets, wipe her forehead with a cool cloth, whisper that I'll be back in an hour.

I love you, I say, and she nods again. As I reach for the curtain, she turns her head and covers her eyes. Her mouth twists. It's truly over.

As I pull the curtain shut, I see she is shaking. From her head to her bare, scarred feet, she is shaking.

angels

My girls are angels, Mom says to the nurse. Allison has arrived and Mom lifts her hand in greeting. She's groggy, and her IV vein has collapsed again. Blood, another change of her johnny shirt. Each time a nurse tightens the elastic crumpling the papery skin on her arm, I wince.

As the nurse palpates Mom's wrist, Mom says to no one:

I have to do the right thing. When the time comes, I have to do the right thing.

Whatever you do is the right thing, I say.

Do what you need to do, my sister says.

My head is a mess. I'll have to make the best of it.

Allison and I exchange glances.

Has the barium been done? A man's voice. The resident has slipped inside the curtain and joins us at the end of the bed.

Just back, I say. I can't shake the image of my mother, barium dripping off her chin, legs shaking as she tried to stay upright, and me, cheerleading behind the protective screen: one more swallow, Mom. One more.

Grace? Mom looks in the direction of the man's voice. Do you know why you had the barium test?

What? I did it, she says. I don't want it again.

I know, he says. Not fun. Do you know why you had it done, Grace?

She closes her eyes, takes a breath. Because doctors need to legit-imize parts of the body. She sighs.

The resident looks at me, lips pursed. I'll come by later this after-noon and perhaps we can talk? He opens the curtain.

Angels, she says, ignoring him. My girls.

You called me a white-haired angel, I say. Last week, when I got here.

I've been in here a week?

But you're the angel, Mom. I throw back the word self-consciously. Our family doesn't talk this way, and I'm still trying to make sense of her comment to the resident. People talk of hospital delirium in the elderly. Whatever it is, it's frightening.

You almost didn't have hair at all! Mom's teeth are out and she slurs her words. I thought you'd be bald for life. Now you have too much!

Punk has the good hair, I say. I turn to my sister.

Mom nods her head. She's the angel.

No, I'm not. Allison laughs, but her head is down. This is dangerous territory. This trip to Winnipeg marks the first time my sister and I have spent any sustained time together since I left home at seventeen. Both of us have made decisions we regret, committed sins our parents can't forgive. And we both know our mother is a loose cannon at the best of times.

Why, at a time like this, can't we break through old family patterns to say what's on our minds? I feel as though I'm on a stage, speaking lines someone else wrote.

Allison smiles. You're tired, Mom. Get some sleep. I have to go back to work anyway. I only popped in to see how the test went.

You were an angel. My mother points at my sister.

But you! Mom turns to me. You're like me. You're a bullshitter.

A small laugh creaks inside her throat. Goodnight, Irene, she says. Goodnight, angels.

She lifts her arm as though she's blessing the congregation. Close the curtain please.

breath

Jennifer pauses at the end of the bed, jaw set, eyes down. They'll sometimes stop breathing for thirty seconds, she says, then start up again. Sometimes they'll sit up, look at you with total awareness, then fall back. It can take minutes, or days. Two minutes with no breath is when they call it.

My sister died this time last year, she says, so I understand. Allison and I exchange looks. I'm sorry, we whisper.

Jennifer nods. Like so many of the nurses here, Jennifer is so young.

The aspirator growls in the background. It looks like an old paint mixer with arms but it clears Mom's stomach and keeps her from choking. I move the tubing to adjust her sheets and the static electricity shocks me.

Jennifer remains motionless. The last person Mom spoke to was Brittany, I say. When Brittany came in with an aide to turn her, Mom held out her arms. Oh, I love you, she said. If ever the word *beseeching* applied, it was then. *Beseech.* From the same root as *seek.* A cosmic muscle, a pull, like divining.

You know she's blind, don't you? Jennifer nods.

Now she's confused.

It doesn't matter, says Allison, whose left hand is against her nose. She is taking her turn sitting near the aspirator. The stench is putrid. Mom has had no food, not even water, for a week.

She hugged someone she thought she loved.

It's the morning of December 25, and the temperature is almost forty below. The sky is the texture and colour of pack ice. Mom's hands are hot. When she was rolled into this room yesterday, a doctor came to introduce himself and held out his hand. I am the palliative care physician, he said. Jesus Christ, Mom muttered, and pulled back her arm sharply.

Later that day, Christmas Eve afternoon, her friend Millie came to visit. Oh, I love you, Millie, Mom crooned, and her arms reached from the bed like a child wanting up.

Soon after, Mom stopped speaking altogether. But late last night, she suddenly sat bolt upright, eyes closed, and gave the one nearest her a ferocious hug. Each of her children in turn approached, embraced her. Then she flopped back on the bed and hasn't moved or spoken since.

As I tell Jennifer this, she smiles a distant smile, gathers her supplies.

Even that scratching thing, I say, that Tourette's thing—that's gone.

She knows you. You're her daughters. Jennifer pats Mom's foot. She averts her eyes, swipes her hand across her nose, opens the door to leave. Don't worry. She's not in pain. Her organs are shutting down. It won't be long now.

Allison and I sit on either side of the bed, each stroking a hand, forming a mother-daughter chain. Outside, smokestacks billow white sheets into the air and cars fret back and forth on the Maryland Bridge. Why so much traffic on Christmas morning? Someone out for coffee cream, perhaps. A family with gifts on the way to Gran's, someone driving home from a party.

The night before, each of us took turns moving from chair to bedside to family lounge to chair again. The only nod to the season was Mom's favourite carol on the stereo: "O, Holy Night." Suddenly, out of the dark corner came Colin's voice.

It's midnight, he said. Merry Christmas, everyone! He got up to kiss each of us, including Mom, whose ragged, huffing breaths laced the air. If there was irony in his voice, I couldn't tell.

How does movement in the room affect Mom, I wonder. How does she know when to let go?

Palliative nurses say the dying need only a suggestion, a gesture of reconciliation, and they signal to us when they are ready: we're to watch and listen. What seems insignificant to us—has the rent been paid? Will you bury me where I want to be buried? Have you told my cousin, called my brother?—can loom large to the leaving.

From the window, I see the Golden Boy glinting on the Legislature. I am so far away from the sea.

The sign on the door says *NPO—nil per os*. Nothing by mouth. The IV is gone, leaving green and purple bruises. Mom's peeling tongue is swollen, rough as the skin of a toad.

Last week—was it only?—we brought in Popsicles and she whooped with delight. The day after, we poured a few drops of Scotch onto a spoon, and watched her drowsy eyes pop open: Oh, my! Well, I'll have more of that!

A song is on the stereo, "Nessun dorma." *O notte. Tramontate stelle.* I rinse yet another washcloth under cold water and begin slowly, carefully to wipe Mom's face and chest. She takes in one deep, shuddering breath; another, then her chest is still. Allison's eyes are wide: is this it?

One corner of Mom's mouth lifts, an almost-smile. I wipe her cheek, her neck, and undo the top button of her blue nightgown to reach her collarbones. Cornflower blue; I'd helped her buy it last year at The Bay in the local mall. She'd plopped down on a pile of boxes while I wove in and out of racks to find an easy-to-button housedress. Take it; that's good enough, she said. Let's go. And I'm paying, so don't try.

We'll take you to Strathclair, Mom, I say, wringing out the washcloth. We'll take you to be with Aunt Laura, your dad, Aunt Bell. Jean will be there. We'll make sure you are under the Glenn stone, with everyone.

I remove the cloth to rinse it in cold water, and it's then I notice.

Her left eye is dry, staring beyond anywhere we can see. But her right eye is bright, brimming with tears that cling to her lower lashes. Her chest lifts. One breath more.

talk to me

Mom and Dad died within days of each other, and a month later I was back in Nova Scotia, in bed with tea, Kleenex, my notebook, and a mystery to solve. At my father's funeral, a thin man had come up behind my chair quietly and offered his hand.

I was dazed, missed his name. Across the reception room, M was holding court. The man crouched behind our table, as though he was trying not to be seen.

Your dad would be glad to know you're all here, he said. He, uh—I think you should know—he had regrets.

And then, a rush of words: We wanted your dad's Legion friends to be here—he gestured to the table of photographs and memorabilia—and something to represent his shortwave radio buddies. We wanted it to be different, but unfortunately—he cocked his head in M's direction—I have to go.

And he disappeared.

After some sleuthing, I'd learned he was my father's former lawyer and perhaps his only friend. I searched for his number in Winnipeg, took a deep breath, and dialled.

We speak carefully. I'm trying to tease out anything about my father's final weeks and months, I tell him. He sounds relieved to hear from me, but wary.

I was fond of your mother, he said. But your father's new wife, well... He left the words hanging.

Can you tell me anything about Dad's last days?

Well, when your dad went into the hospital, M was nowhere to be found. We may never know why, he says. He'd been left in full-time care while she was in Hawaii, and you know, for such an openly grieving widow.... His voice trails off again.

That's what the priest had said at the funeral. She plays the part.

As we talk, he relaxes. He and Dad shared a love of prairie railway history. After the war, my father loaded milk cans on slow freights, trained to be a telegrapher, and took a series of promotions, eventually becoming a superintendent of transportation. The two men had gathered artifacts of those days for the railway historical society. No one knows where the items are now.

When you look at it, your father was always in communications of some sort.

I didn't respond; clearly my father had saved his communications skills for his job.

A pause. Your father's last outing was with me, I think.

I cling to the voice. Decades of my father's absence, and now I'm privy to these details.

We went to Tim's. Your dad inched his way up the ramp, and a line formed behind him. Instead of becoming impatient, people cheered him on. You can do it, they said. One step at a time. And he made it.

His last coffee and doughnut, I think.

Afterwards, your father wanted to see his old haunts. So we drove to the CN station downtown, out to St. Boniface and south to the Symington Yard.

He said he'd wished he'd reconciled with his family.

By now, my heart is hammering.

Your dad seemed more—how can I say this?—spiritually conscious. I think he was referring not only to his children and grandchildren, but to your mother. I sensed he had let old grudges go.

I'm not sure how to answer, so I wait.

Oh, and before we'd gone for coffee, I'd picked up the renewal forms for his driver's licence. He was so proud to be eighty-five and still eligible to drive. But he called the next day to say he'd changed his mind.

venice is sinking

The angel is perched on top of a wooden coat rack outside the anteroom—likely a dressing room for a doge at some point—where my brother has a rollaway cot. We tied her silk ribbons to this makeshift tree, along with silver beads, a red bow, a scarf.

To believe, I guess.

It's Christmas Eve, fifty-two weeks later, seven thousand kilometres away.

The flowered chintz walls suggest the luxury of the original fourteenth-century palace. Overhead, Murano glass chandeliers; between rooms, stone pillars. A warm thick carpet leads to an all-marble bathroom with polished silver fittings and dangerously slick floor.

On the sideboard, a silver ice bucket, wine from the alimentari, olives, a wedge of pecorino and two red-ribboned Panettone we'll never touch. The gilded mirror doubles the single orchid, its long stems pointing toward what little light seeps in from the windows overlooking the lagoon.

Below us, walkers on the Riva degli Schiavoni shrug their shoulders against the cold and damp.

No snow here, but I am chilled to the bone.

None of us has stayed in a five-star European hotel before, let alone a former palace. Our elder son, a hotel employee at the time, booked a suite in the historic Danieli for the price of a secondary-highway motel room in Canada. The opulence, the ancient buildings, lyrical voices in another language, a ride on a vaporetto and a walk down stone streets to have squid for dinner—all create the distance we need, my brother and I especially, to make it through the season.

The angel on the coat rack is five inches of stuffed ivory satin with an implacable face as comical as her fat-booted feet. She's travelled in my backpack across Canada at least twice, passed through scanners at Heathrow and de Gaulle.

I believe in angels, sings ABBA.

Except I don't, not really. I do remember a picnic in Chester Basin where a guy on a flatbed stretched the word *angels* into four nasal syllables above the ka-chunk-ka-chunk of his guitar.

I found this angel last year at the Salvation Army thrift store across from St. Boniface Hospital. Nursing stations and elevators wore garlands, icicles, and cardboard Santas, and holiday Muzak blared in the cafeteria. Brian and I tacked up Mom's nursing photo on the corkboard, along with a snapshot of Mom, her brother Jack, and Gram—Mom looked to be in her teens (I will never know where that oak tree is). We'd found, too, a snapshot of Bob MacDonald, Mrs. Gibb's son who was like a brother to Mom.

The angel cost two dollars, and when I tied her ribbons to Mom's bedpost, she looked to be the perfect symbol for the season.

Since Mom was blind, the photos and the angel were for the hospital staff, who referred to Mom as 5B. A kidney was in 5F, an infarct in 5C, a bowel obstruction down the hall: all the broken, failing bodies bearing only the name of their condition.

5B's condition, at that point, was undetermined.

Venice is bitterly cold. My coat doesn't keep out the piercing damp in the stone streets. Venice sinks two millimetres a year, and in late fall and early winter, tide peaks of the Adriatic called *acqua alta* flood the city, especially around the lagoon. In 2019, we'll see photos of Venetians swimming in Piazza San Marco.

On Christmas Eve day we walk to the Rialto market, the Ghetto Nuovo in the Cannaregio up to the Arsenale and into tiny shops. Long, narrow streets open to small courtyards where we find our bearings; five wandering foreigners—my husband, our two sons, my brother Brian and me—as alien to ourselves as to our surroundings. I wish my sister were here.

At the hotel, we put up our feet and pour ourselves a glass of wine. I hear talk about going to bed early. Brian, who has been quiet all day, says, Okay, where were we at this time? What's the time difference? Six hours? Seven? It was morning. She had another day.

The room is silent.

Suddenly, I'm alert. Mass, I say. Let's go to St. Mark's. The Basilica.

The lineup will be huge, someone says. It's too cold.

It's a starless night and the crowds at Piazza San Marco offer warmth. We arrive a half-hour before mass begins; a wide arc of hundreds waits to enter a single door in the Basilica. We jostle step by step, lose and find one other, shoulder to shoulder, feet tripping on other feet, muffled by wool, fur, scarves, another's breath. A woman tucks her head under my arm like a football and propels herself forward into the vestibule.

Inside, I look up and can't breathe: the ornate balconies, glittering mosaics, massive, lustrous metal pipes whose sounds penetrate my chest. I squeeze AJ's arm and feel the press of the lump of satin in my breast pocket, freed from the coat rack. From behind a pillar several metres away, I see Brian's eyes glistening. This time last year, he was playing "Nessun dorma" on the stereo in the palliative room. Guaranteed tear-jerker.

This time last year I was wrestling with reality: my mother was dying. How fiercely my mind fought the obvious, hung on to thin strands of hope. To believe in this living, as John Prine sings, is a hard way to go.

We are thousands of hours and kilometres from the last Christmas Eve, from the last room my mother would inhabit. All of us a presence in a centuries-old Basilica breathing in the smoky tang of incense and perfume, our pulsing bodies inching toward a sacred centre so distant we can barely glimpse it.

Midnight is moments away. I forget I have a body as I flow into this larger, breathing one, illuminated by countless flickering lights, swathed in the choir's swelling voices billowing harmonies surfing above the billowing organ.

yellow roses

What was it he said?

We don't get many here from the reservation.

Seriously. What an ass.

My sister's birthmark glowed on her forehead. We were hot, exhausted, and half in the bag.

The room reeked of old smoke. We were sprawled side by side on lumpy and musty-smelling single beds. In the corner, a colonial chair with a cushion in seventies autumn hues and a small rabbit-ear television with a turn knob. Around us, mixed-palette particleboard and panelling, curling wallpaper, a fused aluminum slider window, and indoor-outdoor carpet in full-spectrum excrement browns.

The flowered polyester bedspreads were the arm-hair-raising static-makers our mother used to buy. We needed fresh air, but even the corkscrew from our cooler wouldn't budge the clasp on the windows. At least the bathroom was spotless.

After we spoke with the owners outside the hotel, the woman gave us a key and they drove away. We were the only people in the building. Main Street was so empty I expected tumbleweeds to roll by.

Do you think anyone noticed two middle-aged women drinking in the graveyard?

It'll be all over town tomorrow.

Reservation, ha. My god. And then you said to him—huh?

I know. The look on your face!

Between us: the heels of two bottles of wine, Allison's tiny cosmetic mirror-turned-knife with bits of avocado on it, a half-eaten package of crackers and two apples. The coffee shop was locked. Nowhere within fifteen kilometres to buy nuts, a piece of cheese, fast food—anything. Snacks we'd bought at the Co-op in Neepawa were limp and damp.

We weren't hungry, nor were we fit to drive.

Allison fanned herself with the newspaper.

I liked her, though. The woman. She was all right.

She probably does all the work around here. Proprietor, my ass. He just hangs out in the truck, gawking. His shirt was greasy at the neck. And those teeth—

We have a reservation, I said to him. In a deserted one hundred-year-old hotel in a dying town. Jesus. I must have sounded snotty to him. So *urban*. I stretched out the word.

Oh, Punk. This is hard.

I know. I had too much wine.

She's been underground all winter. Frozen. Ashes, but still.

I wonder if she ever stayed in this room when she was younger. I bet she did.

Well, her dad died here—right downstairs.

She'd get a kick out of this, though. Her daughters alone in the old hotel. Not a soul around. Not. A. Soul. This has Stephen King written all over it.

Good thing we booked ahead, huh?

Early Sunday morning, Mother's Day, we'd packed up my sister's Jeep, ready to drive to Strathclair, two hours west of Winnipeg. We'd attended a weekend-long writers' festival, then walked the gravel path of the newly dedicated Carol Shields labyrinth. It was a moving ceremony, serious but not sombre; the air was brisk but the sun appeared from high-moving clouds often enough to warm us. Buds were starting to burst on the trees.

Our great-grandfather Carson Glenn had helped to build this hotel and his son Bill, the grandfather we'd never known, had died here. Last June, after Mom's interment ceremony, my husband, my brother Brian, and I decided to stay in town overnight. We had the hotel suite—two and a half rooms on the top floor where we found a chair with broken legs, ripped couches, and a fist-sized hole in one of the panelled walls.

Hockey tournament heaven, said my brother.

Almost a year later, and I'd been imagining the cemetery locked in thirty- to forty-below temperatures under prairie wind–sculpted snowbanks. Mom's ashes in an urn, under a plaque beside the large Glenn family stone. Just as she had wanted.

All my life I had been torn between intimacy and retreat from my mother—we were both alike and different; we'd fall out of touch for years at a time, but I could always draw on a bodily connection. I was from her; because she moved in the world, I did as well. Her death put me at a threshold. A primitive part of me felt buried with those ashes under the snow. As Megan O'Rourke said: "the people we most love do become a physical part of us, ingrained in our synapses, in the pathways where memories are created."

Punk and I had travelled between Saskatchewan and Manitoba before, and always stopped at the Riverside Cemetery in Neepawa to visit the grave of Jean Margaret Wemyss Laurence. It was near rolling hills and the river, thick with flowering bushes and birdlife. Peggy (nicknamed by the mother she lost when she was four) apparently hated flowers, and her gravestone, next to the Wemyss family marker, is always left clear. Only clover grows around its base, a leaf of which I once pressed between the pages of my journal. Near the grave is the stone angel, the statue that inspired the title of Laurence's novel. The angel is, in fact, a shepherdess, and marks the grave for a man named Davidson.

But no Peggy visit for us this time. We need to outrun the sun. We reached Neepawa in time to buy a dozen yellow roses and the clerk filled a disposable container with water, cut the stems, and wrapped the bouquet.

They'll last longer, she chirped, and I thanked her, knowing they'd be left on a grave to dry in the sun. Months before, our youngest brother had passed the cemetery on a business trip and placed a vase of plastic flowers on Mom's grave.

Better to have wilted roses working their way into the ground, I thought, than a petroleum by-product sticking out of a February snowbank.

Maybe Mom was right; maybe I am a snob.

My whole body exhaled when we turned off the highway into the driveway at the edge of the cemetery.

Mom, I'm here, I wanted to shout, but didn't. A strange, forlorn intimacy had ambushed me, the kind that causes my breathing to quiver and renders me mute. Punk opened the trunk of the Jeep, we opened the swinging gate, and soon spread an old blanket on the grass by Mom's grave. We cracked open the screw-top bottles, raised a toast, dug a small hole by the family gravestone, and tucked in the roses. The wind turned our hair to dervishes and flapped our jackets. Buds on the peony bush were beginning to form, and birds were busy in the tall pines.

Perhaps it's odd to have favourite cemeteries, but I do. The one in Neepawa where Margaret Laurence is buried, the Fairview Lawn Cemetery in Halifax, and a few others across Canada, including one in Selkirk where Métis relatives are buried. The Strathclair Cemetery, however, is my favourite. But do I want to be buried here, thousands of kilometres from where I live now? Who would visit? Does it matter?

As my sister and I sit, we can hear traffic humming on the nearby Yellowhead Highway. This graveyard is set far back, with gently sloping paths, and gives me a glimpse of what the land was like before settlers carved it up. Robert Pogue Harrison writes about what he calls the "dominion of the dead": more humans are buried in the earth than are living above it. Below our feet, second cousins, a few greats and great-greats, aunts and grandparents. Coming from a peripatetic family, having this much of my gene pool in one acre of good dirt would, in Nova Scotia, make me a credible resident.

Here in Strathclair, Allison and I know only our mother's cousin, in her nineties and suffering from dementia. Jean sometimes remembers us when we visit but only if we offer a lot of backstory. Some locals recall our mother, Grace, but only when we connect her to Carson, the Glenn patriarch and ancestor of dozens of local Glenns.

As the sun sets, I lie down to watch the clouds, watching colour deepen in the west behind the trees and near the railway tracks, thinking: this is as close as I can get to Mom. The pull is visceral. As a young mother it felt as though my body was a magnet, that the tiny human in another room or in another part of the city was still tethered, soon to return home. Here there is no body, only ashes below the ground. There is no language for this.

The trees along the back of the cemetery are huge, the smaller trees below them like offspring. Writer Hope Edelman describes the redwood trees of Muir Woods, how the seeds are stored in burls that grow where the tree trunk and its root system meet. When a tree is downed, for whatever reason, the trauma causes burls to release the seeds, creating a circle of new trees around the old one. These daughter trees, as Edelman calls them, grow by absorbing available sunlight, along with moisture and nutrients from the old root system.

What have my sister and I absorbed from this woman whose remains have been placed in a faux-Wedgwood urn? What do we carry forward?

As we sat on the blanket, we told our mother about our goings-on. Generic talk: The boys are fine. Mike has a new job. I'm thinking of retiring. What might I have said without being aware of an audience? What would Punk have said if she were alone? I realized how much I missed the long-distance conversations Mom and I often had on Sundays.

Long distance indeed. Perhaps we are always talking with our mothers, whether they are alive or long gone, whether we love or hate them, have lost them, lionized, abandoned, or escaped from them.

Later, in the hotel, as my sister and I tried to find sleep on the musty beds in the deep quiet of the hotel, I remembered a story Mom told of a maypole dance in a small railway town, the kind of event likely organized by a service group. Long ribbons, a pole, and feet weaving, looping in and out as they circled the pole. Didn't seem to have a point. Edson, perhaps? Or was it Saskatoon? Or was it here, in Strathclair, in the halcyon days before her father died?

Mom once told me she used to feel like that.

Like a maypole? God, it's hot in here. We should have booked the suite.

She wrote that in a letter, after the divorce.

Well, four children. And no help.

Allison's eyes are closed. What a gift to have a sister, I think. I couldn't have done this alone.

I'm never having that much wine again, Allison groans.

I'm glad we saw the grave without snow.

And with buds on the trees.

She doesn't feel gone, you know.

She's not, I think.

just the facts

She doesn't believe in objectivity. Impartiality, yes. Accuracy, most definitely. A serious look at her own biases and assumptions for sure. But everyone comes from somewhere and no one has a god's-eye view. She cannot speak for anyone but herself, on or off the page.

Like so many writers, she returns often to the same themes—loss, grief, betrayal, her mother, to name a few. She knows it's important, as Patricia Hampl says, to mistrust revenge and to avoid mere confession and emotional unloading, even though those can be natural impulses. How much is too much? When is writing mere self-indulgence? Between a writer's seasoned instincts and the reader's openness to another's world, however, the story will find a place to land.

Joan Didion's comment that "writers are always selling somebody out" stings because it rings true. Luanne Armstrong's daughter once said, "We're just material to you, aren't we?" The woman knows her stories are second-hand even in the house of her own memory. She checks facts, calls on her relatives, allows work to sit to be sure she is ready to put it out into the world. And even though many of the people she writes about have died, any license she believes she has to write about them is tempered; she stays with what can be known.

Perhaps in telling stories she finds hope, release, connection with others. The theologian Walter Brueggemann said that "memory produces hope in the same way amnesia produces despair." Telling stories from memory is an exercise in selection and complexity. A writer can't tell everything. "You may not let rip," said Annie Dillard. The woman has to examine her motives. If she uses the work to catalogue petty grievances, to exact revenge, to polish her halo, or to have the last word, the writing suffers. Readers are like sniffer dogs; they detect self-pity and self-righteousness with the twitch of a nose. Let the facts speak, she tells herself, and get out of the way.

where they dance

It was spring in Canada, and although Greece was warm in comparison, the wind had a bite. Our clothes flapped in the stiff wind as we climbed down into the boat, chattering and trying to keep our balance. I found a seat alone at the back and looked up at the clear morning sky, wisps of cloud and the faint outline of the moon.

Once we left the dock, I tied my scarf, zipped up my sweater, and opened my shoulder bag. My friends' shouts and laughter lifted above the wind and the sound of the motor, but I kept my head down.

I pulled out the tiny plastic packet, gripped it between my fingers.

It must have been a friend of a friend of the innkeeper, Giorgos, who offered us this tour of the harbour. Nothing was impossible, it seemed, for a troupe of enthusiastic Canadian writers who'd gathered that spring in Crete. A rocky ride on loosely gravelled switchbacks to the top of the mountain. Songs and endless krasi and plates of olives and graviera at Giorgos's late into the night.

And today, a chance to zip around the waters off Sfakiá on the southern coast, perhaps travel as far as the secluded Sweetwater Beach, a sandy nook tucked under the rocky cliffs.

The few strands in the plastic packet weren't white but almost sepia, in part because of her medications and her lifetime of smoking. During her last days, she'd rip off her johnny shirt daily, scratch her skull and cry out: Off! Cut it all off!

I'd been sitting by her bedside one day, shocked at how small her body had become. Her skin was smooth and had an oily sheen.

Is there any place you wish you'd travelled to, I asked. Even as I said it, I knew the past tense was an admission of what we didn't want to talk about.

That place where they dance.

I could barely make out the words through the sluice of syllables. Her teeth were out; the nurses feared she'd choke.

She'd been off the continent once, to Ireland, where my father felt—or perhaps wished—he truly belonged, and to Scotland, the country she considered her homeland. She treasured her tourist trinkets from the site of the Battle of Culloden and always had a thing against the English.

Dance. Greece? You wish you'd gone to Greece?

She nodded, and her mouth curled up at the corner.

You're thinking Zorba? Now she was smiling.

She coughed. Are you going to cut my hair or not?

As the others chatted with the man at the helm, I braced my feet on the hull floor. Sea spray on my hands made my fingers slippery, so I had to grip the little envelope firmly as I opened it. I turned, pretending to watch the bright white wake behind us and released the strands into the mist.

from the back of a shepherd's truck

Rag mops with bad dye jobs. Strawberry- and dirt-streaked cream puffs on hooves, their daggy ends dangling. I look one creature directly in the eye. His horns are perfectly formed and he holds my gaze before dipping his muzzle to the ground for the kernels of corn Nikos is scattering. What am I looking at? A low-lying canopy of red-veined wool, gathered under a tree Giorgos says even his great-great-grandmother had known as large. The name of the tree? No one knows.

We have lurched up precipitous hairpin turns above Sfakiá in the bed of Nikos's truck, all six of us, unbelted and grinning, clutching our hats. The road's shoulders are soft and the truck's tires bald. Nikos does this run daily, though, so I talk myself down from full-on panic. His dog—a large mongrel, perhaps a German shepherd mix—runs behind us. The dog thunders over the gravel, begins to foam at the mouth, and just as I fear it will drop dead from exertion, Nikos slows the truck, allows the dog to jump in the back with us. Its glazed eyes reveal exhaustion, but it welcomes my hands on its back. My friend Kim and I have organized a writing retreat in the south of Crete and Nikos, a regular in Giorgios's tavern, has invited us to his farm in the hills for a meal. I stand in the back of a truck high in the Crete landscape, catching wind in my hair. Not something I thought I'd be doing in my sixties.

Oh, how I wish my mother had had the chance to do this.

Nikos has stopped to feed the animals. I take another step, aim the camera. The sheep recoil together, a shaken blanket. Mr. Ram turns back to take another glance at me. I have been seen. Human and animal, recognizing each other's wilderness. I bend into the flock, close enough to graze the back of one so intent on separating the yellow kernels from the gravel that a two-legged intruder must seem no longer a threat. Or at least, the risk is worth the food. My fingers touch wool. The creature jumps, rippling the mass.

Strung between sky and sea an hour above Sfakiá, I can see where faded snowdrifts line the broken trails, mountain pastures flecked yellow and white with new growth. The air is a bright mix of thyme, sour blossoms, goat manure, the gin whiff of evergreen, and the fading chill of winter.

Nikos, the shepherd to about ten thousand sheep and goats, killed and dressed one of the goats the day before. He had prepared the stew down in Sfakiá and is carrying it in the cab of the truck, braced between the legs of one of our band of writers. Nikos wears all black, including the sariki, or traditional headscarf, his mother tatted for him. His handlebar moustache is white against his red cheeks.

Here in the hills, traffic is a straggle of stick-legged goats bawling a ragtag baseline under the clank of their bells. Rockfall scrapes the underbelly of the truck, and above the road, circling us like wonder, kites and hawks. From this precipice, and this, and this one, too, we can turn our eyes from the road to the sea and, if the horizon is clear, point at North Africa. You could find us easily on your GPS; you could point to us on a map of the world: simply look somewhere between daydream and myth.

grace house

If we return to the old home as to a nest, it is because memories are dreams, because the home of other days has become a great image of lost intimacy.

Gaston Bachelard, *The Poetics of Space*

The house is lopsided; the east side leans toward the United Church next door. Last night, I slept on stained sofa cushions on the hardwood floor under my damp coat, and this morning I am standing at the sink stabbing at leftover fruit salad from a container in my carry-on. I don't know a soul here; my friend and his partner won't be at their nearby farm until June. I'll clean the cupboards, pick up some groceries, and ask someone if there's a place in town to check my email. Afterward, I'll move the piano from the porch into the living room.

I love this house.

Last night, from the window of the bus, I saw a spring storm rise out of the west, a long dark broom across the horizon. Lightning sliced the dusk and short-circuited something in me, an ache as deep as memory. By the time I stepped off the bus the rain was pelting and the lightning closer. The man from the bus depot waved me into his truck: he'd drive me to the house.

One block? I asked. That's what we do here, he said, as the wipers flapped and spray shot from the wheels in the rutted road. The inside of the cab flashed bright; lightning was at the edge of town.

What am I doing here? Why am I opening the door to this little Depression-era house on the prairie? A wooden storey-and-a-half with bad plumbing and high ceilings, with broken blinds and a porch to the sunset, with an old piano and a runaway garden and rooms ready to be filled—five provinces away from my husband and sons? And why now? It's true that people are more open to new ideas and adventures at turning points in their lives. But do they buy houses thousands of kilometres from home?

I look out the window at the abundance of plant life, dormant but blanketing the yard. The tall pines between the house and the church are stalwart, and they reassure me. One day, the pastor will invite me to read poetry in that church, but I don't know this now.

The open horizon, solitude, all for the price of a modest used car. I'm not sure what I'm doing, but I'm okay with it.

I'd forgotten about the cement-like properties of Saskatchewan mud, and when I return from the store, I sit on the steps and scrape the muck off my boots. Early-spring sun shines in a sea of puddles on the road. I rummage in my suitcase, glad I brought a plug-in travel element to heat water in a cup for instant coffee.

I had braced myself for open curiosity when I walked across the street, up the concrete steps, and through the spring-loaded wooden door of the grocery store. A couple of women at the back chatted with the owner behind the meat counter, and as I squeezed behind them they turned, smiled, said hello. I felt their eyes follow me. I wondered if they guessed I was the one who'd walked into Joe Donald's insurance company-cum-real-estate-cum-notary-public office late last summer, asking about the For Sale sign I saw on Main Street.

Behind the till—the sort I'd used as a teenaged cashier at Safeway—the wall was papered with curled posters, tear-off ads with phone numbers. As I lined up my items on the U-shaped conveyor belt, I talked about the rainstorm with the tiny bright-eyed woman at the cash. A broad-shouldered man stepped into the store as I left and nodded sharply in my direction; on the street, a driver waved at me. Someone home for lunch will likely comment on the new person they saw in the store this morning.

I'd lived in a series of railway towns this size when I was young, and by the time I was a teenager, small-town curiosity inflamed me. Why is everyone so nosy? But here, while I feel self-conscious, I don't feel overly protective of my privacy. In fact, the promise of a house on Main Street in a small town seems exactly right after the winter that broke my life in half.

porch

For years I have wanted a porch, a summer room. When I'm done, the porch in this old house on the prairie will be bright, a place to watch what's growing in the yard—lilies, I hope—and to look down Main Street at sunset to see the sky roar in red, pink, and blue. To taste the breezes through the screen at night. A perch for morning coffee, an evening cup of tea, a word or two through the screen with people walking by.

Right now, it's dismal. I'll have to pull up the stained indoor-outdoor carpet, scrape down to the wood flooring, find the original window openings under the sixties panelling, and open the room to the light. I'll build—or perhaps ask my brother if he will build—a daybed frame to hold a single mattress. Fix the sticky living room door. The porch can then be used, in a pinch, as another bedroom.

In Northern Alberta in the 1950s, the most I could hope for as a retreat was a cool spot on the front stoop where I'd sip Kool-Aid and call out to a friend whizzing by on her bicycle. Later, when we lived in a railway house on Lathlin Avenue in The Pas, what my mother called "the verandah" faced the railway tracks on one side, the Opaskwayak reserve across the river on the other. I don't remember playing in there; all I recall were the grain trains shuddering past, the rattle and clatter of four busy children, my harried mother's dripping arms over a wringer washer, and the occasional sound of my father, going in and out on his way to or from Lynn Lake or Flin Flon or a Mason's meeting.

Verandah, indeed: for women like my mother, time to sit in a porch with a cup of tea would have been as rare as a blue moon.

And yet, I think of summer porches as women's spaces, a means to be both in the house and connected to the community. The word *porch* derives from portico, those covered entrances with columns outside Greek temples. And Latin, *porta*: passage. A transitional space. Women, especially, thrive in liminal spaces, at least the women I've known.

Of course. I think of my friend Pat, who should be here with me.

Pat had driven out here from Saskatoon last fall when I signed the closing papers. We vowed then to return here to write together, and to finally, after decades, catch up. But in the last few months grief had impaled me, I took a leave from work, and Pat underwent yet another round of chemotherapy. Six years of chemo; no one I knew had such tenacity.

Is this only a grown-up playhouse? Am I an impulsive fool? Am I, like my father, indulging in a perilous mid-life dalliance? In my case, not with a younger woman, but with an old house. An affair with my past, the prairie I love and days of bright possibility.

Suddenly, I'm bone-tired and sad. I tell myself it's the months of travelling and minor ailments: the long December in Winnipeg when my parents died, back to Nova Scotia, up to Yellowknife and Whitehorse for poetry readings, then back home with a bout of the flu and bronchitis. But this is more than fatigue; this feels more like psychic whiplash.

I can do this. I will do this. It's only early afternoon and the sun is glorious. Children's voices erupt outside, behind the steady procession of truck motors. Yes, a truck. A truck to search for furniture would help. The local garage must have a loaner.

The house creaks; something ticks in the heat register when the furnace turns on. I drain my coffee cup.

Right. Okay piano, you're on. I use my back and legs to inch the beast away from the wall, then swing it around to position its legs by the door to the living room. It's a tall, solid, century-old Gerhard Heintzman the previous owners left behind, along with a sagging, thread-bare old couch. The piano once belonged to Sadie Doner, a widow who now lives in a seniors' care home about twenty miles away. I'll learn this from the librarian, Velma, whose husband, Dale, once stayed in the house as a young boy. This is the magic of small towns. Forget gossip, prying eyes. Here are interwoven stories.

This is a bloody heavy piano. I stop to catch my breath, heart thumping, and I open the lid, try the keys, plunk a few notes. The sound is a bit tinny, a notch off-key, but the piano is certainly playable.

Down in the cold room, I find a few rags, some folded cardboard, a filthy throw rug. I position the rug under the piano leg, slide down to a crouch, and use my legs to heave. The piano slide-bumps up over the molding and lurches into the living room.

When I manoeuver it against the long wall, I know immediately this was its earlier home. My brother Brian plays, as do friends responsible for my being in this small town. My friend Rose plays. We will have music nights. I sit at the bench for a few minutes and pick with one hand notes to "The Tennessee Waltz," "You Are My Sunshine," and "Mairzy Doats," a few of Mom's favourites. Not bad.

I'll find old sheet music in a thrift store around these parts, I'm sure of it.

for a song

Let me live in a house by the side of the road.
Sam Walter Foss

Piano, done. I have to keep moving, run ahead of the elevator drops of grief, the fissures of sadness. They're gone; they're truly gone. No more words to say, nothing more to be done.

As I curled up on the cushions last night, I could see the moon through the front piano windows to the south. I tried to imagine the families who lived here, looked out at the prairie sky. My heart lifted, thinking of how to furnish this space.

Thrift stores. Already I'm scheming. Mennonite thrift stores are famous in Saskatchewan for their cleanliness and quality, and the driving will be freeing, rejuvenating. Dishes. Old furniture. I will find a Sears catalogue and order mattresses, bedding, small appliances. A new stove, small. An apartment-sized fridge.

I cannot believe I'm here, that I've done this.

The month before Mom died, I'd flown from Nova Scotia to Winnipeg for a poetry reading, and was surprised and pleased my brother and sister would be there. In fact, everyone in my birth family—even Aunt Kay—joined us at McNally-Robinson. Not my father or M, however, not with Mom in the same room. The thought of M at a poetry reading? I don't think so.

The day of the reading, Mom sat in her favourite chair in her apartment, cigarette in hand, drinking tea, her dark glasses on the end table. She wasn't hungry, and in retrospect, I realize how sick she must have been. It was time to find a place where she'd be safe, eat well, be free from daily upkeep. Millie came once a week to do laundry and some cooking, but it wasn't enough.

Don't you dare put me in a home, Mom said. She was reading my mind.

It was mid-November, and I decided then to return to Winnipeg within the month so my siblings and I could check out assisted living homes. Surely Mom would come to her senses.

As she rose from her chair, feeling the wall to make her way to the kitchen for more tea, I blurted it out.

I bought a house, Mom. In Saskatchewan.

You what? Where? Are you moving?

I bought it for a song. Ridiculous.

What will you do? Will Allan move there?

I don't know, I said. It was a snap decision. Maybe I've lost my mind.

She barked her distinctive laugh. Then she coughed and couldn't stop.

The following month, in the hospital, Mom remembered.

What happened to your little house? Do you still have it?

I do, I said. It's like a sanctuary. Or it will be.

I hope you can write there. The prairie is beautiful. You loved tiger lilies.

I did too. And foxtails. I'll give it a name, Mom. How about Grace House?

Really?

Did I just tell my mother she was dying? Was that my awkward way of telling her she'd live on? But I meant it. The house would be a retreat and a gathering spot for friends and family. Giving it a name might be pretentious, but who cares. Months later, I found a hundred-year-old wood-framed classroom slate in the thrift store in Swift Current, bought coloured chalk, and placed the slate with the name on the window ledge facing Main Street. I made a copy of Mom's favourite poem, "The House by the Side of the Road," and put it in the piano bench with the sheet music.

A gathering place. All because a high school reunion prompted me to return to Saskatchewan. My old friend Ed had invited Allan and me to stay at his farm for a few days, the farm his father had willed to him. We came the following year. The house was near a copse of trees with a view to the prairie beyond, and Ed and his partner were in the midst of adding a screened-in porch.

The day after we arrived, the four of us went into the nearby town. While everyone else disappeared out of the high noon heat to do their shopping, I walked the four blocks of Main Street where trees were in bud and spring birds were zany with activity. Every front yard bloomed with colour. I breathed deeply, pointed my face to the sun. The night before, we'd listened to coyotes from the farm's screened-in porch. I could hear meadowlarks. The quiet, the sky, the clarity of the sound—I couldn't get enough of it.

I was overcome with longing. And memories. Is it too late to make new ones? Do I have enough time?

A block ahead, a small sign. *For sale. Inquire at Donald's agency.* The forties-era house was blue, ringed with flowers and shrubs. It had a porch. I walked to the end of the street to the Rec Center and seniors' home, turned around, and walked by the little house again, slowly.

Ten minutes later, with Allan and the others in tow, I was touring the house.

The following morning, I drove into town from the farm and walked into Mr. Donald's office.

I'd like to make an offer, I said.

Offer? said Mr. Donald. He seemed offended. We don't do offers. That's the price. It's final.

Ah, my big-city talk, I guess. He thought I was negotiating.

And I was. But not the price. Something bigger, something I couldn't yet articulate.

My body felt charged, jittery, hopeful. I was on a threshold, the edge of before and after.

if a woman

crush flint

We need some kind of tomorrow.
Toni Morrison

Enheduanna, High Priestess of the Moon, a woman from Mesopotamia who died in 2250 BCE, wrote poems, prayers, and psalms. While she was exiled, she wrote a 150-line hymn to Inanna, the Sumerian goddess of love, fertility, and war, asking Inanna's help avenging her exile, and the power of her hymn restored Enheduanna's position in the temple. Her poems of desire and praise suggest a fluid sexuality; the considerable volume of her works had a lasting impact on Mesopotamian culture.

But since her work was discovered in 1927, scholars have debated whether Enheduanna, the daughter of Sargon the Great, was, in fact, the first author to be known by name.

She couldn't be, people argued—someone else had to have written the work.

She couldn't be—her father put her in charge of the Sumerian temple and she wouldn't have had the time to write.

She couldn't be—she wasn't a significant figure in her own right, only the daughter of one.

But nevertheless, she persisted. Like countless women before and after, she persisted. Writing to Inanna, Enheduanna says, "With your strength, my lady, teeth can crush flint."

writing tosh

As Virginia Woolf said, "for most of history, Anonymous was a woman." Currer, Ellis, and Acton Bell were the pseudonyms Charlotte, Emily, and Anne Brontë chose. As Charlotte wrote, "we did not like to declare ourselves women, because we had a vague impression that authoresses are liable to be looked on with prejudice." *Middlemarch* author Mary Ann Evans wrote as George Eliot because, like her contemporaries, the Brontës, she wanted to ensure her work was taken seriously.

This is not news. Women writers, regardless of the kind of writing they publish, have been given short shrift forever. Our writing is too domestic, too "light," or too personal. Leave the serious writing to us, we're told; don't worry your pretty little head. Keri Hulme, the celebrated New Zealand writer of *The Bone People*, called Booker Prize–winning author V. S. Naipaul a "misogynist prick" and a "slug" for his belief that women's writing was inferior. Naipaul claimed women have a "narrow view of the world," prone to sentimentality. Even when Naipaul's editor, Diana Athill, wrote a memoir, her work didn't escape his sharp tongue. Athill responded, "I was a 'sensitive editor' because I liked [Naipaul's] work, I was admiring it. When I stopped admiring him so much [my own work] started being 'feminine tosh.'"

When Francine Prose read Norman Mailer's comments on women's writing—"the sniffs I get from the ink of the women are always fey, old-hat, Quaintsy Goysy, tiny, too dykily psychotic, crippled, creepish, fashionable, frigid, outer-Baroque, maquillé in mannequin's whimsy, or else bright and stillborn"—she dubbed the phenomenon *gynobibliophobia*.

Francine Prose is on to something, although we could find a simpler term to use. Given the systemic misogyny, sexism, racism, and homophobia women and underrepresented groups have had to deal with for centuries, it is no surprise writing by women would be discounted, dismissed, vilified, and mocked. For years I assumed it was misogyny, the stench of which I find more overwhelming as I age.

But it's also garden-variety fear, an emotion that underlies a lot of hate. Fear that women's concerns and beliefs might challenge conventional notions of "quality." Fear that engaging in the domestic, the so-called personal, or the emotional will shift readers' focus to what are considered "lowbrow" or lesser ideas. Fear that interpersonal realms not marked by conflict or agonistic pursuits—the bare-chested arena of primitive displays of masculinity—will prove to be valuable, connect humans with one another, show humanity in the quotidian details, however startling or mundane. After all, we know works are lauded if they're characterized as "my struggles" and penned by a male author in six autobiographical novels.

And another fear. Men such as Naipaul and Mailer are intelligent enough to realize, however subliminally, what women's writing often reveals: the very inequities they don't want to be reminded of. Dismiss the "misery" memoir of a young mother whose abuse at the hands of her stepfather has broken her; that way you don't have to face the toxicity of male power. Deem women's domestic chores—their mothering, housekeeping, rearing of children—as minor pursuits to avoid acknowledging the critical role they played in your own life. Refuse to accept conventional notions of "realness," as trans writer Janet Mock challenges us to do. Roll your eyes at stories of Indigenous women in the justice system—this *again*? Can't you move on? That way you can ignore the glaring effects of generations of structural racism and sexism. Once, when journalist Connie Walker pitched a story, the producer stopped her: this isn't another poor Indian story, is it?

Gynobibliophobia. There must be a simpler word.

it's always something

The first year of the pandemic I have a cold and ear infection and, despite antibiotics, antihistamines, prednisone, and lidocaine, despite hanging my head above a sink of steaming water, nothing reduces the feeling of fullness in my ear. Or the tinnitus. Have I punctured my eardrum? It isn't Covid-19, but it's something.

My ears have troubled me since childhood. A few years ago I stood in the library at Trinity College, sweating and dizzy, pain piercing my ear as I tried to read a plaque about *The Book of Kells.* The Irish doctor's prescription hadn't helped in the least.

And lately this fullness, this ringing and buzzing. After a few visits to the clinic, I ask to see an ENT. I stop my regular walks, since the lurching feels like trying to stand up in a Tilt-A-Whirl.

Aristotle referred to women's bodies as men's, only with our genitalia "turn'd outside in." Aristotle did grant women the faculty of reason, at least, but he agreed with his teacher, Plato, that women's bodies are weaker. He didn't share Plato's belief that an ideal society would educate women, though.

In medicine, what's good for the gander is not always good for the goose.

Women's bodies behave differently. Our heart attacks often don't present like men's do; our hormones affect us in a myriad of ways all our lives; our reproductive systems alone can be rife with complications and chaos. Women in my mother's generation could be institutionalized when perimenopause symptoms threw their lives out of whack, and too many were placated with "mother's little friends," benzodiazepines and barbiturates made famous in Jacqueline Susann's *Valley of the Dolls*. My mother had her store of Valium handy when my fiancé Gord died, and despite her best intentions, the drug served only to delay my grieving for years.

Ask a woman to tell you how long it took for her endometriosis or chronic fatigue syndrome to be diagnosed. Ask a Black woman if she's been told the colour of her skin has increased her pain tolerance. Ask an Indigenous woman which of her relatives was sterilized without permission after her baby's birth. It's contradictory: politically, socially, and personally, a woman's body seems to belong to everyone but her, yet that claim to her body doesn't require paying close attention to its needs.

In graduate school, I lay splayed in the stirrups on the clinician's table for a checkup.

You're getting on; time to stop birth control, don't you think? the doctor said, and the nurse nodded her head in agreement. In my late twenties, I wasn't happy birth control was primarily my responsibility, but I was too compliant to question it.

Isn't that for me to decide, I muttered. Then worried I'd jeopardized my own care.

When I persist with doctors, research legitimate sources about my conditions, when I make yet another appointment because things don't feel right, I am bringing with me my son's grade-three teacher whose breast lumps were dismissed because she was "too young to have cancer"; the colleague whose pain and swelling was "likely caused from stress in her job"; the former student whose bloody stool was misdiagnosed as hemorrhoids. I bring my friend Pat, whose bloated belly and painful cramps turned out to be stage-four ovarian cancer.

Being the good girl I am, I usually apologize for my persistence. I make my demands in civil language and with a smile, with no hint of hysteria. I offer the doctor "I wonder if" and "do you think we might try..?" Being polite is a good approach anywhere, certainly, but blowing our stack is riskier for women. We're more likely to be labelled obnoxious, to become *that* patient. I've had great doctors—my current GP is one—and I've had others whose eyes glaze over when they see a woman old enough to be their mother or grandmother. The body of an ageing woman is often a motley collection of kinks and quirks, creaks, twinges, and pangs. As Gilda Radner said, it's always something.

This time, the symptoms in my head persist. And I am looking for answers.

foremothers

They're not your people. Don't worry about it.

Don't worry? I was new to writing poetry, working with a beloved poet whose wit, insight, and friendship guided me through the publication of my first collections. He shrugged.

I felt inadequate. I'd been reading the latest award-winning collection of a poet whose work, critics suggested, I must read to be current in contemporary poetry. And the more I read, the longer the list of must-reads became.

One poet's work eluded me, much as I tried. Was I too literal? Ill-read? How could I call myself a poet if I couldn't read all the poetry out there? I was older, having published my first collection at fifty-four, but I had the insecurities of a neophyte. My work had garnered a few awards, so why was I worried?

After talking with my mentor, I went back to my room and sat by the window, looking at the mountain towering behind the residence. The flush of embarrassment was still on my face.

When I escaped from writing academic prose to focus on poetry, I read and found inspiration and solace in the works of Jane Hirshfield, Daphne Marlatt, Marilyn Dumont, Jane Kenyon, Louise Bernice Halfe, Elizabeth Bishop, Maureen Scott Harris, Lucille Clifton, Jan Zwicky, the essayist Nancy Mairs, among many others. I read work written by men, too, and learned from it, but I was drawn to women's perspectives.

Then I found Bronwen Wallace. A few pages into her book *The Stubborn Particulars of Grace* and I was overtaken.

Wallace was a Canadian poet and short story writer who died in 1989 at the age of forty-four. In the pages of *Stubborn Particulars*, I found women escaping to shelters, teenage boys, truck drivers, a talking parrot in the Yukon, and bones upturned in the field. A woman singing alone in the house on a Saturday afternoon.

As a former ethnographer, I'd researched and written about the lives of women at school and work. Wallace wrote their lives with candour and fierce clarity, all in rhythmic, prose-like lines that propelled me from one page to the next. The intimacies of the everyday slow-dancing with philosophy. Wallace was an activist, a tireless political ally of autoworkers and abused women, among others, and her work plumbed their despair and their hard-won joys equally without a hint of preaching or of exploitation.

Later, I learned several of my writer friends knew Wallace personally; a few studied with her, sat around kitchen tables with her. Friends tell me she was complicated, flawed, brilliant, generous, and no-nonsense.

Coming to her poems without any preconceptions, however, I was struck by the lift and sway of her lines, by a conversational voice belying a fierce intelligence, and by her canny attention to craft. And her wit—an open-heartedness that allowed the whole world in.

I began to think of Wallace as a literary foremother, and drew courage from her work. Not long after, I worked with Daphne Marlatt, a poet whose innovative work taught me the body "insists itself" in our words. As someone who studied women's lives, I thought I knew that, but I didn't. Until I read Wallace, Marlatt, and others such as Sharon Olds and Lucille Clifton, I'd been reticent to put experiences considered "private" into words. Now I cleave to such candor; how else to valorize the whole of our lives? I was drawn, as well, to what reviewer Casey Stepaniuk called the "rhizomatic, circular style" of Marlatt's novel *Ana Historic*, and looked for work that disrupted conventional approaches to poetry and prose. Travels and long conversations with Maureen Scott Harris, whose award-winning poetry is a testament to the art of attention, helped me feel at home in the literary community. Later, as I devoted attention to researching my Indigenous background, the work of Marilyn Dumont and Louise Bernice Halfe taught me, deepened my understanding.

While I found inspiration in the work of women writers, I also developed strong friendships with some of the women themselves.

Local author Budge Wilson, for example, was a regular and beloved visitor in my writing courses; our long talks about the Swissair Flight III crash in St. Margarets Bay brought us even closer. Authors' acknowledgement pages in their books remind me it takes a village to create not only a book, but the author herself. How else do we learn to be tenacious, resilient, generous, and kind?

And speaking of tenacious, I'm reminded, as well, of students whose courage and persistence have been both humbling and enlivening. One, Jen Powley, was a young activist whose late-stage MS didn't stop her from completing her memoir. Meticulously, doggedly, Jen dictated word by word the short pieces she called "chaplets" until *Just Jen* was completed. It won an award. Here was a woman who could crush flint.

As surely as my grandmothers have influenced who I am as a person and a writer, so too have writers I've known and loved.

great white way

I have since reconsidered Eliot
and the Great White way of writing English
standard that is
the great white way
has measured, judged and assessed me all my life
by its
lily white words
its picket fence sentences

Marilyn Dumont, "The Devil's Language"

The women were laughing, chattering as they found their seats. When I began to speak, I was hesitant.

Let's start with our stories, I said.

Of course. Those of us soaked in the conventions of mainstream education assume everyone wants to say something about themselves to strangers. We enter classrooms expecting a group to trust us and each other without any work to earn that trust. We encourage the individual's story, especially heroic ones.

The formula: Write (or tell) on demand; work promptly, and on your own; conform to expectations: keep a journal, write multiple drafts, revise, expose your work to others' critique, revise again, publish.

And...go!

Years ago, working with Indigenous women in Northern Canada, I arrived before 1:00 P.M. for the workshop and found the room empty. When women began to arrive, some with children in tow, we dove into the coffee and snacks and began to talk. The empty journals I'd set out stayed unopened as the afternoon unfolded; one woman gave her journal to her daughter to colour in. We laughed a lot, shared thoughtful silences, a few dark moments, and some tears. The women asked me about myself and my children, told me about their communities. We made more coffee, stayed long after the allotted time.

The next day, I suggested we all draw a picture or a map of a place we remember from our childhood. A street, a place by the river, a favourite spot where we always met our friends, the old shed where we buried a treasure. If you're comfortable, I said, talk about them with someone here in the room.

Later, everyone helped each other write down what they talked about.

"I lost my talk / The talk you took away": Mi'kmaw poet Rita Joe wrote years ago about the loss of her language. Many women I've worked with, including those whose first language is not English, are in a liminal place—their language has been deliberately and systematically extinguished in their ancestors' generation or their own. Writing in English means abiding by norms not of their making. They're torn; Great White Way education is both necessary and problematic. How to keep your talk and yet take advantage of opportunities that require a command of Standard English?

Like most women, I've dealt with loss, sexual violence, invisibility, emotional abuse, and silencing. But my Western and colonialist upbringing means I can draw upon any number of cultural, social, and financial resources to support me. What do I know about another's life? Women in a writing workshop may have travelled from a war-torn country with empty pockets, birthed babies at fourteen, become deaf from beatings, lost a sister, dealt with men who run off and keep coming back. They might have had a drug habit, been abused, or lived in a succession of foster homes. They were a farm wife for thirty years before returning to school, or they survived residential school or the Sixties Scoop. Their hair or skin colour may cause them to be followed by store clerks or targeted on a bus. They might struggle with illnesses of the body and the spirit.

And despite this, they persist. They want an education.

Jenny Horsman, a literacy researcher, claims we fail to recognize "the impact of women's and girls' experience of violence on their attempts to learn." But the violence is not only physical or psychological, it's violence in the cultural collisions they face when they step into a mainstream classroom.

Schools can be sites of ongoing judgement and assessment, requiring a certain degree of self-assurance to survive. Even when teachers are supportive and emphasize the positive—"this part works, but here you could—"; "have you tried X?"—they are still reinforcing a mainstream standard of writing quality that doesn't apply to all students or all cultural groups.

A climate of judgement and fear douses the spark writers need to connect with their thoughts and with each other. Maya Angelou wrote about the agony of carrying the burden of an untold story. That burden can include the belief your story isn't worth telling.

Years of listening to women's raw and candid stories in church basements and community halls have taught me this: the "perfect" prose that would earn an A or an audible sigh in a university class-room would pale against these tales of blood, bone, and sinew.

I recall one session when children gathered around their moth-ers, waiting for them to finish reading so they could pounce on the cake and cookies. There was an ineffable presence in the room then, a sense of affinity and calm I can't put into words. We all stayed after-ward that day, talking and laughing. The long afternoon stretched like a satisfied cat, a glint in its eye, knowing more than we could know.

anne on the beach

The ocean is all sparkle and glitter this morning, the last day of sum-mer. I step across the rocks to the expanse of smooth sand and spot a moving red dot at the other end of the beach. Must be Anne. She bikes here from her home in Riverport most every morning and, regardless of weather, walks, meditates, and does yoga, then rides the five kilometres home. She is several years younger than I am, and I'm awed by her tenacity and discipline.

She has to do this, she says. Years of crippling spinal problems have plagued her and one day, on a trip west to see a friend, Anne emerged from the plane in a wheelchair only to be greeted by a tongue-lashing: Anne, you are not to do this. Her friend was adamant. You're too young to lose your mobility.

Although I walk a lot, stretch and meditate now and then, I need to do more than admire Anne's initiative. My ageing body needs to move more.

A day like this, however, is about spirit, not body. What the ocean offers the heart.

When Anne and I reach each other on the sand, we both throw up our hands and yell.

This is magnificent!

How lucky can we be?

Heaven!

A moment of shared joy—the warmth of the sun, diamonds cascading in waves, the hop and rollick of seabirds.

And life. Life.

storyteller

for Joan

As the class packed up their materials, including the copies of her book, Joan and I continued the conversation we'd begun in front of the group. Outside, the snow was falling and the teachers who'd travelled a distance needed to be on the Trans-Canada Highway before dark. I was looking forward to our dinner later, weather permitting. For almost fifty years, our friendship had been interrupted by our respective moves across the country and so we kept up with each other over long phone calls. Joan lived in St. John's and because I travelled to teach courses in Newfoundland and Labrador several times a year, I relished any chance for us to catch up in person.

The difference is that I'm a storyteller, Joan said.

For a moment I was at a loss for words. What difference? The class had been discussing the degree to which a novelist draws on their own life when they write fiction. As a celebrated novelist, Joan knew fiction inside and out. I marvelled at Joan's insight into the human heart, and the places she took her characters, narratively and emotionally. She was an instinctive, driven writer and I envied the trust she had in her work.

I waved as the last person closed the door, and the meeting room fell silent.

Don't get me wrong, Joan added. You're a terrific writer. A poet. But I'm a storyteller.

I felt stung. What did she mean by storyteller? Someone who can spin tales, create fictional worlds? If that's what she meant, she was right. I could never do what she did, ever. The class had been talking about her latest novel, *Latitudes of Melt*, not about my writing.

Decades before, Joan had been a guest in my writing class at what was then Mount Royal College. She and I worked alongside Edna Alford at *dANDelion*, the magazine the two founded in Calgary. I felt out of my depth reading submissions; my only writing credentials at the time were a thesis and book reviews and columns in news-papers. I read constantly, but I wasn't writing fiction or poetry. When Joan visited my class, her down-to-earth and reassuring comments inspired every person in the room, including me.

Then, almost twenty years later, after I'd moved to Nova Scotia and she'd moved to St. John's, Joan and I were at a workshop in Fredericton. She was the fiction instructor and I'd enrolled in the non-fiction workshop.

No one is publishing non-fiction anymore, said our instructor when she returned my work that week.

What?

When I told Joan, she was furious.

Don't listen to her, she said. That woman has difficulty with other writers.

Joan was right. I watched this woman belittle a man from Toronto whose heart attack on the 401 had caused him to move to the Maritimes and take up freelance writing. Don't waste my time with this kind of work, the writer said. I've dined with Ondaatje. The man blanched. Another woman in the class, who'd documented the stories of women in fishing communities, was bold enough to speak up about the importance of encouraging novice writers. The room fell silent.

Soon after, Joan and I met again, this time for a writing retreat she led at the abbey in Rogersville, New Brunswick, where she urged me to write poetry. Joan was what writer Sheree Fitch calls (and is herself) a *permissionary*.

I'll never know what Joan meant that snowy afternoon in St. John's. That she was a storyteller and I was a poet is a straightforward statement of fact. Was she talking about differences in how and what we imagine? Imagination is often thought of as "making things up" when it is far more than that. It's observation, insight, and reflection as we create the unknown and recreate the known. But it was late in the day and we were both hungry; I didn't have the energy to parse these things.

What matters, after all, is our commitment to our work and support for others. Few were more committed to writing and to the Canadian writing community than Joan.

This morning I learned Joan died. I'd tried calling her in St. John's before the pandemic, but learned her family had moved her back to Alberta by then. She was in long-term care. Her daughter, I see, uses the word *dandelion* in her counselling business. The days in the basement of the Alexandra Centre with her and Edna are long gone, but I am forever grateful for my friend—a foremother, a guide, a consummate writer.

Once, when Joan had finished a reading in Halifax, a member of the audience picked up a book left near the front of the room. The person was horrified. Joan, she said, someone has written all over the pages of your book.

Joan laughed. Oh, it's my copy, she said. I never stop editing my work.

how to kill her

Chaque jour et partout dans le monde il y a des hommes en cercle autour d'une femme, prêts à lui jeter la pierre.

Annie Ernaux, *Mémoire de fille*

Here's how you do it. Toss the food she cooked in her face, or climb aboard her sleeping body after a night out with the guys. Make a snide crack about her to the cashier at the grocery store. Walk in with muddy boots, blame her for the mess of clothes and dishes you leave behind. Mock the way she speaks to your son; show him how to keep the upper hand, keep her alert, jumping at sharp noises. Smack the table, raise your fist.

Or, speak over her in a crowd. Stand at her office door and tell her what she should be reading in her field of expertise. Ignore her suggestion in a meeting but bring it up later as your idea. Scream at her in the science classroom, then send a three-page email detailing your outrage. Be granted tenure by those who remain silent about what they know. Use her shoulder as an armrest at your professional gathering. At an appointment about her disabled son, show her your book about childhood disorders and ask her if she'd like to sleep with you.

Help her with her writing, compliment her craft, her ideas. Take her for a drink to talk about revisions, suggest journals certain to accept her work. Give her a signed copy of your book. At the wrap-up party, watch as she leans on her friend, sobbing, intoxicated with wine and with you. Lead her out to the third-floor balcony for a smoke, then take her up to your room. Watch as she picks up your award-winning book from the desk and clutches it to her chest, then take it from her, murmur as your liver-spotted hands reach for her buttons—oh her talent, you tell her, her bright eyes.

If she's drunk, if she's with the band, if she has nice tits, if she wouldn't friend you, if she's new around here, if she's a cop, if she's at a grad party ten miles from home, if she's alone in a bus station, if she's your stepdaughter, if she's disabled, if you feel like it, if she's on a street corner, if she's passed out, if she's vomiting, if she's from the reserve, if she watches hockey, if it's about time she got nailed, if she sexted, if she didn't, ask your buddy to hold her down. Then hold her down for him. Post a photo. Spread the word.

Knock her out, then stab her with four knives one hundred and four times. Knock her down, step on her head, throw away the blood-stained sneakers the cops will find in the bush, strangle her and stuff her body in a hockey bag, then throw it into a Cape Breton river, the Red River, the ocean.

Rape her at the back of the bus, all of you taking turns, use an iron bar until her soft core breaks open and her entrails begin to fall out of her body. Kidnap her, along with three hundred more girls, leaving families to mourn while you put them to work on their backs, force them into sexual acts with men twice their age, auction them off into slavery. Behead her, burn her, cut her legs off, choke her with your cock, with your hands, with the handle of an axe.

Oh, we've seen your crocodile tears, heard you apologize for the bruises, listened to the same promises again and again. It's because you love her so much. You need her. She started it. You were just kidding. If she had only, if those bastards hadn't fired you, if she didn't make more money than you, if the neighbours didn't speak so highly of her, didn't insult you by giving a second-hand jacket to your son, offer to mow your lawn. If she hadn't read that book. If she hadn't gone to school. If she didn't have a mouth on her. If she hadn't laughed.

Write a poem to attack a poet; tell her to drink piss, but call it a joke. Publish a poem about her story without permission. Lie. Use wordplay as a shiv in your reviews. Put sticky notes on her door at a writers' retreat, and hover outside her room all night. You don't hate women; women have no sense of humour. This is not violence, not bullying, this is not abuse for fuck's sake—why can't women just get over it?

Send death threats to her, because she's Black, because she's new to Canada. I'll ram it through your throat, you say. I want to hate-fuck you, you say.

Start your men's rights group, with your claims that women are violent, too. Argue you're a humanist, not a feminist. Remind your friends women use sex to destroy you. Send death threats to women gamers and journalists. Decapitate your mother and store her in the freezer. Trumpet your support for women from the couch while you wait for dinner.

Shove, force, plunge, ram, strike, beat, choke, punch—
until she is silent.

not all men

Picture this. Christmas Day, we are packing up dinner to take it to the flat rock at the far end of Nelly Bay on Magnetic Island off the coast of Australia. Dinner is a simple picnic at the beach instead of the usual North American turkey dinner gorge-fest. A friend, Sharn, who lives nearby, has found a small house for us not far from the beach. No malls with their canned carol loops, no large tree to trim, no frantic late-night wrapping. No baking.

As a family, we've agreed not to spend more than five Australian dollars on each other. We've wrapped our small gifts in banana leaves or scarves.

It is hot, too hot.

I relax; this is the easiest and sanest Christmas I've had yet with children. The martini Allan mixed for me is large, tasty, and so cold.

The others head out before me with a tablecloth and utensils, and I follow with the chicken and salad. The sand is scalding, my feet sink and slide sideways; the alcohol has kicked in and I am woozy. As I start to fall, holding the platter of food high above, I am scooped up from behind by two young men with remarkably quick reflexes.

You're right now, they say, grinning their wide grins as I regain my footing. They turn away to their own goings-on as if nothing has happened. No eye rolling, no sniggering.

As I reach the picnic rock, one of my sons calls out: what happened?

Nothing. It's good, I say. Saved the food! Thanks to those lovely men.

I lay the platter down on the tablecloth, push the chicken back to the centre.

Lovely, I repeat, regretting my decision about the martini. Such lovely men.

Allan and the boys share glances and snort. *Loorvely minn,* they say, in their worst imitations of an Australian accent.

For years, I am teased about this.

I've always known lovely men. I am lucky. The phrase might sound condescending, even emasculating, and might cause anyone to wince. Perhaps *mensch* is better. The Yiddish word suggests honour and respect, a man with a big heart, with integrity, a sense of what's right. Although mensch originally meant "a good person," it's come to be used most often to describe men.

As I age, my feminist convictions deepen. And the more I see misogyny and systemic sexism around me, the more I value the good men in my life. Men I can trust; friends (friendship the only benefit); men who never patronize me or mansplain, who look me directly in the eyes, who listen as much as they talk. Men who behave as though I am as capable and intelligent and as worthy as they are. Men like my husband, my sons, and several friends and colleagues.

To me, the word *feminist* has never meant hating men. I don't hate men. As with anyone of any gender, there are some whom I don't respect or trust, and I'm lucky to be able to keep my distance, a privilege I don't take lightly. I'm enraged or deeply saddened when anyone who identifies as a woman is kept from living a full, safe, and productive life.

The world can be wonky, dangerously tippy. Mostly I wish everyone helped others find solid footing.

what matters

What matters is what is out there in the large dark
and in the long light,
Breathing.

Gwendolyn MacEwen, "Let Me Make This Perfectly Clear"

Annie Ernaux, whose work had been celebrated for years, recently won the 2022 Nobel Prize for Literature. The jury commented on "the courage and clinical acuity with which she uncovers the roots, estrangements and collective restraints of personal memory." I toast this recognition, but I wonder about two descriptors in their citation:

"courage" and "clinical acuity." Writers of autobiographical work are often asked about the courage it took to write it, a question that has always perplexed me. Why is revealing ourselves risky, especially if readers can find themselves in the work? What if being candid and unvarnished is necessary in order to honour the experience? Ernaux herself says she writes to "make things exist." Women readers I know are grateful she does.

And "clinical acuity"? Precise, skilful language is the mark of a good writer. Clinical, to me, suggests dispassionate, unfeeling. Ernaux, who writes in *The Years* that "one day we'll appear in our children's memories, among their grandchildren and people not yet born," seems anything but dispassionate.

Ernaux isn't afraid to write about what poet Gwendolyn MacEwen calls "the large dark" and the "long light." She illuminates. As do Maria Campbell, Amber Dawn, Katherena Vermette, Elly Danica, and Shani Mootoo, to name only a few. Margaret Laurence's evocations of the Manitoba landscape, along with her indelible characters have never left me. I understood Carol Shields's anguish as a mother and am deeply affected by Miriam Toews's writing about depression. Sylvia Hamilton's poetry offers a glimpse into the difficult lives of early Black Nova Scotians, a population I know too little about. Women's stories can allow me to imagine their characters' lives and circumstances as if I were living them. It's those "stubborn particulars" Bronwen Wallace wrote about. All our ordinary lives are, once crafted and brought to the light, shown to be extraordinary. Women exist on the page and in the flesh. We are out there, breathing.

fireflies

As the sun sets, my friend Rose and I walk down the gravel road to the shore. We've been friends for almost twenty-five years and it's rare she can spend time out this way. I want to show her the fireflies in the woods near here.

Rose is a singer-songwriter, beloved for her many albums that focus on Maritime life, on human joys and woes. Her clear and simple lyrics are beautiful, yet never sentimental, and move people deeply. On occasion we've written a song together, a novelty tune or two.

Once she fell asleep reading and woke in the morning with the book under her.

Oh my god, I slept with Leonard Cohen last night, she said, and spent several hours composing a silly tune we'd sing at a writers' event. My singing is enthusiastic, but not always on key. She's patient with me. Rose is patient with everyone.

One year, I learned a few basic chords on the guitar, determined to learn enough to amuse myself and give my word-bound brain a break from print. Around that time, my mother's health was failing and an opening line came to me: *She sits alone with the TV and a fresh pack of smokes.* It revived my dream of being a country singer in another life.

Rose and I have spent countless hours talking about our siblings, our children, and our health concerns, the quotidian joys and dramas that make a life. We share a love of thrift stores and bad puns. We call our check-ins about ageing and health our "organ recitals."

Rose has a sense of wonder most of us lose by the time we are adults. She stops on a walk to examine the colour of a leaf or the shape or texture of a stone; she dwells more in her body than I tend to. She has taught me so much.

Dacher Keltner, writing about awe, says it can pull us out of our "self-focused, threat-oriented, and status quo mindset to a realm where we connect to something larger than the self." Perhaps awe is the birthplace of faith.

One evening, Rose and I watched as fireflies sparked between the trees until the night was pitch dark and we could see only fireflies ahead and stars above.

I no longer see fireflies in the woods; they may have moved farther inland or, like other species of lightning bugs, their numbers across the world have declined. Urban growth, artificial light, and climate change have destroyed their habitat.

Even stars are becoming more difficult to see.

I cling to the memory of our firefly walk, however.

I cling to wonder. To awe.

dreams

For a time, whenever I was alone, I'd blast The Cranberries' "Dreams." The tune has the same propulsive energy as Wolf Saga's "Keep Dancing," Metric's "Gimme Sympathy," Mavis Staples's "I'll Take you There," or Lucinda Williams's "Can't Let Go." Start-up fuel. Better for me, it turns out, than too much caffeine.

But that's not what I meant to write. I was thinking of Dolores O'Riordan, lead singer of The Cranberries, who died far too young (as did Kirsty MacColl who sang with The Pogues—I am drawn to stories about women who die too young). Of Dolores's lyric about things never being what they seem.

When I woke this morning from a dream, I didn't know where I was for a moment. I rarely dream and so I felt as though I'd left a gift behind on the pillow. It was digressive, as dreams often are. I was taking a test along with other people (don't ask me who). I was given a sheaf of papers with handwritten notes in a variety of colourful scripts, pell-mell across the pages. Nearby a voice gave instructions. The questions are near the end, someone said. I flipped through the pages but couldn't find the questions. I walked through several rooms (where? I don't know), puzzled but not panicked, curious but not frightened. And I resolved to interpret the handwritten notes on the papers, to find the questions and answer them.

I turned over and went back to sleep, hoping, as sometimes happens, I could resume the dream. Not this time.

Of course, I jumped to cheap analysis: life is mysterious, you never know where you're going, you're always searching for answers and the main questions come at the end. The handwriting styles represent the influences of people you've known and read. I've often dreamed about searching a house with several rooms—including a hidden one—looking for my bag, certain I am going to miss the plane. My youth was filled with dreams of flying—not so much being airborne, but the exhilaration of liftoff, of "getting air."

Better minds than mine can sort those out.

Today's dream reminded me of the process of writing itself. I begin writing about X when Y pops in and takes over, leading me to W for some reason. Something drives me, like the beat of a good song, and I have to keep moving. On a good day, the momentum can be intoxicating. After a while, what appears on the page suggests a sense of direction. Then, when I wake from this dreamlike state—yes, let's call it flow—I step back and analyze. Where am I going with this? Is it worth pursuing? If it is, I explore it, this time with focus and intention.

And it changes every day. Yes, in every possible way.

best summer vagina

That spring morning, a magazine piece online: "How to Get your Best Summer Vagina Ever."

God, another thing to worry about.

I clicked on the article.

OB/GYN and author Dr. Sherry A. Ross explains summer heat can make your vagina drier, making it sensitive and temperamental.

Dr. Calhoun suggests spraying bug spray on our underwear to prevent vulvar bug bites at night.

Sitting for prolonged periods of time, especially in tight clothing where heat gets trapped, can lead to both vulvar irritation or yeast infections, she says. Apply Vaseline ointment to the labia—but not inside the vagina—two to three times a day. Finally, Dr. Ross recommends staying hydrated while in flight to keep your vagina happy.

I'm left wondering what an autumn or winter vagina is like, what drugs can help a temperamental vagina, and what would be going on that I couldn't feel bugs in my vulva. And until I reread her advice and realized she likely meant drinking more water during air travel, I considered the challenges of applying Vaseline to my labia thirty-three thousand feet in the air.

Women in my mother's generation were urged to use Lysol to clean their nether regions or risk their marriage. Their mothers were encouraged to use Lux to avoid the horror of smelly underwear: "That's why we can't get a man for Edith!" Lux was the recommended treatment for our "mimsy," and a daily wash with Lux Kebab soap would "freshen up your flaps and stop it stinking like an old kipper."

Old kipper?

My generation was urged to hide every odour: body, menstrual, vaginal. Feminine sprays made us doubt good old soap and water. Back in the day, an ad in *Summer's Eve* magazine offered young women ten pieces of advice for getting a raise. Top of the list? Shower and make sure you clean your vagina. No mention of the vagina's resume.

How many years have women been told we're too fat, thin, pale, red, hairy, bald, with too-sparse or too-thick eyelashes, brows, or lips, too-dimply thighs, too-wrinkly neck, skin too dark, pores too large, complexion too oily, hair too thick, too coiled, too kinky or too wispy, too coarse, too dry, too there. We're always too much or not enough. Shame on us.

Fuck that.

it didn't occur to me

Rebecca Solnit often puts into words what I can't. Writing about her youth, particularly her responses to the men around her, she says: "We often say silenced, which presumes someone attempted to speak. In my case, it wasn't a silencing because no speech was stopped; it never started, or it had been stopped so far back I don't remember how it happened."

When I was young, a lot of my actions were instinctive; I acted within the constraints of my limited imagination and knowledge of the world. I believe we act according to what makes sense wherever we are in our lives; later, we think differently. My parents weren't well-off financially and were emotionally ill-equipped for much of life's demands, so what limited their worlds limited mine. My mother was never silent, however, about the differences between what men and women were allowed or expected to do. As a teenager, I was embarrassed when she spoke up, and vowed I'd never do that. Now I see her anger and frustration were, in fact, the feminist beliefs she couldn't articulate.

Like Solnit, it didn't occur to me that anyone, male or otherwise, had any obligation to respect my wishes or my comments. Solnit says she became expert "at fading and slipping and sneaking away, backing off, squirming out of tight situations, dodging unwanted hugs and kisses and hands." She learned the art, as she describes it, of nonexistence.

Some women have more strength or wherewithal and they refuse to be quiet and fade away; crissakes don't kick up a fuss here in public what are you doing? Before my parents' marriage began to disintegrate, I lived in a relatively safe and stable home. My father wanted to leave behind his working-class roots, and, as far as I know, my parents expected me to be capable and resilient, to do better, whatever better was. I wonder if that stability affected how I allowed myself to be treated as a young woman, and then, as an adult, how comfortable I became about speaking up. I had advantages galore.

Once, a colleague of mine in an abusive relationship took the man to court and wanted to prepare an impact statement. Her first draft was good, but general. We talked about specifics—his behaviour when he was drunk, his lies, the money he owed her, how small he made her feel. Her revised statement was replete with vivid details and when she went to court, she prevailed. I've learned that women often don't know what they know. One of the gifts of writing and working with writers is to see what happens when they find the words.

lookin' back

For the love of god, for the love of that nubile young woman—do you remember her? The one with long blond hair, the one who never needed a lick of lipstick, who wore any old thing because everything fit and nothing is as beguiling as smooth skin, bright eyes, a lithe body, and the energy of a gazelle.

Decades on, she notices she isn't noticed; she could be a rock or a stump, no one looks back to see if she is looking back to see; she's no longer the muse for a poet, a fertile prize, the spirited gal in the lyrics of a Buck Owens song.

Men look at women. Women look back to see if they're looking.

She learned to move, dress, gesture, paint herself for the male gaze. To subject herself to being an object. Later she'll read an interview with Neko Case who asks: how much of my life was wasted in the tractor beam of the male gaze?

The woman realizes she can pry off the clammy fingers of scrutiny, stride past a whistle-free construction site. One day, if the mirror pleases her alone, no one else matters. No sorrow for her changing face.

And you? Yes, you. Your eyes glide past her in the grocery aisle. You pay her no mind; she's free from the unwanted touch, sly leer, the eyes' swift assessment at chest level. And almost free from the awkward, breast-smashing hug. Almost.

She strides past the coffee shop, a fugitive from fuckability. Even if you were the rare soul who desired a lived-in body and wise eyes, it's too late. Time is short; she's off to do things it took her years to realize she wanted to do.

She has picked up a paintbrush, or she takes walks in the forest alone. She's writing a book, arranging flowers, knitting for babies in the NICU. She's reading philosophy, organizing an environmental movement. She's living with another woman, shocked at the joy of it, or travelling the Canadian North or writing disability policy or volunteering for medical research.

Listen.

Can you hear that deep sigh of contentment? Can you see the corners of her mouth lift lightly?

She's not looking back to see if they're looking. She's focused on a new horizon: dwindling days glow brighter. She looks at the moon in the sky, as Rumi said, not the one reflected in the lake.

She is reaping a harvest she hadn't known she'd planted. She is crushing flint.

Nothing to see here. Only a woman looking forward. Taking stock, making lists. Naming names. Finally, yes, finally. Not only does she have a room of her own, she has become the room.

And now she can get some goddamned work done.

waning crescent

afterlight

*We are being asked to be consistent as humans
over great swathes of time.*

Zadie Smith

There's no material as variable as moonlight.

Alice Oswald, "Full Moon"

I head out to the country when the moon is a waning crescent. The pandemic continues to take the lives of several people a week in Nova Scotia. Visits to specialists about the Thing growing in my head prove less than helpful; the last neurologist pronounced his verdict, twitched his pen impatiently, and ushered me out as I was trying to form a question.

At this late stage of my life, I'm grateful for the love of family and friends, so grateful, and I relish the time to write, read, think, and feel. My two sons are fledged. Given the rocky years of their youth, this is a huge relief.

I was born when the moon was in its waxing crescent phase, four days after the new moon, when light was growing. The people who raised me are all gone; my parents, aunts and uncles, including my Aunt Kay, the last and dearest. If I think of moon phases, I'm waning. That sounds dreary, but I'm not; I still burn with intensity, but differently—quieter, calmer.

In her memoir, *Two or Three Things I Know for Sure*, Dorothy Allison claims she'd rather go naked than wear the coat the world has made for her. It's a lesson I wish I'd learned earlier. Too often,

events and people who governed my youth and early adulthood affected what I believed I could do, how I related to others. Shoulds
were etched in my psyche; my worst fear was to be rejected. I was my
parents' first-born child, the promise of the future, loved unless, until,
and except when. Allison says she knows what it means "to have no
loved version of your life but the one you make," and I understand
this. She adds, "we cannot know beauty in any form" unless we are
beautiful to each other. It's finally all about love.

It was Allison's aunt Dot who said, "'Lord, girl, there's only two or
three things I know for sure. Of course it's never the same things, and
I'm never as sure as I'd like to be.'"

And that's where I am. I've spent my life trying to open my mind
and fill my brain with as much knowledge as I could, piling my book-
shelves with the thoughts of the brilliant and provocative. For years,
my need for knowledge equalled my need for water and air. Not as
a cudgel to wave around at gatherings or to populate the reference
pages of others' work, but simply to slake my thirst for learning about
ideas, their roots and effects on the world. I will always be curious,
want to know more.

Why? Perhaps my upbringing, steeped as it was in high expectations, instability, and tall poppy warnings, made me believe if I
excelled academically, I'd gain my parents' approval. Perhaps a
constant diet of criticism ensured I'd never leave myself open to being
shamed. Or maybe I've known all along this immense world offers
far more than I can know, and the more I learn, the more I'm hum-
bled. But book-learning has often come at the expense of attending
to my emotions. Thinking is my refuge; my emotional self remains
a work in progress. Even so, those deep chasms of grief and pain,

those moments of joy and contentment have given me a full life. I'm surrounded by beloved kin, age has (I hope) given me a sense of proportion, and I am less in the grip of the me-me-me-ness that characterized my youth. I'm moving into a phase of feeling less like a fraying knot of personal preoccupations and more like a part of a larger mystery.

What more could anyone want? To adapt a lyric from the old Waterboys song, a mind may know the crescent, but only a heart can see the whole of the moon.

And what do I carry into my final days or years? What matters?

In the last phase of my life, I have the chance every day to start again.

scrim

Suddenly, it's summer. I wake to a warm ocean breeze on my face, my body damp under the quilt. Outside, the early-June greenery appears soft, bursting with promise. I've slept long, with churning, vivid dreams, the likes of which I haven't experienced since childhood.

When I pull my sticky body from the bed and pick my way down the stairs to make coffee, I reach for one of the ripe bananas from the bowl, and find they're not there. Ah, yes, they were in the dream. How slippery and fluid consciousness is. Ripening bananas, images of a house with many rooms, and the woman who spoke with a Minnesota accent, enunciating each word roundly, hard R's, front of mouth—insistent, she was, very Frances McDormand, but I can't remember what about. How easily mental illness or dementia could draw a thin curtain between what we think of as real and what blooms in the mind. Is reality the wraith I wake to, or what I leave on the pillow?

I could ask the same of writing. After decades of learning and teaching about writing, of crafting poetry, essays, and books, I still find the enterprise mysterious. It's an exercise in wandering in the dark tracking small points of light, of using grit and hope to brush away fog and reveal insight. A state that feels not unlike dreaming, another reality that seems limitless and unconstrained, a kind of floating.

Outside, the Maritime breeze is a light breath on the tree branches. Crows hover and I see more of their white droppings on the barn roof. A family moved in this spring—one always perches on the larch near the shore, on the roof, or on the pine tree behind the garden shed. Yesterday the big one was so raucous I mimicked its squawking; the bird cocked its head and the dog turned to stare at me.

This is downtime. After more than a year of too-frenetic-too-long, of emotional upheavals, illness and loss, recuperation, round-the-clock keeping on keeping on, I've carved out a week without the usual avalanche of work clutter. Although I've been looking forward to the break, I'm unsettled—who am I when my mind isn't filled with must-dos and shoulds? Am I, like so many, suffering from workism?

The house is quiet, only the hum of appliances. I open the computer and pick away at an essay, and two hours later, realize I need to use the washroom and the dog is staring at me, telepathically demanding a walk. It had been a long time since I allowed myself to fall into the bright and altered state of writing.

When the dog and I walk along the shore, the tide is out as far as it can be—I rarely see that many shoals reachable by foot—and so we walk across the shale and the seaweed, the tide pools of periwinkles, the black rock heaves, the seagrass. We walk as far as we can toward the ocean itself, a hundred or so metres from shore where, just a few hours ago, a lobster boat might have passed, making its way to open water.

It's as though I've peered into the ocean's subconscious. Seawater covers 71 percent of the planet yet it's said we know more about the surface of the moon than the bottom of the ocean. That's a lot of mystery. We have only one global ocean: so much life is underwater yet most of us see only the surface, its skin.

But at low tide, when the thrash and slosh of water are gone, look at this. Colours—umber to cadmium, putrid green to glossy black, nodes of bright white and handsome grey; shells of sea snails, entire universes gathered in clusters. Everything exposed to air and sky, to sounds of trees and shrill birds, the breath of the early summer wind. Vulnerable to our footprint, to small seismic shifts.

This is under, behind, beyond, before. This is the sea, dreaming.

carrots

Why am I growing old?
Bashō

September is the new year. Unsharpened pencils, pristine pink erasers, fresh foolscap. Wrapping my school texts in clean brown paper.

Later, as a young wife and from-scratch mother, September called on me to chop, simmer, stew, boil, can, and bake to fill the freezer; to stuff school bags, fill out forms and organize fundraisers, my body sprouting extra arms like an Eastern goddess. Those days are long gone.

Last year, off the highway exit, I spotted a truck on an empty lot, its bed stacked with huge orange mesh bags: *Carrots, 50 lbs $6.*

Six dollars?

Cake with cream cheese icing, muffins, frozen coins to drop into a stew in winter's dark days. Carrot sticks to snack on.

The man lifted the large bag into the trunk.

When I reached the shore, it was dusk. By the time I had picked up the bits of cardboard raccoons had shredded by the garbage bin, night had fallen and fatigue had turned my legs wooden. I left the carrots in the car.

The next day my jacket flapped in the warm sea breeze as I walked along the shore. Seabirds were noisy, and the sun played on the waves.

Carrots! I almost forgot.

As I opened the trunk, I saw our neighbour at his mailbox.

Can you use some of these?

Carrots? He grinned. Out this way, people are more likely to share eggs from their chickens. I filled a plastic bag.

The following afternoon I took a break from writing and drove across the bay to see a friend.

You know how people leave zucchinis at the door?

You have zucchinis? Her light hair was a puff of curls in the sun.

Even better, I said.

By this point, I had not baked, boiled, or peeled a single carrot. Later, I filled a pail with flaccid carrots and tossed them with abandon under the canopy of trees where the deer sleep.

Were you planning to get a horse? Allan said when he saw the bag.

They were a bargain. And for reasons I can't explain—don't ask—I have an urge to do some cooking.

Later that week, our elder son dropped by, and stepped around the bag.

What's up with this?

Hang on. I'm sending some of these with you.

Most of the carrots were firm, so I lopped off the black tops and filled two plastic grocery bags.

My fall bounty was becoming a rotting Giving Tree, I realized. Brother Love's Travelling Carrot Show.

For two nights in a row, I peeled and steamed carrots, ignoring Allan's careful silence. The orange bag of regret was more than half full.

Oh, the waste! I could rationalize my purchase, at least. I'd already used six dollars' worth of carrots at store prices, but it's criminal to waste food. Those carrots grew for nothing; I'd disrespected their purpose. Worse, this proves I've lost my mojo; I'm a slacker who can't even keep a promise to vegetables.

Daucus carota sativus.

I googled carrots. Originating in Central Asia, grown by humans for one thousand years.

And now turning to mush by my door.

Fall is a wistful time; loss is everywhere. I had to face it: gone are the days I thrived on superhuman challenges. Every season in my life has had its own imperatives; was I trying to be forty again?

The next time I passed the intersection where Carrot Man plied his wares, I winced. Why hadn't I taken the bag directly to the food bank?

Later, I sat on the deck beside a bucket, removing as much decay from the carrots as possible. I cast the peels and dead ends along the deer paths. I went back inside, cranked up the radio, and peeled and chopped for two hours. I culled, shredded, blended. Soon a dozen muffins and a large pot of carrot relish were on the go. My hands were orange and carrot bits mottled the floor.

Still, a small pile of carrots remained. They had black veins in their cores. Goners. A James Joyce quote came to mind: "My mouth is full of decayed teeth and my soul of decayed ambitions."

I hissed, hurled the leftovers off the deck.

That night, noises in my dreams seemed to be coming from the open window.

I woke up. Chitters, scrabbling, snarls and whoops—

Raccoons.

Ah, thank you, I whispered, and pulled up the covers.

who's the fairest?

I did a double take. Is that her? That elderly woman? Can't be.

But it is.

The woman in my mind is twentysomething with long curly hair, an often-dreamy expression on her face. She sighed a lot and made wry comments that caused her mouth to curl up at the corner. She was kind, and her face lit up easily in laughter. But the woman I see on social media—is that her?

German researchers say recognition is an embodied sense, based on countless small signals and markers that imprint on us in person, and which we can later pick up, even in a photograph. My friend looked like a stranger at first, then suddenly she didn't; all of her presence returned to me.

The older we are, the more faces we've encountered; we store a staggering number of face combinations in our memories. My husband or I will comment on a stranger's face—her smile is like Jane's or his eyes are like Charlie's. And we'll disagree, too, which suggests we each recall our friend's characteristics differently. No, those aren't Charlie's eyes, not even close. More like Greg's.

Our brains go through several processing stages and access parallel routes of information to recognize any single individual. Not only is it complicated to recognize anyone, it's remarkable we can do it at all.

Years ago, columnist Rose Madeline Mula wrote about a strange old woman who moved into her house. Whenever Rose looked in the mirror, the old woman was there, keeping Rose from seeing her own gorgeous face. When Rose renewed her driver's license, the woman followed her and jumped in front of the camera.

It's true. Lost in thought, I opened the bathroom door the other day only to glimpse a white-haired, wrinkled old dear who'd clearly been hiding in there. I waved at her and she waved back. Apparently, she lives here. I wonder if she knows my friend.

steps

Today, I take the walking stick. After the storm, boulders thrown by waves crowd the path, some the size of a curling rock. In the last few years, violent storms have reshaped the shore near us, ripped out two century-old apple trees, and gradually washed away a retaining wall at a cottage farther down the road.

During Hurricane Juan, my writer friend Budge in Northwest Cove saw her dock clawed from its posts and land across the bay, only one of countless jaw-dropping effects of the storm. In 2022, Hurricane Fiona devastated Cape Breton and the west coast of Newfoundland, resulting in weeks-long power outages and loss of life, homes, and businesses. The power of the sea shocks and destabilizes even the most inured. Nova Scotians shake our heads in disbelief when visitors to Peggys Cove walk to the edge of the rocks, assuming the playful waves licking at the granite won't pull them under.

The seaweed is slippery so I hug the edge of the path where my feet have better traction. By my measure, it's a wobbly day, maybe a six or a seven out of ten; most days are a one or a two and I try to take advantage of them. As I pick my way along, I'm suddenly stabbed with sorrow. I miss being able to run. I miss the stretch in my legs, the rib-expanding breathing, the moment when the effort was forgotten and I felt closer to flying, even at my slow pace. When I wrote my first book, I often ran the loop around the coastal community where we lived. Not only was running a way to collect my thoughts, I used that well-worn device to open the book; as I ran along the route, I introduced the area and its residents.

As I tap my walking stick on the seaweed, my mind wanders. When I was in graduate school, my professors encouraged me to turn my research into story. It felt transgressive, but I relished the chance to enliven the work, to write from where I was and not from the god's-eye view that often marks academic work. I wasn't alone. At the time, the fields of medicine, education, and the social sciences began to see the value of stories *for* and *as* research. Oncology nurses in one of my qualitative research classes claimed if they gathered stories of women with breast cancer, those stories could add the richness of human experience to the statistical data often reported. But it was the nineties and there were barriers: could women's stories (considered too subjective and emotional) be truly credible? The standard clapback at the time was that narrative accounts were anecdotal, one-of-a-kind, biased. But we need to explore phenomena from all angles, I thought, using many approaches.

Steps. Steps in learning, steps in erosion of this shoreline, steps in my efforts to keep moving while this Thing grows in my skull.

Just keep moving, I tell myself. Good life advice. Keep moving.

When I was in graduate school in my twenties, I fed cards into a room-sized machine that spit out numeric results two days later; that was research. It's taken decades to expand our ways of documenting the world, to blur the lines between practices, disciplines, genres, and more. Categories contain, but they also constrain. Dichotomous thinking marked my youth, but the older I am, the more allergic I am to absolutes, to either-or. After all, where does the water meet the land? Where is the edge of a cloud?

A wave moves the sand, collapses a castle, rearranges seaweed and the shore; in the world of ideas, shifting practices reshape intellectual landscapes, too. Step by step. Everything in increments.

But always moving.

grasp and hold

Writing finds the sore spot, the unresolved issue, the open wound. And despite wise advice about separating ourselves from the work we send out into the world, most writers feel vulnerable. Some take criticism of the work so personally, they quit writing. The more I've written, the more I've understood a critical distinction: thanks to countless hours of hard work, writer friends, wise editors, and a thriving writing community, I have developed confidence in my own possibilities, yet, depending on the project I've undertaken, I may at times feel uncertain, unsure. Doubting the work at various stages—a healthy doubt that pushes me—can be productive; doubting myself is time wasted.

Once the work is out in the world, it's impossible to know how a reader will respond. I cherish books and treat them well, yet once, after reading the first twenty pages of a mystery that sold eighty million copies, I threw it out. Other books I savour; I read each page slowly, dwelling in the ideas or the language. I want to stay inside the writer's mind and the world they've created.

When I reached late-middle age, I realized I felt the same about people. It took me a long time to understand I don't have to love them all and they won't all love me.

As writers and as people we can receive bouquets, but it's that one leaf of stinging nettle that stays with us. The one bad review. The one unkind comment. Reviews are meant to introduce books to readers, but sometimes they're a platform for the reviewer's unresolved issues. I have found the same in a community or in a family. It's not about you, psychologists say. Or, to quote columnist Regina Brett: what others think of you is none of your business.

That sounds cavalier, and in publishing at least, a bit unrealistic. Reviews—print, online, on blogs, word of mouth—help a book reach a wider audience. I won't review anything I can't say positive things about, says one writer. My job is to situate the book in the context of other works, says another. Yet another insists there are standards to uphold and they are obliged to point out the failings.

But failings by what criteria? Most "standards" of literary excellence have been based on Eurocentric notions of "quality," on what a segment of the readership values at that point in the culture. Reviewing literature has too often been marked by agonism, a combative approach to ideas and practice.

There are as many responses to a book as there are readers of it. Even the opinions of so-called expert readers differ. Who among us hasn't ignored reviews and found a jewel of a book or a film?

I go back to something basic, perhaps even old-fashioned. Writers often quote Rilke's statement: Works of art are of an infinite loneliness and with nothing to be so little approached as with criticism. Only love can grasp and hold and be just toward them.

One of the kindest men I've known, Stan Dragland, was blunt about reviewing: "If I elevate myself to shine as a beacon to others, that just makes me a bigger prick."

None of us love everything or everyone. Writing has taught me this: When I approach works—or a person or a community—with respect and humility, I honour them.

pilgrim soul

A field of sunflowers, heads turned to the sky as geese slice through the clouds. I am alone on an open road. My heart feels light.

The Yellowhead Highway, three hours' drive ahead. Perfectly formed bales of hay roost on the rolling landscape. As a child I wondered if they were the source of shredded wheat cereal. Now I think they were the inspiration.

Summer is leaving and I haven't made the best of it.

I'm coming, I whisper, as if she could hear. I have so much to tell her. How I burned years on cramped focus and petty urgencies before I realized what's truly important. How I spent years fearing her when she was the one hurting. All those worries arising like bad weather, then moving on.

I swerve to the shoulder, park by the ditch, wait while slipstreams of semis and trailers buffet my body as they pass, then run across the highway to the fence. I can't get enough prairie greens and blues and whites and umbers. That expansive clarity. If I could enter that field and become it, I would.

I fill the camera with colour and line to take home. To look at when the wind from the north seeps into my core for days on end and the ocean looks like hammered pewter. Half my life was big sky and a horizon that demanded humility, and the other half has been steered by the sea and its lessons in mortality. Both have shaped me, their presence in every cell of my being. The thought offers a kind of exquisite comfort, a deep equanimity.

On this, another long drive across the land of my past, the obvious comes as a flash: my history is my both my destination and my future. The years I drove north to track my Swampy Cree ancestors, then south along the Red River where car wheels drove on what were once rutted dirt roads, the river plot for which my Métis grandmother received $240 in scrip from the Canadian government, now a golf course for the well-to-do in St. Andrews. This year, farther west again, to the farmlands of my mother's people, their emptied-out businesses, desolate roads, old railway stations given tenuous new lives as museums with dusty telegraph machines, yellowing photographs of men lost to wars, tatted baptism blankets, scythes.

More fields of sunflowers, heads bowing deeper as the sun drops. The sky is layered in heavy greys, and, in the distance, shafts of light spear the earth. Of course—a god sky. I hold back tears and speed up, pass a slow flatbed. I want to arrive by sundown.

By the time I pull in front of the gate, the tall pines have cast long shadows. The sparrows are jabbering. I see her family stone has been righted; the last time I was here it tipped precariously. Desperate to pee, I grab a tissue from my bag, call out, Be right there, Mom! and dash behind the peony bush near the Morrison plot. She would have laughed at that.

It's a plastic-flower-only zone, but I retrieve the store-bought brown-eyed Susans from the car and place them across the plaque anyway. She is my story and I am hers, for better or worse. Twelve years now. I lie on the grass and settle in to wait for dusk when the world withdraws, birds are silent, and the two of us are alone.

you first

No, you won't, he'd said to me. I'm going first.

Allan was zipping up his coat as we searched for the right boots and hats to walk the dog in Nova Scotia's uncertain weather.

No you're not, I answered. Not at this rate.

After yet another visit to the doctor's office I was indulging in a rant. I'm clearly not ageing like Aunt Kay. I have so many conditions, some of them have surnames. Kay had lived a century before she reluctantly agreed to take what she called a "water pill," and another year still before she used a walker.

Our conversation began with a stop at the drugstore to pick up another prescription. My husband and I are well into the Age of Loss: friends, family members, colleagues. My sister and two close friends have recently become widows. The word comes from an old English word with Indo-European roots—*widewe*—meaning "empty." Widows, who outnumber widowers three to one, are thrust into a strange new world: one poached egg instead of two, a half-filled hall closet, a single movie ticket, an empty passenger seat in the car, not to mention years of birthdays, holidays, and family rituals filled with an absence. Dozens of adjustments and reminders every day.

Some compare losing a spouse to losing one or more limbs; Sylvia Plath's poem about a widow describes a spider at the center of spokes, absent of love. A common feature in old Nova Scotia coastal homes is a widow's walk, a top floor or rooftop enclosure where those left behind could look out to sea waiting for a mariner's safe return.

Whether or not I die before my husband—I insist he's in better health than I am—I don't wish loss on anyone. I don't know how anyone survives the loss of a child. I'm confident my husband, with the help of friends and family, would manage after my death.

It has me thinking. More than 117 billion people have lived on this planet up to now. The odds of being born are estimated to be 1 in 400 trillion. Infinitesimal. Hundreds of years ago 50 percent of humanity didn't live past childhood. Every day I marvel: how lucky is it that any of us are here at all.

the old bone house

When the movie *Harold and Maude* was released in 1971, many viewers praised Ruth Gordon's lawless and irreverent Maude. The cult hit portrayed an intimate relationship between a death-obsessed young man and a woman decades his senior.

Other viewers were horrified. What could Harold have found attractive about an old body, its sagging breasts, age spots, and skin hung like laundry on frail bones? Those seashell-rough toenails. And what about, um, you know, down there?

As a young woman, I was one of many in my generation who resigned ourselves to the fact our bodies were watched, monitored, assessed as objects for others' consumption and desire. At this age, my body has become an invisible backdrop. But misogyny knows no age limit. Older women's bodies are often reviled, our lack of sexual worth scorned and weaponized. We become caricatures: the desperate, lusty biddy who stalks the only man in the long-term-care home and probably thrusts her hips against the washing machine during its spin cycle. We're *grannied* in news stories, *deared* in stores, and spoken to slowly, loudly, and in simple sentences.

Any freedom a woman's body earns comes at a price.

Elizabeth Bishop's poem "One Art" reminds me I lose something every day. My once sturdy bone house is crumbling and becoming contrary. Hair that disappeared from my legs now pops up any damned place it pleases. The smooth palette of my face is crosshatched. My once-thin, graceful hands have grown knobby joints and my waist has been gone so long I've forgotten where it used to be.

"The art of losing isn't hard to master," Bishop claims, and claims again. She knew losing was hard, often disastrous. Learning to lose teaches me to adapt. Gone are my close-up vision, the stamina to run a 10K, and countless nouns. I can't dream of living on a desert island: I need a pharmacy. Gone are an inch in height, a molar or two, some hearing.

The list grows; and so far, the workarounds I use seem to, well, work.

Ageing has gifted me other losses. The need to please, my knee-jerk Yes-impulse, a few grudges. My filter. I cull friends and acquaintances who weigh me down, jettison boxes of dusty belongings. I've lost FOMO. Except for maintaining my health, I am less interested in my body and more in the quality of time left to me.

Each loss makes what's left matter more. Things *mean*. My blue-veined hands recall my mother's. My sore ankle tells me I can still hike. My scars are stories; one across my belly brought me a son. My knobby fingers have produced books and countless syllabi, casseroles and salads and crocheted scarves, the same few chords on the guitar, letters to aunts and cherished friends. I now inhabit this body as mine alone, aware of its material presence in a way that feels grounded, self-contained.

This body will die one day (psst: yours, too).

I'm grateful it's taking so long.

i believe

Like a lover, your life bends down and kisses your life.
Jane Hirshfield

It's the middle of July and the writing workshop has ended. My mind is numb with words and voices and I look forward to the shore, to the sounds of birds and water, the salt in the wind.

I am on the couch, resting my burning eyes, when my cousin Ray calls from Winnipeg. Ray and Shirley have been caregivers for so many—their adult son whose diagnosis of Epstein-Barr made him a wheelchair user, both of their mothers, and now, since they are the only ones who live nearby, Aunt Kay.

That year, when Kay turned one hundred and six, I sent a card and flowers to her, but for the first time, I didn't call. Her hearing loss had become so severe the call would mean shouting for me and con-fusion for her. She rarely left the apartment. Her daughter, Eleanore, suffering with emphysema, couldn't take her shopping on Saturday mornings anymore. The pandemic kept everyone inside. After sur-viving the flu pandemic as a child more than a hundred years before, Kay was trapped indoors again.

Years before, Kay had organized her own one-hundredth birth-day party, an epic gathering we all remember to this day. Kay rallied the other residents on her block and brought together more than a dozen family members from across the country to celebrate. As she moved about the seniors' complex common room that day, dressed smartly in her wine-coloured suit, her short grey hair freshly cut, she made sure to speak with everybody. All the while she kept an eye on the food and gifts, dispensing orders to Ray and Eleanore: the sandwiches go here; your homemade wine goes over there; this is the basket for cards. It was hard to believe that spritely woman of one hundred would be one hundred and six now.

Everything all right? I say to Ray.

Well, he says, when I opened the apartment door today, Kay was lying on her loveseat in her living room. She hadn't eaten, for how long I don't know. I helped her to the bathroom, which was in bad shape. You-know-what was everywhere.

Ray made her a little lunch, cleaned up what he could, and helped Kay return to the loveseat, where she lay whispering, I can't remember, I can't remember.

She wasn't making much sense, Ray said. He called Eleanore, then the paramedics.

After a hospital stay, Kay recovered from a lung infection and surprised everyone by regaining some strength. But, like my mother, she'd left her apartment on a gurney and never returned to it. Her daughter Eleanore sorted what to keep and what to throw away, sent tchotchkes and housewares to the thrift store, found homes for items Kay would never touch again. Barely able to breathe herself, Eleanore worked doggedly to empty the apartment.

After Kay had rallied somewhat, she was moved to a care facility in the south end of Winnipeg, giving me hope I could visit her again, once the pandemic eased. In the last decade, Kay had become a lifeline to me, the last remaining member of an entire generation of our family. With her gone, my siblings, cousins, and I move to the front of the queue.

But I didn't see her. Aunt Kay passed away quietly at the end of November. The following April, Eleanore, whose condition had worsened, died in her car as she was leaving for work.

On his last visit to the care home to see Kay, Ray heard her whisper, *I believe.*

you did well

You good? That too tight?

Nope, I say. My skull is cradled in a plastic cage snug against my ears. I insert the ear plugs, and pads clamp on my head. My throat feels itchy so I clear it, hoping I don't have to cough while I'm inside.

Ten minutes, he says, and waves as the bed slides me into the metal tube. I take one more deep breath, my heart pounding more rapidly than I'd like. One more breath. Calm down, I think. Calm the fuck down. It's not as though I don't know what to expect.

I've never minded the noises, beeps and grinds, screeching and blaring, as though the gears and levers behind the waking world have found speech. I listen intently, follow their patterns, the knock-knocking, then the long whine. When the bed moves again, a new sound begins.

My breath calms. I can do this. This is easier than being in an underground parking garage. A touch of claustrophobia plus too many cop shows, I guess.

One sound drones for three or four full minutes and I wonder, Does this mean they found it, or they need better images of this part of my brain? Odd.

I refuse to let wonder turn to worry.

Years ago, I don't remember why, I learned to stop resisting in times like these. The "be here now" mantra is overdone, but when I'm in the middle of an unfolding tragedy or struggling with pain, I lean into that state. I've heard it described as radical presence. I no longer fight what's going on: I count, or listen hard, or breathe and watch. I attend closely, suspend judgement, and stop thinking about the next second or the next minute.

The bed is sliding out. It must be over.

You did really well! The young technician's face crinkles above his mask.

Really well, he adds.

You sure did. The technician on the other side asks if I want her help getting up.

No thanks. My balance is good today. Quite the noises in there.

Sure are.

I wouldn't want the whole album, though, I say, wondering if people use the word *album* anymore.

She laughs.

You sure don't seem your age, she adds, as I slip into my shoes and she hands me my phone and health card.

In the change room, I fight back tears.

An A in MRI, I think. Great. Do they feel badly for an old woman, or are they reassuring me because of what they saw?

life at all

Monday morning. Fog lifts on the coast to another hot, hot, hot summer day. The land here in Nova Scotia is parched and, across the continent, fires ravage the West Coast. I refill containers of water and put them out on the deck for what few birds are around. We took down the feeders this year because of a dangerous virus killing the bird population. Where are the bright goldfinches, the bevy of robins that bounced in the grass; the family of crows that gathered on the larch waiting for me to throw scraps off the deck? When we first came to this part of the province, I checked local bird-watching sites to see what species people had spotted in the area. Early mornings I'd wake to raucous bird action on the roof and in the trees, listen for the whistle of the northern cardinal. Something has turned.

The silence is unnerving.

All my life, the natural world has seemed to me, as it did to biologist Louis Agassiz, a sacred text, every creature a thought of the Creator. It wasn't romantic: it could be harsh and unforgiving. In childhood, I always lived in or near the bush; ravaged nests, broken shells, and feathers scattered with blood taught me about predation and helped temper my ignorance and naivete. But in the ensuing decades, the global environmental crisis has perverted what we thought were the laws of nature; a 2019 study revealed that more than 3 billion breeding birds in North America have been lost in the last fifty years. I have no illusions about which species is the deadliest predator on the planet.

As I watch the sea lift its grey veil, I scan the shore for a gull, a heron, even a crow. On the computer, I see a five-minute clip of Joni Mitchell, Brandi Carlisle, and Wynonna Judd. There she is: the woman known in my high school as Joan Anderson, who had graduated before me and was the first president of the school's Writers' Club. Our English teacher Mr. Smyth claimed she'd "never amount to anything."

I turn up the volume. Joni, who's had health problems, sits in a grand chair and leans in to sing "Both Sides Now," slowly and with care, her smoke-darkened phrasing a stark contrast to the sweet and light sounds of her 1969 album, *Clouds*. Every word she sings brings the past with its lost dreams into the present. Like the moon does with the tides.

People around Joni are weeping. I am weeping.

What we knew is gone.

No, that's not true; we really didn't know it at all.

story

I spend half my time making story, and the other half trying to unstory myself—or, rather, trying to value the parts of lived experience that do not fit into a narrative shape.

Kyo Maclear

When I look up at the moon, I think about the fact she has repeated herself for countless millennia, been seen by billions of creatures on the earth. She carries all the old moons in her arms and none of us knows when her story will end.

Mine, I know, will end sooner rather than later. My life bursts with stories, memories I can shape into narratives with an arc and a sense of an ending, but most I cannot. Writer Jane Alison looks at our conventional approach to narrative and says, "Something that swells and tautens until climax, then collapses? Bit masculo-sexual, no?" As readers and writers, we are used to stories with a beginning, middle, end, to delayed gratification, to plots that pull us along to a resolution, to main themes or points, so much so that when stories drift or straggle or move in a circle, we can feel groundless, unmoored. Yet many cultures, including Indigenous ones, share knowledge and experience in non-linear forms, with no grand denouement. When I think of pleasurable moments, like glimpsing a shaft of golden light, hearing a strain of music or the rush of waves washing ashore, I don't think of story. No crescendo, no explosive release, no plotted narrative, yet these experiences enrich me, as do moments of struggle.

Our experiences have a "what" and a "so what," I often tell students, even if we don't plot them. The writer Vivian Gornick calls the "what" the situation (our experience, the circumstances) and the "so what" the story (its significance, what it means, why it matters).

So what matters in all I recount here? The list is too long. The lives of my grandmothers, my mother, my birth and present families, my aunts and distant relatives, my friends and lovers and mentors and colleagues—their histories, their wisdom, and their teachings. The land and the water that have borne me for decades, taught me humility and constancy, the strength, cruelty, precarity, and beauty of life. Wonder. Awe. Writing to record this beauty and wonder, these relationships. If there's a lesson for me here, it's one of kinship: when we forget we are interrelated, that we rely on and affect one another in our small and larger ecosystems, we jeopardize the world that sustains us. That is what I've come to say: We are the richness, the silk threads woven through each other's lives. We are the prose and poetry of one another's stories; we compose our lives with others. We are here because of each other and the earth that carries us.

Recently, after a heavy rain, I went outside to feel the soil under my feet, the wind's cool touch. I looked up to see a rainbow, one end dipped into the ocean, the other arching across the sky and down to the land. I could have shaped the moment into a story, perhaps, the earth doing that thing she does with such flair and grace.

But with the sun filtering through clouds like light through gauze, petrichor in the air and a pastel sky, I was left wordless. In awe. That was enough.

at night

One keeps forgetting old age up to the very brink of the grave.
Sidonie Gabrielle Colette (1873–1954)

Death being shy: I've heard sleep described that way. Macbeth said sleep is the "death of each day's life, sore labor's bath / Balm of hurt minds"; the notion of balm and bath certainly appeal more than death does.

It's common for older people to wake because a plane flew overhead, they need to pee, or birds are squawking in the early dawn. I can wake for what seems like no reason at all. I lie in silence and when the silence becomes unnerving, I turn on a podcast. When I drop off again, my mind's not around. Which could, incidentally, be the perfect way to die. Unaware. In my sleep, dreaming.

Before the electric light was invented, people often slept in two phases, what's called a biphasic sleep pattern. Birds do it; in fact, a lot of animals do it. People who have long afternoon naps do it; a nap gives them energy for the rest of the day.

Poet Louise Bogan wrote that, at night, "more things move / Than blood in the heart" and, it's true, when I pull my mind out of its self-involved stew, I am better able to sleep. I fall into what Carol Ann Duffy calls the "wide night," both awed and comforted by its vastness, its evermoreness.

When I was a child I understood what "the dead" referred to in The New Testament, but had no idea who "the quick" were. Yet I was one, still am, and each day find myself filled with inexpressible awe.

And so at night I try to dip my consciousness into what we call eternity to quell the noise of petty peeves, what the late writer Steven Heighton called our "grimy little workshop of the ego." I think of my ancestors, of their lives in landscapes and seascapes hundreds of years ago.

Eternity's sunrise, as Blake called it, is out there.

attention

To pay attention,
this is our endless and proper work.

Mary Oliver

A gust of wind tugs at the truck door as I try to close it. On the old road to the public beach, I notice flash-frozen flowers on a grave. At first I thought it was Marie's grave, the woman who sold us the house years ago, but it's not. The cemetery is filled with long-standing residents of this quiet corner of Nova Scotia. German settlers mostly, now spending eternity overlooking the ocean.

Only one other car is in the parking lot. In the distance, the surf rises beyond the seaside growth, foamy white against the paler white of the sky. The wind pierces and I'm tempted to put on the N95 mask I keep in my pocket merely to keep warm.

Walking on slick beach rocks takes care, especially in winter, but keeping my head down allows me to take in their colours, from black to rust to speckled white. I've picked up countless rocks from this beach. When I walk, I examine their flecks and folds, imagine the long lives they've had tumbled in salt water, polished for thousands of years. Before I leave, I drop them elsewhere on the beach, give them new neighbours.

Today the water looks more foreboding, colder, deeper. The wind is ruthless.

Halfway down the beach, my fingers ache and my legs are numb. The rockpiles are higher and far too slippery to navigate, and so I turn back. I resisted the temptation today to set a goal—walk to the first cliff or the big rock—remembering a walk is different for the one who receives rather than the one who projects. I will learn to receive, I tell myself. But not today. I'm bloody freezing.

And that's okay. It's all part of paying closer attention to my body and the world it moves in. Attention is receptivity. I am alive to risk cold, biting wind, to feel all the minor inconveniences my body encounters.

My stiff fingers drop the truck keys. I pick them up from the gravel, fumble as I unlock the door. Inside I turn on the heater and watch the waves, rubbing my hands to bring warmth back into them. Every sensation, even the ache in my fingers, attests to the gift of being.

Philosopher Simone Weil writes: "We must not wish for the disappearance of our troubles but for the grace to transform them." For Weil, the grace of the divine is what causes a person "to grow against the gravity of their own ego."

Ego. And that's it. Weil claims true attention to anything requires us to empty ourselves of ego. Attention isn't the focused effort to examine a phenomenon closely; rather, she says, it is our willingness to empty ourselves. Complete attention fills us up with the other— a landscape, a person, a problem.

Later that night, I wrap a blanket around me and step out on the deck, as I often do. The wind has died down and the sky is so clear I can lose myself in the moon and stars.

I look up, imagine beyond.

heirloom

Our son and his wife wait for me as AJ—already thirty; how did that happen?—adds a few logs to the wood stove, my husband of almost fifty years refills everyone's coffee, and the dogs pace between everyone, hoping for a ball of tissue paper to fetch and rip apart. The Pogues are in the background, then Chris Rea. We typically empty stockings before opening the "main" gifts.

The box is large. I take off the wrapping slowly, careful to salvage what paper I can. Everyone is patient. I'm a string and paper saver, a habit I picked up from my mother and her mother, Gram.

When the layers of tissue are off, my hands fly to my face and I burst into tears.

On one of my trips to Winnipeg, Aunt Kay disappeared into her tiny, overstuffed bedroom and emerged with a plastic bag filled with fabric.

Here, I want you to have this, she said. She was giving things away. Inside the bag was a trove of cotton quilt pieces.

This was mother's, she said. She died before she could finish it.

Kay's mother, my grandmother Eleanore, had quilts in every room of the house. I remember her huge vegetable garden, the cellar filled with preserved fruit and meat. At night, I slept under one of her quilts, but was too young to appreciate her handiwork.

These hand-stitched creations take countless hours, and when Aunt Kay handed me the bag of quilt squares that day and asked if I'd be able to finish it, I paused.

I'll try, I said. I didn't want to disappoint her, but I feared I couldn't do it justice. The pieces sat in my closet for a year or two. After our elder son married J, a talented woman who designs and sews, I brought out the bag, hesitant to ask. Someday, if she had time, and only if she had time, I asked, would she perhaps sew these pieces together?

And here it is, now, backed, stitched, from Eleanore's hands to Kay's, to J's, to mine. An heirloom, whole and beautiful, a part of the family. Before Kay died, I told her J finished the quilt for us and sent her a photo. It was Kay who prompted my search for our grandmothers, a search that gave me roots on this land. By giving me the quilt pieces, she gave me tangible remnants of our past, threads of an old story still being written.

beaver blood moon

Passed years seem safe ones, vanquished ones,
while the future lives in a cloud, formidable from a distance.
The cloud clears as you enter it.

Beryl Markham, *West with the Night*

We drive home in the dark, stuffed with Thanksgiving bounty, more delicious food than we needed. The first time in recent memory the meal wasn't at our house.

Oh, the decades of planning and orchestrating a big meal. As our sons grew, they learned to peel, cook, bake, and clean up. But even with their help, I found timing well-risen popovers, lump-free gravy, hot-but-crisp vegetables, and an edible yet photogenic bird a challenge. It all seemed so excessive. By the time I sat down to dinner, I could barely taste the food.

Suddenly, I see the moon. Startling. Look! Look at the moon!

AJ squirms in the back seat, trying to see out the window. The dog perks up, wondering what the fuss is about.

There it is again! When the highway changes course the moon moves across the sky, but we're in the thick of Nova Scotian trees and for a while, we can only catch glimpses. The moon looks ten times its usual size.

Full moon, full bellies, full heart.

That day, AJ had joined us when we drove down to the South Shore to have dinner. AJ now lives in an apartment in Kjipuktuk (Halifax) with the cat companion he'd always wanted. He loves his job and has regular assistance from an agency to help organize his life. We're in touch daily, but meals, transport, and appointments are all his to handle now, and he is acing it.

And after years of renting, our elder son and his wife have found a house on a wooded acre outside of Mahone Bay that is, in their words, "a dream come true." They love to cook, and are looking forward to growing their own food. After years of scraping by, they are managing. I think about Allan and me, the houses we've turned to homes during our half-century together. We're in what we think of as "our last house," a small place in the northwest end of Kjipuktuk. After having lived in more than a dozen towns and cities, more than thirty houses, I find staying put offers comfort.

As we near Tantallon, the landscape opens up and we can see her, the whole of the moon, low on the horizon, looking for all the world like a colossal orange sun. The sight is galvanizing. I know I'll remember the present moment with joy.

Have you ever seen the moon that large? Ever?

Nope.

Nope.

I haven't either. Ever. I'm serious, AJ. Never in my long life have I seen the moon that size. It's huge!

That's a long time, Mom, AJ says. A long time.

Very funny, dear.

It's breathtaking. I learn later it wasn't a supermoon; it was a Hunter's moon, a Falling-Leaves moon. A Beaver Blood moon that seemed as though she had completed herself, become all a moon was meant to become.

We followed her all the way home.

a word is a shore

Snow, I say to you, and in the word are two-metre drifts, my red wooden sled, the shock of ice down my neck in the schoolyard. Moguls at Norquay, the milky sheen of prairie fields in the sun, White Juan, a snowman AJ and I made overlooking the ocean. Snow is filthy, hard-packed berms on Winnipeg streets one long, dark December as I lurched a cold car to and from St. Boniface Hospital. My snow isn't your snow, but the word is a gathering place, a space where we bring snows together, the same, but richly different.

Sea, I say, and we do the same. The neighbour leaves his house at 5:30 A.M. to put his boat in the water, I've looked out on the Atlantic for forty years, snorkelled on the Great Barrier Reef before the influx of tourists like me killed the coral, walked along the shore in Cambridge Bay in the Arctic to a shaman's grave. My neighbours along the South Shore dip into the bone-piercing cold of the sea every New Year's Day.

And the moon? Do you mean the silvery moon or the harvest moon, the hunter, corn, wolf, buck, or the strawberry moon? The moon that lit your walk home in the cold when the bus broke down or the moon casting light across the bedclothes that hot summer in the North. The barely visible wafer moon at dawn when you turned the key in the ignition and left for good.

How many memories and experiences, how vast is our collective knowledge of snow, sea, the moon, or of love, peace, hope, loss? Or of the earth itself. We saturate each word with how we found it, lived, felt, and used it. Writing, hummingbird, ecstasy, evil, cinnamon, joy, family, pain, grief, Métis, woman, gratitude, writer, feminism—we try to carry all we know and all we don't in a word. We meet in a liminal space that moves and changes with the tides of our lives, a space for the time being where we bring those words to life.

epilogue:
beside the glowing bars

It's been a time. Rain and fog for three days, and night
comes earlier. A walk by the shore, the brimming sea,
and I carry inside pots of herbs, frost biting

the muffled air. A fistful of wooden matches, sticks
of cedar, crumpled tissue, sparks. A half-hearted flame,
smoke, breath to coax, a flicker of life, then: gone.

Outside, sea and sky fuse in quiet repair. None of us
knows what's coming, but we pay attention, reach—
fingers, eyes—wrap our tongues around what is true,

what brought us here. What now. At the edge of death
are beauty, awe. Whisper salvation to each other, where
to find winter fuel, our bones between earth and water

means to track light. *Peyahtak*: go slowly and with care.
The sky gauze, starless, the moon waiting. Set down words
and a lick of flame rises, opens a bright eye in the stove.

acknowledgements

The list of family, friends, colleagues, and readers who made this book possible is long.

I'm grateful to the close and extended family of remarkable women, some long gone, who compose my life. They inspire, support, and challenge me. I am because they were, and are.

My thanks go to early readers of parts of this manuscript, including Mary Jo Anderson, Binnie Brennan, Carol Bruneau, Susan Glickman, Jennifer Haigh, Donna Kane, Ramona Lumpkin, Kim Pittaway, Maureen Scott Harris, and Jane Silcott. Their feedback has been vital. The foursome known as Gritz (you know who you are) continue to be my rock.

For many reasons, I also want to thank Ray Adam, Shirley Adam, Janet Barkhouse, Lawrie Barkwell, Kimmy Beach, Brian Boggs, Anne Carter, Lauren Carter, Pauline Dakin, April D'Aloisio, Stan Dragland, Marilyn Dumont, Sheree Fitch, James Fisher, Ariel Gordon, Roetka Gradstein, Sylvia Hamilton, Juniper, Rene Kastrukoff, Theresa Kishkan, Jeanette Lynes, Allison Marion, Daphne Marlatt, Tanis McDonald, Don McKay, Dianne Miller, Jen Powley, Margaret Primeau Nielsen, Shelagh Rogers, Maureen Scott Harris, Susan Siddeley, Anne

Simpson, Marilyn Smulders, Christian Smith, Tara Dawn Solheim, Rose Vaughan, and W. B. Yeats. And so many more—my apologies if I have missed anyone.

Some names have been changed in the interests of privacy. Any errors in this text are mine alone. I've been true to my memories, but perhaps they may differ from those of others.

My thanks to editors of the following anthologies, journals, and magazines who published pieces that have been excerpted, adapted, or expanded here, sometimes radically: *Apart, Good Mom on Paper: Writers on Creativity and Motherhood, Gush, How to Expect What You're Not Expecting, The Nova Scotia Book of Fathers, Prairie Fire, Sharp Notions: Essays from the Stitching Life, Slice Me Some Truth, The Malahat Review, This Magazine, You Look Good for Your Age, Waiting.*

Organizations and retreats where I have learned and/or taught and whose opportunities have supported my writing include The Banff Centre for the Arts, The Writers' Federation of Nova Scotia, Sage Hill Writing Experience, Lios Dana, Los Parronales, St. Peter's Abbey, and the University of Saskatchewan. Mount Saint Vincent University, where I am Professor Emerita, has been a leader in supporting women. For the last decade, The University of King's College MFA program in creative nonfiction and its remarkable students and colleagues have continued to inspire me.

Thank you to the astute and generous Whitney Moran and to Nimbus Publishing, including Jenn Embree for the beautiful cover art. I couldn't have asked for a better team to work with. After I'd finished a draft of this book, I opened Jane Munro's *Open Every Window* to see a chapter titled, "New Moon with the Old Moon in Its Arms." Coincidence and the moon are everywhere.

I am grateful to family and friends who have trusted me with memories I've shaped here into prose. My sons and daughter-in-law, along with my husband, Allan, are everything. Allan has my heart.

Works Cited

Prologue

An earlier version of this piece, "Footing," was published online at EssayDaily.org, August 6, 2018.

"With every step, the world comes to the walker." Trinh T. Minh-Ha, *Lovecidal: Walking with the Disappeared*. New York: Fordham University Press, 2016.

"All the lives we ever lived and all the lives to be are full of trees and changing leaves." Virginia Woolf, *To the Lighthouse*. England: The Hogarth Press, 1927.

Origin Stories

ANOTHER COUNTRY
"Childhood is another country but also a waiting-room, a state of accommodation and acceptance." Antoine de Saint-Exupéry, *The Little Prince*, translated by Irene Testot-Ferry, Wordsworth, 1995.

Sylvia Moore. *Trickster Chases the Tale of Education*. Dissertation submitted in partial fulfillment of the requirements of the Degree of Doctorate in Educational Studies, Lakehead University, 2011, p. 165.

CUTTING OUT HEARTS
"Time makes room…" Ursula K. Le Guin, "Hymn to Time." *Late in the Day: Poems 2010–2014.* Oakland, CA: PM Press, 2015.

O'CLOCK
Greta Gerwig quote from "What Greta Gerwig Saw in 'Little Women': 'Those Are My Girls,'" *The New York Times,* October 31, 2019. nytimes.com/2019/10/31/movies/greta-gerwig-little-women.html

WHAT SHE DOESN'T KNOW
Excerpt from "Peanut Butter" by Eileen Myles from *Not Me.* Los Angeles: Semiotext(e), 1991.

SEVENERS
Amma Theodora excerpt from *The Sayings of the Desert Fathers: The Apophthegmata Patrum,* translated by Benedicta Ward (Collegeville, Minnesota.: Liturgical Press, 1975), pp. 83-84.

FRAIL THINGS
Virginia Woolf quote from *To the Lighthouse.*

Note: John Watson as Ian Maclaren: oldest known instance of the quote often attributed to Plato appears in MacLaren's piece in the 1897 Christmas edition of *The British Weekly.*

Orbits

HANDICAP
AJ has granted the author his approval to write this essay.

HOMING
Rilke, Rainer Maria. "No Place that does not see you" from the poem "The Archaic Torso of Apollo" from *New Poems,* translated by Edward Snow, 1907. San Francisco : North Point Press, 1984.

THAT'S YOU (YAASS)
Liz Phair quote from *Newsweek*, September 9, 2022.
newsweek.com/singer-liz-phairs-defense-queen-elizabeth-ii-sparks-de-bate-feminism-1741584

THE MOON INSIDE
Joy Harjo quote from *Crazy Brave: A Memoir*, New York: W. W. Norton, 2013.

SCAR
"I like to Kiss Scars" by Rosa Chavez, translated by Gabriela Ramirez Chavez in *Poetry* magazine, February 2022.

THE LAND IS KIN
Quote from Patty Krawec in *Becoming Kin: An Indigenous Call to Unforgetting the Past and Reimagining our Future*. Pine Bush, NY: Broadleaf Books, 2022.

THE GOLDEN LEGEND
"A god should be smarter than that." Robert MacFarlane, *Underland: A Deep Time Journey*. New York: W. W. Norton, 2019, p. 67.

WINTER IN HADES'S BED
Lines of poetry from Louise Gluck's "Persephone, the Wanderer" in *Averno* (2006), New York: Farrar, Straus and Giroux, 2006.

YELLOW ROSES
"the people we most love do become a physical part of us, ingrained in our synapses, in the pathways where memories are created" from *The Long Goodbye: A Memoir* by Meghan O'Rourke, Riverhead, 2012.

GRACE HOUSE
The Poetics of Space by Gaston Bachelard, New York: Penguin Classics, 2014.

WRITING TOSH
Naipaul quote from "V.S. Naipaul's attack 'just made me laugh' says Diana Athill" by Alison Flood, *The Guardian*, June 13, 2011. theguardian.com/books/2011/jun/03/v-s-naipaul-diana-athill

Mailer quote from "The Lingering Scent of a Woman's Ink" by Macy Halford, *The New Yorker*, June 9, 2011. .newyorker.com/books/page-turner/the-lingering-scent-of-a-womans-ink

Connie Walker from CBC Radio One's *The Current*, May 10, 2023.

GREAT WHITE WAY
Miigwech to the women in a range of settings—Indigenous communities, immigrant organizations, women's shelters—across the Maritimes, Newfoundland, Western and Northern Canada who have taught me, and many others, about what matters in education.

Lines of poetry from "The Devil's Language" by Marilyn Dumont from *A Really Good Brown Girl*, London, ON: Brick Books, 1996.

"I Lost my Talk" by Rita Joe from *Song of Rita Joe: An Autobiography of Rita Joe* Sydney, NS: Breton Books. © 2007 by the Estate of Rita Joe.

Jenny Horsman, *Too Scared to Learn: Women, Violence, and Education*. Mahwah, NJ: Lawrence Erlbaum and Associates, 2000, p. xv.

HOW TO KILL HER
Annie Ernaux, *Mémoire de Fille*. Paris: Gallimard, 2018.

WHAT MATTERS
Excerpt from "Let me Make This Perfectly Clear" by Gwendolyn MacEwen, *Afterworlds*. Toronto: McClelland & Stewart, 1987. Copyright to the estate of Gwendolyn MacEwen, with the permission of David MacKinnon, executor for The Estate of Gwendolyn MacEwen.

"...one day we'll appear in our children's memories, among their grand-children and people not yet born." *The Years* by Anne Erneaux, translated by Alison L. Strayer. London: Fitzcarraldo Editions, 2018.

FIREFLIES
Dacher Keltner quote from *Awe: The New Science of Everyday Wonder and How It Can Transform Your Life*. New York: Penguin Press, 2022.

IT DIDN'T OCCUR TO ME
Rebecca Solnit quote from *Recollections of my nonexistence: A memoir*. New York: Viking., 2020.

LOOKIN' BACK.
An earlier version of this piece was published in *You Look Good for your Age*. Edmonton: University of Alberta Press, 2018.

Waning Crescent

AFTERLIGHT
Zadie Smith quote from *The Guardian* "'Identity is a pain in the arse': Zadie Smith on political correctness" by Claire Armistead, Feb 2, 2019. theguardian.com/books/2019/feb/02/zadie-smith-political-correctness-hay-cartagena

Alice Oswald, "Full Moon," from *A Sleepwalk on the Severn*. London: Faber and Faber Ltd., 2009.

Dorothy Allison quote by Aunt Dot from *Two or Three Things I know for Sure*. New York: Penguin, 1995, p. 5.

WHO'S THE FAIREST
Rose Madeline Mula. *The Stranger in my Mirror and other Reflections*, iUniverse, 2003.

GRASP AND HOLD
Rilke quote from *Letters to a Young Poet: The Norton Centenary Edition*, translated by M. D. Hertern Norton. Translated variously in other volumes, for e.g. "Works of art are of an infinite loneliness and with nothing to be so little appreciated as with criticism."

THE OLD BONE HOUSE
An earlier version of this piece was published in *This Magazine*, March/April, 2022.

"One Art" by Elizabeth Bishop. *The Complete Poems 1926-1979*, New York: Farrar, Straus and Giroux, 1983.

STORY
Kyo Maclear quote from "It bears repeating: The stories we tell about dementia," the *Globe and Mail*, April 28, 2023.
theglobeandmail.com/opinion/article-it-bears-repeating-the-stories-we-tell-about-dementia/#:~:text=I%20spend%20half%20my%20time,caring%20for%20people%20with%20dementia

ATTENTION
Mary Oliver quote from "Yes! No!" in *White Pine: Poems and Prose Poems*, New York: Ecco, 1994.

"We must not wish for the disappearance of our troubles but for the grace to transform them" from Simone Weil, *Gravity and Grace*, translated by Emma Crawford and Mario von der Ruhr, London: Routledge, 1952.

BEAVER BLOOD MOON
Beryl Markham, *West with the Night*. New York: Warbler Press, 1942.